RED PASTURE

HIGH RIDING HEART

RED PASTURE

Book One

Joan
enjoy the Ride in
the Red Pasture!

Kathryn Bartow

Kathryn Bartow

Rev. date: 12/19/2014

To order additional copies of this book, contact:
Xlibris
1-888-795-4274
www.Xlibris.com
Orders@Xlibris.com
695827

CONTENTS

Thank you for choosing to read my book. I hope you enjoy reading it as much as I have enjoyed telling the story. This is a work of fiction; should perhaps there be a likeness of name, location, or event, it is completely coincidental.

To all who love their families and their family histories, have known the meaning of the love of an animal, or have found love in their lifetime, this story will hold all of this and more for you. See you in the Red Pasture!

Kathryn Bartow

When God pushes you to the edge, trust Him fully,
because only two things can happen.
Either He will catch you when you fall
or He will teach you how to fly.

—Author unknown

PART 1

The Drive

"The snow in the canyons has reached a record depth this year." That was what the newsman on the radio morning program reported as the 'top story'. The thought of riding out to bring in the herd was not comforting at all. Outside the window of their small bedroom, the overnight snow had again insulated the earth under a blanket of white. Unable to put the thoughts of the previous evening's love shared between them out of her mind, Sara crossed her arms against her body, holding to her heart the quilt her grandmother had hand-sewn for her when she was an infant. She snuggled closer to Samuel. The awareness of his muscular body so close to hers after all these years could still arouse her in both flesh and mind.

Sara's procrastination had to end. She did not want to leave the warmth and comfort of their bed or pull away from the feel and scent of her husband. Slowly, she lifted herself forward, with one arm behind for support. She smiled as she looked at Samuel. "Any more handsome and I just wouldn't know what to do!" she whispered to him as he lay face down in his pillow, trying to block out the morning light. "Oh yeah, you say that now, how about in thirty years?" he mumbled into the pillow. She knew that a lifetime of years would never be enough for them in their love. She bent down, and with the gentleness of a butterfly, tickled his back along the center muscle line. With a soft moan of pleasure, he rolled over and drew her to him.

She lay beside him, and with a knowing of his pleasures, she gently stroked his awakened maleness. He was hers. She was his. Though his hands were strong and calloused as he softly caressed her breasts, she felt only the heightened desire to make love to him. She rose over him, lowered herself, and with her rhythmical movements, he succumbed to her without abandon. Afterward, as he kissed her, she felt the intensity of him; the truth of how he felt for her needed no actual words.

With a sigh, she rose back up again "What happened to the old saying 'when the cows come home'? It sure would be nice if the herd just decided to up and walk right into the barn, would sure save us all a lot of trouble!"

"You just want to stay in bed longer. I know . . . we could arrange for that . . ."

"Why, Samuel, you are frisky this morning! Now just get your big bad self up out of this bed, and get the fire started—it's chilly in here." She was slowly inching her way out from under the warm blankets. "I can keep you warm enough, come back here . . ."

"Oh, Sam, I love you so much."

"Does that mean you're coming back to bed?"

"You just don't ever stop, do you?"

"Ah, you say that as you giggle. I know you love my teasing."

"Yes, I do, now get up! We have a lot of work to do even before we get to the trailhead."

Samuel could not help but think of just the two of them on the trail . . . when they rode together, he kept behind her not only to have the optimum look out for her the protection, but also he loved to watch her ride. Sara was truly a 'horsewoman' in and out of the saddle. He would watch her maneuver Jazzy so silently, as if by thought she could transmit her instructions. The mare would listen and work with such obedience that he was almost jealous of their relationship with each other. Samuel's horse, on the other hand was not as cooperative as to the finer aspects of training. Tonk's reputation as a solid trail horse was well earned. He was known for his 'levelhead' and for being a trustworthy mount.[1] Most of the hands preferred him to the other horses in the corral.

OK, so he was not able to perform a flying lead change, a 'half halt'[2], or that fancy side pass execution, but get him on a mountain and he's as surefooted as a mule and willing to accept any challenge a ride or Drive[3] presents to him. Samuel was proud of the hard work he had put into the rangy colt when he was orphaned at just seven weeks after his birth. Despite the tough start in life, he matured into a fine ranch horse.

Sara always made the best of camping and sleeping out under the stars. She loved to sit on blankets around the campfire and snuggle together. She knew all the constellations and would find each one to show him. Her awareness of the earth and knowledge of it never ceased to amaze him. She was in 'her element' his grandfather had told him years ago when she had helped their son Michael to earn the first place ribbon at the Brandon Elementary Science Fair.

---

[1] Refers to the horse

[2] A half halt is a Dressage movement whereas the horse not quite stops within a transition of gait.

[3] When a herd is moved from one location to another using mounted riders and dogs. It usually refers to a long distance move of a herd.

"The tent . . . you just keep in mind the tent tonight, we'll pick up where we left off!" Sara smiled as she blew an air kiss to him. She was not sure which of them was more excited at the prospect of spending the night paired in the sleeping bag. Neither of them ever tired of the pleasures they shared while camping. A long day's ride was well deserving of a good meal cooked on the campfire, a bit of stargazing, and the heated retreat to the tent.

A smile came as she thought ahead to the evening. This ride would be especially grueling as they would be far outnumbered by the cattle, and then of course, the prospect of temperamental weather just added to the uneven equation. The hope was to get just more than halfway to the herd by nightfall. She said an extra prayer that the weather would hold out and that the herd would cooperate. It would be a tough enough job for an actual drive of riders. Knowing there would only be the two of them wrangling[4] and at last count, there were still about 300 head of cattle. Sara winced at the odds against the success of the journey. Most any other time, there would be a half dozen or more outriders[5], but the storms had kept the men needed at their own ranches, and she just could not bring herself to ask them to leave their families so close to the Christmas Holiday. She and Samuel would be able to get the herd home. They had ridden together enough years now that they knew the movements of the other and could understand and communicate without actual words. Knowing that the Border Collies Rex and Bandit would be acting as the outriders, she had confidence in them as a foursome to get this drive home safely. She had to keep reassuring herself and trust in Samuel, the dogs, and God.

Propped against the pillows, Samuel watched as Sara dressed for the ride. Ten years of marriage and she still looked good to him. Her figure had matured, and he realized he preferred the newfound curves to the slimness of her youth. As she donned her favorite pair of pink thermal 'long handles'[6], his gaze wandered to the photos that she had meticulously placed in frames around the mirror above his clothes bureau.

---

[4]   Wranglers are the cowboys and cowgirls riding on the Drive.

[5]   Outriders are the wranglers that ride the sides of the herd keeping the herd following the lead riders also known as the point riders.

[6]   A term used for insulated thermal undergarments.

To the left she had hung the photo of her parents—Scott and Marie Bloom—tragically killed in a blizzard, and her brother Mark, still hoping to find the right girl over in East Dale while he enjoyed the life of an underling at the law firm of Miles, Miles & Welderman. Facially, Sara looked much like her mother. Yet, she had the muscular frame to work like her father, and then of course, her occasional blatant stubbornness was definitely a known trait of the elder Bloom men. With her brother being far more passive, they were often teased as to the role reversal.

Under her parents, she had placed Michael's school pictures. The photograph of him in kindergarten was Samuel's favorite. His parents were to the right in the old barn wood frame. John and Mary Moore married forty-five years this past anniversary. He sure hoped that he and Sara would have that many years together. He then looked at the photo of himself, taken at the Brandon Fair years ago with the Heavyweight Champion Steer. Sara had insisted that was her favorite of him; so when he had made his choice for favorite, she had no winnable argument for its exclusion from the wall. She had repeatedly voiced objection as to his choice, but in the end, there she was—wearing her 'Daisy Dukes' as she called them at a cattle auction in Huntston. He still laughed when he remembered how he, as a newly licensed auctioneer fumbled his 'bidding call' when Sara walked in the pen. It was to the entertainment of the crowd as they jeered for the young man who so obviously was love-struck the instant he saw her. As if she knew his embarrassment, she winked at him, and he knew at that moment he would love her for his lifetime.

"Hey there, handsome . . . time to show off that bod of yours and get out of the bed!"

"Just rolling memories through my mind of the auction."

"Oh, and here I thought that smirk was directed to my long handles."

"I know we have to get going . . . wait, there is an update to the weather report . . . Sara, it seems as though the storm system may take a more southern route. I think we will have that luck you were hoping for after all."

Sara was already in the kitchen, working on the first of several cups of coffee she would drink before they left. She needed to address the day and 'ready the stores'[7] that would be needed to fill the panniers on the pack

---

[7]   The stores refer to the utensils, dry goods, and personal items that will be packed in the framed canvas pouches fastened to the pack saddle known as panniers.

mule for the long ride to the North Grazing Lands. The canyons were the least of her worries; it was December, prey for the wolves and the wildcats had long since dwindled, and the 'hunters' were hungry. They needed to get to Anglin Pass to push the herd through the Draw[8] and down to the lower riverbed. This time of year, the ice on the river was still at a manageable and travelable stage; waiting much longer would allow the snow and ice time to increase, making passage dangerous for the cattle and nearly impossible for the horses. The cattle, having tougher hide, are far more resilient to lower limb injury due to 'cutting' the ice layer of the snow and the frozen waters.,

Sara knew this would be a hard ride, her fortitude would be tested; the ride to the Pass would be the toughest. They had decided to take the shortcut through the east Red Pasture gate up to the Old Tree Line Trail Head. From there, they would try to keep to the old trail to cross Hobb's Ridge and then drop down to the Pass. It would save many hours and miles of riding time. The herd could not navigate the rougher terrain. Therefore, the drive home would be through the Pass and into the River Bottom, they would then make their way back to the Red Pasture on the west end. She hoped that Jazzy was up for it and that it was not too late. They just could not lose more cattle this year. The spring blizzard had taken nearly 100 head off the Brandy Gulch herd. There was no room for more loss physically, mentally or monetarily.

Samuel walked into the kitchen and though still very sleepy, put a hand on her back and kissed her shoulders. "We really need to ride don't we?"

"Yes, Samuel, we do. The reports have not been good for the North Canyons, and we can't afford anymore loss." She handed him his coffee mug and plate of eggs. "Oh, Sara, however did I find the one true love that is so much a part of me and my life . . ."

"Talk like that could delay our leaving, Mr. Moore!"

"Yes, Mrs. Moore, you are right, I will hold back for now . . . just keep in mind the tent tonight!" Smiling, Sara thought of how her friends always commented on how her marriage was better than a romance novel. She agreed.

"I'll head out to the barn to start getting the horses ready." Standing in the doorway looking back at their bedroom, Samuel could not help but

---

[8]   The widening area before and after the actual Pass, the Pass being the narrow route through mountains, steep hills, waterways, or the like.

notice his reflection in the mirror surrounded by the photos of his family. He stood there smiling at the man he had become due to the love of the people framing him there on the wall. The smiles and the laughter of his life were all there in stationary form. Yet as he looked at each photo, the remembrance of each moment still very much alive in his mind.

He reached into the lower left drawer and retrieved a letter he had written for Sara as an early Christmas gift. Tucking it into the inside pocket of his flannel-lined shirt, he closed the door behind him and headed for the barn. As he passed by the kitchen, he held out his mug, and with precision, Sara was already there with the coffee pot ready to refill it.

He thought of himself as the luckiest man in Brandon. With a tap on the chest pocket with the letter, just making sure it was still there, he donned the full suit coveralls, opened the backdoor, tipped his head to shield the biting early morning wind, and through the powdery overnight snow made his way to the barn.

Samuel was 'at home' in the barn. Granmam Etta and Granda Malcolm told him once that he was a true rancher from "way back," and they were sure he would always stay on the land. He fulfilled their hopes and dreams as heir to a heritage of honor and prestige in that he proudly respected it with hard work, honesty, and fairness.

Part of that heritage was the fine string of horses the ranch was known to produce. This year's foal crop was one of the best yet: six fillies and ten colts, each with the signature head of the red dun overo Paint horse stallion 'Captain'. As he opened the heavy carriage doors to the stall barn, he heard the familiar nickers of hope and anticipation of the feed wagon. "Are you ready, Tonk? It is gonna be a hell of a couple days for us!" Content with the feed, the horses had quieted in their stalls.

Samuel decided that a double check of their tack might help relieve the uneasiness he just could not shake. Sara's saddle was all ready. He grinned as he handled the two flashlights she insisted to always carry. "You just can't be too prepared," she would say. He turned to the rack his saddle rested on; rubbing his hands on the leather forks, his mind remembered the birthday that Sara gifted him with it. He had never had one with such fine tooling and the breast collar and bridle to match was definitely a 'first'. He had thought it too extravagant for a 'simple ranch cowboy'. She almost cried thinking he did not like it. The moment he sat in it, he smiled so wide she knew that he did. They both started to laugh at each other, he at her for doubting the gift and she at him for finally showing a more proper turnout. He had not ridden any other saddle since.

A slow reach for the letter in his pocket, he patted the outer layer of his jacket. He had it all planned out. His romantic side seemed always to please her, and tonight, he would not let her down. The candles were packed hidden in his cantle bag, two collapsible wine glasses inside his raingear in the near saddlebag, and then, he retrieved the letter and carefully rolled it into the blanket and tucked it into the offside saddlebag. Satisfied that all was prepared, it was time to saddle the horses. Sara would be arriving in the barn soon and in her usual state of excitement. He loved her spirit of enthusiasm and candor. It seemed always to be contagious to everyone around her.

"Hey there, handsome . . . ready for a ride with your bride?" Sara had been unseen as she entered the barn, and Samuel had hoped she had not been there long enough to witness his packing of the saddlebags. "Uhhh . . . how long have you been standing there?"
  "Just got here, why? Are you hiding something?"
  "Me? Oh noooooo! Would I do something like that?"
  "Your snicker and 'kid-in-the-cookie-jar look' is a giveaway, Mr. Moore!"
  "I was deep in thought, you startled me—that's all."
  "If you say so." Her laughter echoed in the aisle of the barn. With open arms, he motioned for her to come to him, and then he drew her in to a bear hug. "I love you so much. I could not bear to live without you."
  "I love you too, more as each day passes." They stood there wrapped in each other's arms. A nicker from Jazzy reminded them of the importance of timing and their need to ride out. "Are we ready?"
  "Yes, ma'am, we are!"

The crunch of the snow underfoot was a sure sign of the cold front moving through the valley. Sara had warned him of the weather predictions for the next few days. His refusal to be discouraged was more ego than common sense. Sara too knew the weather; her knowledge was well respected, as many times her 'predictions' had come to be. She saved a great many head of cattle three years earlier when had they waited just two days to bring them down from the canyon, they would have perished. Her insistence that they be brought down saved their lives and saved the calves as well.

Samuel felt the bite in the wind, it was difficult to breathe and the hair of his mustache was beginning to show signs of freezing. "Yes sir! This is going to be a really cold ride up to the canyons!" Silently, he agreed with Sara's questioning of why the herd hadn't been moved in October. Reaching for the barn door, he heard the howling of wolves fearing their hunger yet fearing the closeness to the townspeople more.

***

"Seems as though Miss Jazzy has a bit of hesitance today! That's not like her." Samuel had been watching Sara in her difficulties settling the mare. He was glad Tonk was his usual trustworthy self and willing to push forward. "She'll quiet down, just wait and see. An hour in this snow is a sure attitude adjustment" Sara did her half-giggle at the mare and even though she did not want Samuel to see her concerns, they were deeply embedded as she could feel the discontent of the mare, and Jazzy was always a good judge of situations. "Well, at least the wind is at our backs and not blowing directly in our faces!"

"Always finding a 'positive' in everything aren't you, Mrs. Moore!"

"Absolutely, Mr. Moore!"

Arrival at the 'Red Pasture' gate was a welcomed event. The trail through was heavily treed and would provide much needed shelter from the winds and snow. "Here, my dear, let me get that for you . . ." "I married the last true gentleman!" Sara and Jazzy slipped though the gateway, and Samuel still astride Tonk replaced the latch bar on the gate and followed up behind her.

"Do you see the tree line? I'd like to say it is just ahead a couple hundred yards but this snow is deceiving and we know it is quite a bit farther!" Just then, they heard the cry of a wolf, and if they were not already cold enough, the shivers that ran down their spines told them that the mule and the dogs needed to keep close and to get their rifles readied. Sara was vehemently against the shooting of wolves, but in this case, it might just have to be necessary.

Jazzy was well aware of the presence of the wolf. Sara had hoped the mare would settle in; this did not seem to be a possibility. As they approached the tree line, with sudden flight, she was at a hand gallop[9] with increasing intensity. Sara was startled by the abruptness in gait change but not unseated[10]. "Hang on, Sara! The girl is really movin' now!" Samuel picked up the dally rope[11] on the mule, and with a "Yaw," the trio of man, horse and mule were in pursuit of Sara, Jazzy, Rex and Bandit. The dogs had been keeping at heel for the most part, but when the excitement of a running horse came about, they both lit off through the snow to join the race.

Sara was able to rein in her mare just at the edge of the pasture. "Easy there, girl . . . just what got you all shook up back there? Do not tell me a wolf, I know better than that or don't you remember when we chased them off the herd last autumn . . . You can still surprise me even after all the years we've had together."

"Hey there, Lil Miss Speedy, just what was that?" Sara could hear Samuel as he and the 'boys' approached. "I wasn't sure old Roy here was going to kick it up, but he did. I don't know when last he got to run like that, and I don't think he particularly wants to do so again!"
"Tell that to 'Miss Speedy' here." Sara was rubbing Jazzy's neck when the wolf cried out again.
"OK, that's it, stay here. I am going to check this out. I'd give you the mule, but there just seems to be a great difference in attitude right now. Rex, Bandit, you stay here with Sara." Not wanting a confrontation of wolf and dogs, Sam insisted they stay back with Sara. "Be careful, Sam, if nothing else the poor soul is probably just starving, and we look like a darn welcomed meal"
"The only part of a meal you are going to be is dessert in the tent tonight!"
"Oh, Sam, I love you, now please be careful."

---

[9] A hand gallop is a gait faster than a canter but not quite the stretch in stride of the full gallop.

[10] Unseated—loss of balance in the saddle leading to possible fall from the horse.

[11] The dally rope is the leading line between the lead horse and the pack animal that is following. A dally tie is the loop around the saddle horn of the leading line, or when roping calves, to "Dally" is to tie the rope to the horn after throwing the loop over the head or the horns.

"I will." And with that, he rode off in search of the wolf. Jazzy was not the least bit content with staying behind and let her opinion be known by prancing, and just before an actual rear up, she bolted off for the comfort of her friend Tonk.

"What do you think about staying together?" Sara smirked as she asked Sam. "Doesn't look like our opinions are going to account for much of the decision now does it. Jazz is really a handful today. We're not that far out, did you want to go back to the ranch and change horses?"

"We are far enough that if we go back now, we will have lost half a day's ride and we just can't afford that much time loss getting to the herd."

"Your call, if it were me . . ."

"It's not you, and we're not turning back. Just keep your eyes out for that wolf!"

"You realize that the longer we track this wolf the farther off the trail we are getting, don't you?"

"If we don't see it soon, we'll head back toward the tree line entrance. Just a little detour through the woods over there and we will be right back on the trail."

She knew he was right; they were not far off the main trail, and if they could get to the wolf soon, the time loss would be minimal.

"I don't see any more sign of him."

"Me neither."

Halting the horses, they looked around and saw no tracks in sight. "How'd we lose him? There is snow everywhere. We should still be able to see his tracks."

"I gotta admit it, Sara, I haven't ever lost the track on a wolf, but this one has up and disappeared!" "Let's hope he stays that way! Shall we return to the trail, Mr. Moore?"

"I do believe that is what we shall do, Mrs. Moore." He reached over to her and drew her to him, embracing her. Enveloped in his arms she felt his strength and his love for her. She was safe. He would never allow her harm.

Sam checked the dally rope on Roy and then turned Tonk back to the tree line. Rex and Bandit were content to follow close to the horses. The snow was still fierce and deepening quickly. He was thankful that Sara had sewn in a face collar to his coveralls; sure was better than tangling with a scarf. The collar joined the ear protectors she so proudly 'fashioned' for him last year when he had finally agreed to a shorter haircut.

Sara watched him as he fastened the snaps; a smile of pride came over her. She enjoyed taking care of him. He was appreciative of all the 'little things' she could think of to help him and that she had the ability to complete her ideas with the projected end results.
"Nice muffs!"
"Yeah, Carhart[12] wants the patent on them but I told them it wasn't for sale!"
"Hmmm . . . a patent . . . huh . . . Maybe I should look into that!" Sara giggled at the thought of her idea as a new income. "So what should we call them?"
"They're a collar and a muff! Would that make them a 'mollar'?"
"How about since they cover your face too, a 'mug rug'!" They both laughed, and taking his hand in hers, they rode side by side toward the old trail.

****

"Gramp! Hey, Gramp!" Michael stood in the doorway of his grandparents' bedroom wearing his cowboy pajamas and moccasin slippers. He knew to wait until he was sure Gramp and Gram were awake before he sprung onto their bed between them.

"Well, hello there, you early riser you!" John Moore smiled as the boy entered the room. Preparing for what he knew was Michael's next move; he and Mary made room between them in the big feather bed. As soon as he knew the landing spot was properly prepared for him, through his laughter he shouted, "Incoming!" With the grace of a deer, he leaped from mid-room through the darkness, and with precise timing of his aerial twist, managed again to astonish his grandparents as he landed between them; sitting against the feather pillows. "Just how do you do that, young man?" John often recalled how Samuel would wake them the same way. He reached over to Michael and hugged him. "I don't suppose there might be a hug in there for me too!" "Oh, Gram, of course there is!" Michael smiled as his grandmother embraced him.

---

[12]   Carhart is a brand name for a line of outdoor wear.

Mary Moore had been reserved in her opinions as to Samuel and Sara riding out for the herd. It was not only the pending weather systems; it was that they would not have the added help from the ranch hands. If she had learned anything from forty-five years of marriage to a rancher, it was to have all the help possible when it came to moving those darned stubborn cows! Knowing they were in *that* Pass was unsettling to her.

Angling Pass was well known for being unforgiving to those who crossed through the cascading canyon walls of unstable shale slate. Many a traverse through the Pass had led to loss of cattle, she shuddered as she recalled the stories John had told her from his youth when the Pass avalanched while the wranglers were still in the North Grazing Lands; retrieval of them was a somber impossibility, and they all perished in the winter snow. There had been a few cattle that made it through the Pass just moments before the snow slid. When the men did not return, the search party managed to drive the cattle home in the Great Blizzard of '42. It is said the souls of those men still cry when it snows.

Mary knew to keep her concerns to herself as the pride of the rancher would not permit a 'doubting.' She had let it be known that she would have been more in agreement had they had more help. She had faith in Samuel as a horseman and a cattleman and his love for Sara. She knew he would never place her in harm's way. Yet she still had grave misgivings as to their ride out this morning.

*****

Still hand in hand, Samuel and Sara approached the tree line. "The good news is we got to the old trail!"
"And the bad news?"
"Bad news is I saw paw prints." Sara quickly looked around and peered as well as she could through the falling snow into the trees. She had had enough of the wolf back in the pasture; Jazzy had had enough too. The mare did settle down soon after they were heading back to the trail, and Sara was hoping for her to stay that way. She knew the horse would be able to feel her concerns so she tried her best to keep them at bay. "Steady girl . . ."
"Which 'girl' you trying to convince?" Sam could hear the apprehension in Sara's voice as she talked to her mare. "No need to fret yet, we can't even be sure it is the same wolf."

"Oh, that makes me feel better; could be more than one!"

"Ride, Sara, just ride." He took her hand and gently kissed it. He placed her hand over his heart and smiled. Placing it back on her thigh, they each took up their reins, and with a quickened step, they moved forward into the woods.

The trees were heavily laden with the newly fallen snow and dodging the lowered limbs became increasingly more difficult as the day progressed. There were deer trails recently used as the hoof impressions had yet to refill with snow. Samuel took notice of a set of tracks that gave way to his thinking that the deer had an injury. Probably taken down by a wolf and managed escape. He knew the relief would be short-lived, as soon the wolf would return to reclaim the quest. Just the thought of a wolf nearby was unnerving to him. He knew that Sara was worried, and truthfully, the horses and Roy were tiring; response and reaction would be compromised for all the animals, dogs included. He and Sara rode in silence as they made their way on the trail. The dogs had ceased their 'play' and had resolved to stay 'at heel.'

"Sara, look at Bandit, do you think he seems a bit 'off' on the right forepaw. I sure hope he hasn't got frost bit." Samuel reined in Tonk and patting his knee, Bandit quickly was on his hind legs with forelegs on Samuel's calf. "Well, I don't suppose the snowballs he is sporting in his feathers are helping matters. Try getting them loose, and we'll see if he gets better. We need him, and if we have to turn back, well, we just can't, Samuel. You know that."

Not that he wanted to, Samuel took off his gloves and held the dog's paws between his hands to warm the snow that had accumulated within his toes and pads. When the last of the snow had melted, Bandit voiced his happy bark, wagged his tail, and as if there had never been a problem, ran to catch up with Rex. "There you have it, Mr. Moore! Once again you are the hero."

"I wouldn't quite call me a hero . . ."

"Ask Bandit; he will agree with me!"

"Just as long as you think I am *your* hero." Samuel smirked as he reached up to kiss Sara.

He felt the wind pick up as the snow began to fall with increased intensity. He had not told Sara that when he was in the barn, there had been a revision to the newscast. He had told her that the weather was going to hold off, and yet it seemed as though it was actually going to come in sooner than originally expected. He truly thought that they would be able to have the herd on the move before the front came through. The weather was changing and changing quickly; he was beginning to doubt their arrival to the herd in time.

The continuous blowing of the snow accumulated more rapidly than the original prediction they heard on the newscast earlier that morning. The horses were tiring quickly, and the dogs were beginning to show sign of fatigue. They were riding into the wind. Slowly leaning forward, Sara patted Jazzy's neck, and in a soft whisper spoke to the mare. "Well my girl, this is turning out to be a bit more contrary than we thought! Are we still up for it? Sure we are! This team hasn't been defeated yet and we're not going to be now!" Each step became more labored as the mare worked her way along the hidden trail, as if she understood Sara; she nickered and tipped her head to enable the meeting of eyes by the two of them.

"I swear, Sara, that mare knows what you tell her! It is like she understands your words and your movements! I have been a cowboy all my life and have never seen the likes of the bond that you two share!"

Samuel smiled as he recalled the hours he had sat on the top rail of the fence watching Sara as she 'executed' those fancy 'transitions' and all the other terms she used for her Dressage exercises. Dressage—he just could not understand it, but he sure liked watching her ride, and Jazzy seemed to enjoy it too.

"I'd be jealous, but I know for a fact that I kiss better!" "That you do, Samuel . . . that you do!"

The hours of fighting the fierce winds seemed an eternity. Slowly, the miles toward Anglin Pass were lessening. To themselves, Sara and Sam recited silent prayers in hopes of a reprieve from the weather. Sara recalled with a smile the intimate morning shared beneath their quilts. Samuel turned toward her and with a cold stutter. "We're j-j-just s-s-s-south of H-Hobbs Ridge. I can s-s-see the outline of R-R-Rob's R-Rock." He hoped she had understood him. He looked back and could see only a hunched figure blanketed by snow in the trail behind him. He had decided to ride the lead to try to shield her from the gusts as much as he could.

Hobbs Ridge. It was there that the Slide of '42 had fallen. Everyone in the state knew about Hobbs Ridge. Local history told that back in the

1920s, Rob Hobbs had settled there; he soon became known to all as the "Hermit of the Ridge." The stories of the old men in town say that he died in that perilous snowslide when so many of the ranchers lost herdsmen and cattle. After the avalanche cleared way, the Ridge had changed formation and with little use of imagination an onlooker could nearly make out the profile of a man's face seemingly carved into the rock—a face with a downtrodden look, as if it was of Rob Hobbs himself. A man lost in a travesty and with no loved ones to grieve for him. Samuel shuttered at the thought of riding through there. Not that he was superstitious, but it was hard not to hear the moaning of the trees and the cries of the winds in the rocks as you traveled through the Pass. There was not an explainable reason other than instinct to define the behavior of a horse while in the Pass. There was always fright. No matter the horse, there was always fright. All who ride through there, as if in respect to those lost, fall silent, unable to speak.

"Please, God, as we travel through this night, let us be in your arms of love. May you know our need. May you ride beside us and care for us. And, Lord, please give us all strength and wisdom so we may achieve that what we have set forth to do. Lord, you have blessed me with the finest woman I could have hoped to love me. Please, Lord, I pray for her safety above all others. And, Lord, may the travels past the Ridge in Anglin Pass be safe and swift. Lord God, I pray to you in Jesus's name. Amen."

Sara raised her head just enough to have sight of Samuel riding just ahead of her. Walking to his side, Roy leaned into the wind with head down. His long ears were unable to hold position as the winds whipped them about. She could see the struggle showing in the mule's stride yet his determination was still strong. "Hey, up there! You're riding like an old man!" She tried to keep a light tone to her voice to shield the truth of her concerns. Having noticed that for some time Samuel was not his usual talkative self; actually, it alarmed her a bit that he was riding hunched over the saddle horn. "You OK?" No answer. She did not realize that he was in prayer to God for their safety. Had she known, the fears she felt clear through would have been even further justified.

Always the 'upbeat' one, Sara thought it a good time to take notice of Roy's ear situation; perhaps that would enliven Samuel a bit. "You think I should patent an ear muff for Roy too? He just can't seem to decide which way to turn them to get them out of the wind!" Samuel smiled as he heard the words. Sara's voice was soothing to him and she always knew when he needed a good dose of jest. "And just how do you propose to muff those muley ears. Huh?"

"I'll use 'mule slippers' you know, like the ones your dad wears. Sew them together and call them 'mears'—no frost fears when your mule wears mears!" It was just the distraction from the situation they both needed—a good laugh to release the pent-up apprehension they both were harboring.

"Mrs. Moore, I do declare you have yet again devised a much needed accompaniment for the 'equine inclined'!" "Oh . . . just something else those city folk will know they will just have to acquire! Picture this: A tack store clerk standing with a woman all dolled up in the latest riding apparel trying to convince her that her horse needs Mears to finish the 'look'!" Sara laughed at the image she was creating. Samuel too began to see the amusement. "There's just no end to your imagination, is there, Mrs. Moore?"

"Nope!" He turned his head to look back at her. He noticed Roy's ears blowing in the winds; he was unable to hold back his amusement.

Their laughter shortened to a halt as the sound of tree fall filled the air. Tonk bolted sideways in an attempt to escape the path of the massive Pine that was swaying uncontrollably ahead in the trail. Picking up on Tonk's fears, Jazzy stopped on the forehand, and as Sara was pushed into the forks of her saddle, pain searing in her groin, she saw Tonk lose his footing and his haunches slide down over the trail edge. He was scrambling to regain his footing, unable to find earth under a hoof; he tried to lunge in the air. Samuel was frantically untying the dally rope that held Roy. "I've let Roy go! Catch him Sara!" Tonk tried again to regain his footing, down now on his knees. Samuel knew the only way this would end was not good. He had to get off the horse. He had to let Tonk use his every muscle and all of what strength was still there to get back on the trail.

Why had they come this way? He knew the trail was dangerous even on a good day. Sara had been insistent that they get to the herd quickly. No, he could not place any blame on Sara. It was his decision to ride this Ridge and his alone. She was counting on him to keep her safe and to get them back home. He heard her scream. But Sara doesn't scream while astride he thought to himself. He heard her scream his name again as if she was calling from far away. And then . . . he heard silence.

He had thrown the rope to her. She was trying to maneuver Jazzy to make way for Roy who was approaching quickly. Even the mule felt the urgency of what was transpiring. Sara had never known Roy to be unnerved, and yet now he brayed with an almost mournful tone. Just as she caught the rope, Jazzy slid to the downside of the Ridge, narrowly catching her balance and recovering. As Sara regained her seat in the saddle, the grunt from the horse in the trail not a dozen yards ahead broke the sound of the winds with a piercing cry. Sara screamed as she watched Tonk fall over the edge, unable to regain his footing.

"Samuel!" Her heart pounded so hard she could feel it pulsing against her breastbone. She started to scream again just as the wind blew, as the air sucked into her lungs and the extreme coughing ensued, she felt the tears cascading her cheeks. "Samuel!" The man and horse were falling farther from her sight until soon through the snow, it was impossible to see where they had gone.

As the man and horse began to plummet down the Ridge, Samuel's thoughts were dreamlike. It seemed as though they were falling in slow motion. He could see every downed tree, could feel every rock that his body hit, and he could hear the moans of Tonk, his trusted friend as he too felt the rocks and the logs. Samuel knew his leg was caught in the stirrup; his only hope of survival was to free himself. Yet in the dreamlike sensation, he had no ability to do that what he must in order to survive. He heard Sara's screams, her pleading for him to come back to her. The voice he so loved and had listened to for so many years was fading into the distance. "I love you, Sara" was just a whisper in his mind as he slipped into darkness.

"Oh God, Please make it stop snowing! I can't see where they have gone! I have to help them! Please!" The tears were beginning to sting her cheeks in the cold wind. "Think, Sara, do not panic! Think. Fast, but think!" she was reassuring herself, or so she hoped. The dogs were barking; reluctantly maintaining their positions held at heel. Sara knew they wanted to run after Samuel, but she did not want them to add to the fright of the horse if he was to have any prayers of recovering his hoof hold. She did not know where Samuel was and was hoping that the dogs could help lead her to him. He had been trying to get out of the saddle as they fell over the edge; her every hope was that he was separated from the weight of the horse and the hooves that were no doubt scrambling in the panic-stricken 'flight mode' that a horse resigns to when instinct for survival kicks in. Her husband needed her. She had to find him.

Sara rode farther up the trail until she found the spot where Samuel and Tonk fell; she carved a heart in a tree with her knife to indicate it was there that her own heart went over the edge as she watched them fall. The tree would be the marker should there be a need to return. She could make out a small opening in the woods just ahead that would be a good place to tie Jazzy and Roy while she and the dogs tried on foot to find Samuel. The idea of descending this slope frightened her but not doing so and losing all hope of finding Samuel frightened her more. She had the dogs. They would be her guides. She had to do this. She is a strong woman in spirit and physically. Her heart racing, she dismounted and, in swiftness, did have one of the flashlights securely fastened to Roy's pannier. She knew that he would be the calmer of the two and less likely to bolt if left alone there. Jazzy, well, she had her moments of discontent and was not adverse to let her opinions be known. Sara unsnapped her saddlebags from the mare, placed them in the panniers for safety and then put the horse blanket on Jazzy and the windbreak sheet over Roy.

"Just why is it, Sara, that you insist on packing those darned wind covers. They are horses! They have winter hair! Why I never seen the likes of your 'new ideas' regarding pushing a herd! That Sam of mine loves you, and he seems to think that the new ways are better than the old! My horse never had to wear a blanket out on the trail, he had his own coat!" John Moore was a man of few words and great opinions. Sara thought about that conversation in the barn with him. He thought she over-packed. Even Samuel snickered at the two flashlights. She was glad to have them and the blankets now!

Satisfied that she had tied the horse and mule securely, with the flashlight on high beam; she tied the rope, knife, and a blanket around her waist. She took a hesitant step toward the rifle. "Oh, Lord, please don't make it necessary for me to use this! Please!" She knew she had to take it with her. If Tonk's injuries were too great to survive . . . she would have no choice. And . . . what if the predators got to them before she did . . . She had to be ready for whatever she was about to find.

Sara called the dogs, and together they started down the hillside. The winds had answered her prayers and subsided. Or was it just that she was deeper below the tree tops? The snow seemed to be letting up, and she was able to keep a track on the path of their fall. She heard a wolf howl. "Boys, stay close. This is going to be harder than I thought." The dogs had a good scent and were eager to follow it, as Sara tried to keep up with them.

The snow on her left had blood. She could feel her heart pound faster, and her tears were a reflection of her fear. Was it Samuel's or Tonk's? She saw only hoof prints or at least that is what she thought them to be. A few steps farther and she found a tear of Samuel's coat. She knew then that he had not been able to free himself from the saddle before the fall. "Samuel! Where are you?" Unable to hold back the anguish in her voice, she called out to him in a plea for him to answer.

The terrain was changing to a rockier base, and the downed trees made foot travel difficult. She turned and looked back up the hill to make certain she could still see the light on the mule. Jazzy had ceased her protest of Sara leaving her and seemingly had settled down. Reassured that she herself was not lost, Sara turned back to the down slope and continued to follow the indentions in the snow left behind by Samuel and Tonk.

"Samuel?" There was more blood in the snow under freshly broken branches. She could make out the imprint of what looked big enough to be from Samuel as he finally freed himself from the stirrup. "Samuel?" Rex bolted to the left and came back with a torn boot. He dropped it at Sara's feet and ran back again to where he had retrieved it. Sara and Bandit followed him this time; hearts racing. "Rex, you found him! You found him! Good boy!" Her elation was short-lived as they approached the place where Rex had picked up the boot; there was no sign of Samuel. She could see the disturbance in the snow but no Samuel. In her heartache, she sank to her knees in the snow, bending over to shield her tears from the bite of the cold air, she cried.

She regained her composure when Bandit's cold nose touched her cheek in his attempt to console her. He circled her, all the while whimpering as if he too were weeping. Without notice by either Sara or Bandit, Rex had restarted his quest to find Samuel. Sara heard him bark. "Bandit, I do believe he wants us to follow him." Her legs had weakened from tromping in the snow and climbing over the downed trees, and her lungs ached from breathing the frigid air. She had heard the stories of how a person or an animal could freeze their lungs to a point that they could die. She recalled being told it was very painful and with how she was feeling at that point, she could not help but worry just how much more it would have to hurt before she would be in trouble. "Stop it! Do you hear me! Stop It! It matters not how I feel right now. I have to find Samuel!" Sara pulled her wild rag[13] back up over her mouth as she talked aloud to herself. Strength, she had to keep her strength. "Rex! Where are you, boy?"

Off to the right, she heard another bark. Was it truly from the right or was it an echo off the trees and cliff side distorting the tones. "Rex! Bark again, buddy!" Usually well adapted to sounds in the woods, in her current state of near panic, Sara found herself questioning what she was hearing. As she turned around several times, she tried to focus on her surroundings while she waited for him to bark again.

This time she was certain that it came from the right. With a newfound energy, she and Bandit quickly rose and were in motion toward Rex. She stumbled over a tree limb and caught the toe of her boot as she tried to regain her balance. She did not see the other limb under the snow; and as she fell from the trip over the first limb, her foot snared in the crook of the limbs. Her sudden scream of pain rang out into the silent stand of woods. There was no one there to help her. Rex and Bandit ran to her side and with their muzzles pushed the snow away from her leg, and with precision, they each bit into the second limb and pulled it to the side. She marveled at the assimilation of the two dogs. They were the best dog team anyone could have.

She pulled her leg out of the hold and tried to stand. Pain searing through her leg, she took the first step. "Oh my! Guys . . . we have a situation here! Hang on . . . Don't run off on me now!" Having regained her balance, she looked back again to see the beam of light on Roy. It was fading; she hoped that was due to distance and not battery life. The dogs were back at her side, and as she looked ahead, she could see the ravine. At this point, all she could see was the open span between the sides. She had no idea how deep it was or even how long. She just knew it was there, and her entire body trembled. Her every instinct was warning her.

As she approached the side-drop, she stopped, hoping to hear movement that would indicate Samuel and the horse were still alive. She heard only the sound of her heart and the panting of the dogs. Just a few more steps and she would be at the edge. Each footfall more labored than

---

[13]   The wild rag is the neckerchief folded and tied in such a manner that, if needed, can be pulled up to cover the lower face; used often for dust and weather protection.

the one before, as if in slow motion. She wanted to run, but she couldn't. "Samuel! Samuel! I'm coming! I'm here! You're safe now!" At the edge, she stopped and looked down. There they were. Man and horse; twisted together. Lifeless.

"NOOOOOOOOO!" Screaming and running without notice of the pain still in her leg, she was over the edge and on her way to them. The steepness of short slope went undetected as she leaned back for balance as she ran. The dogs reached them first and started to push the snow off Samuel. Bandit had his nose under Tonk's haunches; he began digging into the snow to relieve the weight of the horse on Samuel's left arm. Rex was digging at the log that lay over Samuel's legs. "Oh God! Please! Please be alive! Samuel!" With no response from him, Sara raised his right arm and tried for a pulse. It was there! Ever so slight, but it was there! Her heart pounding, with a newfound hope fueling an energy she thought was spent, she said, "Samuel! Wake up! It's me, Sara! I'm here!" She and the dogs frantically tugged and pulled on his torso until at last they had him freed from underneath the horse.

His weight was difficult to hold as she raised him to her. With arms around him, she rocked back and forth, all the while kissing him. "Please, Sam, please! Come back to me!" She was having difficulty holding him upright, so she laid him in her lap and continued to rock him and warm him with her closeness, her eyes swollen from the tears as she begged him to awaken. A solitary teardrop fell and landed on his lips. At that instant, she saw his mouth quiver. He was coming back to her; she just had to keep him warm! She had to help him! The dogs seemed to understand, and they too were holding their bodies to him to give him warmth.

"Sara?" She felt the intensity of that moment, the sheer need to have heard and not imagined his voice. "Samuel!" She was barely able to speak through the relief of him waking. "Sara . . ."
"Oh, Samuel . . . my love, my heart." She held his head to her, still rocking gently as if comforting an infant. Her mind racing as she looked around her at the terrain and the falling snow. They had found him, and he was alive. He could sense her weeping, and in a labored whisper, he spoke her name again.

Sara and Samuel huddled together wrapped in the blanket with the dogs at their side. Tonk lay lifeless next to them. The snow was slowing, giving way to a better view of just how far they had wandered from the trail and from Jazzy and Roy. Sara tried to find the flash light beam hoping that the batteries had held out. At last, she saw a faint glow up the hillside. Relief.

"Oh my god . . . How am I going to get you back up this hill?" She knew the question would not be answered by her husband. It was more a question to herself and to her own strength that she was about to truly test. "I have no idea the extent of your injuries, and you can't seem to stay coherent long enough to tell me." Not knowing if he could actually hear her talking to him, she spoke more to comfort herself and to try to mask the rising intensity of fear that was trying to overtake her. Again, looking around, she was acutely aware that they were alone in the woods.

Rex and Bandit had removed themselves from Sara and Sam and were nudging Tonk. "Boys . . . he's gone, the great Tonk's last hurrah was to save Samuel's life. We just have to believe that. We have lost a really good friend and a really good horse today and there is no rightful way to repay him." Overcome with her own grief for Tonk, Sara knew that Samuel too, would be 'broken' from the death of his friend. Samuel was a true cowboy and as such felt a greater bond with his horse than he did most people. There could be no grave for Tonk, and that was very difficult for Sara to accept. He was here in these woods, and she vowed they would return to rename this hillside for the great horse who gave his life to save Samuel.

"Bandit . . . Rex . . ., here boys! Stay here with Samuel while I try to get the saddle off Tonk." She knew that once she did manage to get Samuel back up the hill, he was going to have to ride the mule. The dogs lay next to Samuel as Sara worked on releasing the cinch straps. "Sara?" She could hear the labored effort as he spoke her name. "Yes, Samuel . . ." she went back to him and bent down close as he tried to speak.

"Is Tonk? . . ." Tears cascading her cheeks, she said, "No, Sam . . . he didn't make it." Her heart sank as she saw the pain in his eyes and heard the heartache in his voice. She pulled him close as he wept for his friend. "My saddlebags . . . get my saddlebags, please, Sara!"

"I'll try, Sam, I'll try." She had a difficult time loosening the billets but was able to release them. Moving to the far side of the horse, she took hold of the horn and the cantle and pulled. As Sara freed the saddle the offside[14] saddlebag tore and was wedged under the haunches[15]. She then

---

[14]   The off side of a horse is the horse's right side. The near side is the left.

[15]   The haunches refers to the hindquarters of the horse.

removed the breast collar. She placed the saddle next to Samuel. She could see in his eyes, as he ran his hand over the leather, all the memories he was reliving; her heart knew all too well his despair. "Sara . . . help me up . . . I want to be the one to take the bridle off." That 'Cowboy Code' that they live by . . . Tonk was his horse; he should be the one to take the bridle off for the last time.

Symbolic . . . *Cowboy.*

Sara was in love with a man that was a 'true man' and she knew exactly why he had to get to his horse. She sat next to Samuel; she took his hands in hers, leaning in to kiss him. She stood back up and contemplated just how she was going to get him on his feet. Rex came back with a fine walking stick to help balance Samuel's weight. "Good boy! Rex the wonder dog does it again!" Sara smiled as the dog wagged his tail and nudged Sam. "Darn Border Collies anyway!" Sam gave Rex a pat. With the help of the walking stick, Sam managed to get upright, and with Sara on one side and the aid of the stick on the other, he hobbled to Tonk.

Sam trembled as he stood over his horse. He cared not that he was crying. Sara stood back to let him have his time, knowing that he would never forgive himself for Tonk's death. She knew Samuel needed to say goodbye his way. "Sara, please help me down." She went to him and supported him as he knelt next to Tonk's head. He placed his hand on the strong jowl[16] as Sara backed away. "My friend . . . So long we have been together. You were just a scruffy little colt . . . but it was me to whom you came to . . . it was me that bottle-fed you . . . it was me that put the halter on you the first time . . . I remember the day I saddled you . . . it was July 4 . . . figured if you threw me, I would see real fireworks! But you didn't even buck, not once. You trusted me. You trusted me . . .." Sam spoke with a broken heart, and Sara could not cease her weeping. "You have always trusted me, and you have been more friend and partner than any cowboy could hope to have. I've heard it said that each man has one great horse in his lifetime and maybe a good one or two, my friend, you were the greatest! I feel as though I have let you down. I cannot begin to tell you how sorry I am. I . . . Oh, Tonk . . .."

---

[16] The jowl is the large jaw area of a horse head.

Sam retrieved his pocketknife from his jeans pocket; taking hold of Tonk's forelock[17], he slid the blade through the jet-black tuft of hair, all the while sobbing. Sara had anticipated this and held out a small baggie that had been previously been filled with trail mix. "Here, Sam . . . put his forelock in this." "Thank you, Sara." Sam placed the hair in the bag and tucked it into his inner vest pocket. "I know just what picture to place this in the frame of . . . remember Tonk . . ." He had his hand on the horse's neck, running his fingers through the mane. "Remember when Sara gave me the shiny new saddle . . . Remember how you snorted at it . . . even you thought it was something special! You sure were proud to sport it about though! Sara took a great photo of us in our 'finery' as she called it! She said we 'showed a good turnout' . . . Yeah, she uses all those highfalutin terms . . . we just knew that we looked good!"

"Good choice, Sam, good choice." Sara spoke softly, leaning forward and putting her hand on his shoulder in comfort.

Placing one hand on the bit and one hand on the crownpiece, Sam slowly removed the bridle, taking extreme care as he pulled the bit out of Tonk's mouth. "Last time, buddy, last time . . . be free my friend . . . Find your mother . . . she is sure to be waiting at 'the Gates' for you . . . you are with God now, and He has the finest horse in his 'forever pasture.' I have liked you and I have loved you my friend. I have needed you, and I have wanted you. I *will* see you again." Sara watched as he fell over the neck and embraced the horse. She knelt next to him, and with her arms around him, the two wept.

Sara heard Jazzy whinny, followed closely by Roy's bray. Startled, Sara picked herself up from her kneel and feeling the lack of blood flow in her legs, nearly fell back down again. She had not realized the length of time she and Sam had been there with Tonk. "Sam . . . we need to go. It is getting late, and the woods will be darkening soon. Jazzy is getting nervous up there. I can hear it in her whinny." Sam, still with arms on Tonk, knew she was right, but he did not want to leave Tonk there. "Oh, Sara . . . to have to leave him here for the carnivores and the birds just is so wrong! I hate it!"

"Sam, please understand what I am going to say and know how and why I say this . . . Tonk's body is here, yes, but his spirit and his soul are in

---

[17]   The forelock is the tuft of hair between the ears that flows over the face.

heaven. He is safe there. Never to be hurt or feel pain. He is already running with his mother. My parents I am sure have helped him already adjust. He is at peace and will be with you always and is patiently waiting . . ."

"I know Sara, I know. But it is just so hard."

His attempt to stand was hindered by not only by the length of time in the kneeling position, but he had lost a great amount of blood in the fall and that too was posing a problem. Sara went to him to support him as he stood. "Gee, we look like a couple of old people" she said, with an attempt at breaking the solemn mood. She knew that for Sam to make it up the hillside, he was going to have to focus on physical strength that she was in doubt of being there. He would need to pull his mind away from Tonk and concentrate on his need to get back to Jazzy and Roy. Rex and Bandit had stayed their distance while Sara and Sam were with the horse, now they were awaiting cues for the trek up the hill. Rex brought the walking stick to Sam and then ran ahead to catch up with Bandit.

"The saddle . . . how are we going to get the saddle?"

"I got it Sam . . . it might be a bit scratched by the time we get to the top, but I got it! If you can get the bridle, we'll be good." She handed him the bridle and he placed it over his neck, keeping his hands free to hold the stick and to balance himself if needed. She had the rope around the horn, under the saddle, and back on the horn, acting as a sling so she would have her hands free. Starting out with the saddle on her back, she looked at Sam and noticed he was wincing a bit as he walked. "I shall forever be more understanding of Jazzy when she is under saddle!" Sara smiled toward her husband. "Hate to tell you this, Sara, but Jazzy holds a saddle way better than you do!" She was glad that he was trying humor and smiled back at him.

It was just minutes into the climb that Sam knew something was wrong. "I need a little rest here, Sara." She looked over to him and noticed the grimace in his facial expression. With newly pounding heart, she replied, "Are you OK, Sam?" He did not want to worry her any more than she already was, and his reply he feared was not as convincing as intended. "Yes, just taking inventory on the aches and pains from the fall down the mountain. It seems I have a few good bruises coming on." "Well, as tough as you Moore men are, those bruises don't have a chance at taking you down!" Though she was trying to be positive and keep the spirit up, it was difficult as she watched him slowly kneel and then turn to sit on a downed tree trunk. Had he really been truthful with her or was he just trying to placate the situation? His face and body language falsified what he was saying to her. She called the dogs and together they rested.

"The wind is picking back up Sam; we really need to get to Jazzy and Roy."

"You are right, help me up and we will get up this darn hill!" Lifting under his right arm, as she knew the left had been under the horse, she could feel the looseness in the ribcage. "Sam, your ribs are broken aren't they?" "You want the truth?" She looked at him with dampening eyes. "Give it to me straight, Mr. Moore, what are we looking at here as far as injuries . . . I want details, do you hear me. Details. Internal and external. This is not the time or place for heroics"

"No hero today, that is for sure! Yeah, several ribs are broken, and my left shoulder is darn near dislocated. Got a hell of a pain in my left chest, right here." He pointed just below his heart. "Left ankle twisted in the stirrup I think, and the left knee is headin' west. Other than that, I guess I am OK . . . it's just this pain in my chest, and it is hard to breathe." He was relying on the walking stick and grabbing branches for support and balance as he made his way up the hill. Sara labored under the weight of the saddle, but she knew Sam's hardship to be far greater than hers. She shifted positions often and several times had to set the saddle down. Tiring rapidly, she pushed herself upward as darkness was approaching and soon the night predators would be lurking. Sara wanted to get back up to the trail, get to Jazzy and Roy and ride far away . . . far away from the place that nearly took her Sam and did take Tonk. The realization of all that had just occurred was settling in, and the feelings of desperation to be away from here were starting to become consuming.

Jazzy whinnied when she heard them approaching the trail. Rex and Bandit ran to the horse and mule as if they wanted to be the first to tell of the rescue. The flashlight dangling from the pannier had dimmed, but to Sara and Sam, it was a beacon of hope. They had made the climb despite all odds being against them. Out of breath and energy, they both slumped onto the level trail. "What are you doing, Sara?" Sam asked when he noticed Sara on her back moving her arms and legs. "Making snow angels . . . It was by God's grace we made it up that hill, and we both know the angels have been on our shoulders." "So true, Sara . . . so true." He knew it would take more than snow angels for him to continue to the herd; the pain in his chest was intensifying, and it was becoming more and more difficult to breathe. The thought of riding Roy was unsettling as well.

"Here I am again, Lord, talking to you . . . praying to you . . . Please watch over Sara and give her the strength she will need to push toward Anglin Pass. Keep Jazzy sound[18] Lord . . . we lost Tonk . . . she just couldn't handle anything happening to her mare too. Please God . . . hear me. Hear my pleas to you that this pain in my chest will subside and that I will be able to help Sara. Lord, I do not know what all is amiss in this body of mine, but what I do know is that I hurt bad and that scares me. I need the strength to hide my anguish from Sara and to get done the work that lies ahead of us so we can return home safely. We need to get that herd in and she can't do it alone. Please, I pray to you . . ."

"Sam, Sam . . . you OK?"

"Just having a little chat with God."

"I understand." Sara started to look over the panniers trying to decide just how to saddle the mule and keep the storage as well. She had been thinking about this on the climb up the hill. She concluded that there would need to be sacrifices as to parcels in the packs if they were to be tied to the cantles of the saddles. Not just for the sheer size but for the weight distribution as well. Jazzy and Roy were already demonstrating fatigue, and the added weight was going to be a burden they were not prepared for and as Roy was not often ridden and had in the past expressed his opinion on the matter, dispersing the added weight had to be of an acceptable change for the mule. "Here, Sara, let me help you." She noticed his trouble getting up and walking to her. "Are you OK? I mean it, Sam, be truthful. I need to know what we are facing here. Do we need to go back? 'Cuz I will go back. The herd is not worth risking your life if you need medical attention." He could see the concern in her eyes and the quiver of her lips as she spoke. He knew she was scared. Scared for him and scared for them out there so far from home . . . alone . . . he could read her face . . . she knew whatever he was about to tell her that it was up to her to see the ride through. She was in the lead now whether she was ready to be or not.

They rearranged the saddlebags and tied the pannier packs to the saddle; the braces of the panniers folded inside. Sam looked at their workmanship and shook his head. "Damn! Woman, you sure figured that bumble out!" Sara looked over her shoulder and said, with a forced smile, "And you had doubts?"

"Nope, not at all! You never cease to amaze me Sara."

---

[18] A sound horse is not lame or injured.

"Put me on 'Deserted Island' . . . no, better yet this seems to be more like 'The Amazing Wilds . . . I don't want to eat worms though, OK?"

"No worms, huh . . . then I guess you're cooking tonight! Besides, I couldn't find a thing now that you repacked it all!" With all that had happened and so quickly, he nearly forgot about the candles and wine glasses in his saddlebags. "Sara . . . where are my saddlebags?"

"In the left pannier . . . you and those bags . . ."

Sam smiled, as he knew that after today, they were both going to need the candles and wine. The pain in his chest was not subsiding, if anything it was getting worse and more often he felt a sharp spasm along with it. He put his fist to his chest and pushed hard on his sternum. Sara turned just at that moment and saw the anguish in his expression. "I love you, Samuel Moore!" She could not help herself from the feeling of dread that again had come over her. "I love you too, Sara Moore"

In the waning light of evening, they were heading north. Sara took the lead position, as Roy was a follower. "Sam . . . we're passing Robb's Rock on our right, we ought to be past the Ridge soon." She waited for his response, and when it was not audible, she turned to see him slumped over the saddle horn. "Sam!" She halted Jazzy, which in turn set the stop on Roy, and with a sudden jerk, Sam sat up. "You are scaring me, Sam." She was unable to hide the fear in her voice. "Sara, I just fell down the face of Hobbs Ridge, I believe I am entitled to a few aches and pains and maybe a quick nap or two while old Roy and I follow you." His shortness and tone of voice surprised her. "I'm sorry, Sara, I didn't mean to be so hard. Yes, I do hurt, but we have to get the herd, and the boys will help you and I will do what I can. I'm not thinking that Roy here is going to be much of a ranch hand through this ordeal, but if he gets my butt home that is all I can ask for."

Sara knew that Sam's 'Cowboy' had been injured as well. You cannot really call it 'ego' as it is a way of life—his beliefs, his manners, his mannerisms, his actions as well as reactions. How his heart hurts, and how it rejoices and what makes it do either. How he loves his family, his need to protect all that he loves and cares about . . . his true nature. The physical injuries were hampering there was no doubt about that, what concerned Sara was the emotional state that Sam was falling into as the realization that he would not be the lead on the drive and that his assistance would be limited at best. She knew she had to 'buck up' and just do what needed to be done. The sooner they got the herd, the sooner they would get home and to a doctor. She had to be his 'rock' for the next couple of days; she just had to be. She was petrified.

Just ahead, she saw the high cave. With a shudder from the cold, she tried to speak. "Sam . . . Sam? We are nearly to the cave. Do you think we should make camp here tonight? Sam?" She looked behind her, and again, he was slumped over the saddle horn. Slowly he raised himself just enough to tip his head and reply. "Please, Sara, yes, let us make camp here." Sara heard the anguish in his voice. In a low murmur, she asked God to see their plight and have mercy on this fragment of 'Drive Riders'. The wind was again howling; they reached the mouth of the cave as the snow fell with a greater force.

Jazzy hesitated as Sara tried to ride her into the cave. The mare's snorting and balking at the scents of previous inhabitants left no doubt in Sara's mind that a bear had been there recently. She saw the scrapes on the trees just outside and the scat[19] on the cave floor. "Jazzy . . . Easy there, girl . . . we really need to rest here tonight. The weather outside the cave is too severe for you to stay out there. You will be safe and warm in here with us . . . Really . . ." Patting the mare's neck, she was not sure whom she was trying to convince. To both Sara and Sam's surprise, Roy had no hesitation at entering the cave, and with his influence Jazzy gingerly entered.

Sara pulled the rope from Roy's pack and tied it between trees at the cave opening to prevent Jazzy and Roy from leaving the cave. She had enough length to cross twice. "We need a fire . . . soon. Stay here, Sam, I'll be right back." The handsaw John had given her as a gag gift years back was always in her saddlebag; she smiled, as she again needed it. He had laughed as she opened it and said it was her 'little girl' saw. Sara cut several downed limbs and dragged them to the cave. Sam had arranged a rock ring for the fire. "Sara . . . I am so sorry . . ." His voice was faint. "Sorry for what?" "That I cannot be of more help to you." She heard the pain as well as saw it. "You just rest Sam . . . as you yourself said you fell down a mountain today. I think you are entitled to a reprieve on the workload."

"I love you, Sara."

"I love you too, Sam."

The horses were standing together on the west wall of the cave as she finished building the fire. Jazzy had settled and Roy was already dozing.

---

[19] The scat is the fecal elimination of a wild animal.

Sara noticed that Sam was fading in the warmth of the fire. "Hold off that falling asleep Mr. Moore until I get the bedroll, OK?"

"You had better hurry, Mrs. Moore! You get that bedroll, and I won't want to sleep!"

"It just don't matter how bad you hurt does it?" She laughed.

"Nope!" She retrieved the bedroll, and as she returned to him, she could see he had already fallen asleep. Sara carefully placed the blankets next to him and gently nudged him into a rollover; when he was on the oilcloth and the base blanket, she lowered the quilt. "Sleep well my love. Lord knows that you need it. I love you. We will get this herd home, we will. I promise you."

She wept as she stood up and returned to Jazzy and Roy to unsaddle, brush up a bit, and set the well-deserved feed out for them. She did not like the direct ground feeding; the pans had been one of the sacrifices when she repacked. "Sorry, guys, as hungry as you are, I am sure you won't even care." Sara placed her right hand on Jazzy's neck and her left on Roy's. "If you had any idea of how thankful I am to you two, Jaz . . . you did a lot of growing up today-- and, Roy, thank you so much for accepting Samuel as a rider. I know you aren't too keen on being ridden, and you really came through today. This is not going to get any easier tomorrow. That wind is really kicking up out there. We'll be safe tonight." Jazzy nickered as Sara set the feed on the ground. "All we can do now is hope Samuel sleeps well, the weather clears and the herd cooperates."

She returned to the fire and stood there; eyes befallen on the man she loved and his two faithful dogs seemingly sitting as a sentry between Sam and the outside world. "Boys, you lookin' for this?" Setting their kibble next to them, they greedily ate the meal.

Slowly, so as not to disturb him, she snuggled beside Samuel. She was cold and hungry, but he was warmed and asleep, and she thought that was more important. They would wake and have a good meal before heading out. Sara draped her arm over Sam, drew herself to him, and as she drifted off, a tear fell when she heard the rattle in his chest and felt the difficulty he had breathing.

"Sara? Sara? You need to wake up." She opened her eyes and smiled at him. She was just so happy that he was still alive, she didn't hear the tone of his voice. "Good morning, handsome!" "Good morning to you to my love . . . look outside."

Sara turned toward the opening, and as she did, she realized the urgency of his voice. Close to a foot of snow had fallen overnight. "Well, the good thing is the sun is shining today! How do you feel this morning, Sam?"

"Hungry!"

"Me too! Stoke the fire and I will get cookin'!" She set a bit more feed out for Jazzy, Roy and the dogs. "They will have a good workout today, hope they're up to it!"

"If the snow depth decreases by the time we get to the Pass, we just might be able to reach the North Grazing Lands by nightfall". Sam could feel the pain in his chest deepening with each breath. His ankle had swollen in his boot and the shoulder was just plain 'cold'. A night on the cave floor had not helped his injuries. His 'will' on the other hand, was steadfast. He was determined to see this ride through. He had to. For Sara.

They ate their breakfast without conversation, listening to the sounds of the animals in the cave with them and the waking of nature outside the cave. An occasional smile shared beween them.

They had done this so many times that the routine was smooth. Sara repacked the cookware as Sam doused the fire. He had planned so well to every detail how he had wanted their night to be. The feeling of dread was overwhelming. "Sam . . . you have a really strange look about you. Are you sure you are OK?" "I am, Sara. I am. Just doesn't seem right to have had this whole cave to ourselves . . . and I fell asleep." His attempt to be jovial played on Sara's heart. It was true, they both enjoyed camping and the togetherness of the shared sleeping bag. She sensed the anguish of a lost night of loving and the pain of injuries together in each word he spoke. "I suppose, Mr. Moore, we can always return to this cave. I think it just might be willing to wait for us. Just one request . . . maybe when the weather isn't as bad?" "Oh yeah, like when Mama Bear wants to have her cubs! Why, there may be a far back sub cave we don't know about, and she just might be in there right now!" "Oh, Sam . . . shush about that . . . you don't want Jazzy thinkin' there's a possibilty of a bear in here with her, do you?" "Would that be worry on her part or yours my dear? Huhhhhhhh?" Sara brushed her hand in the air to him. "Before you get *her* all worried . . . I'll saddle our trusty steed and steedette. Meet me at the front door of our lovely abode and we'll ride out into the sunrise"

As he walked to the mouth of the cave, he felt the pain in his ankle increase. Bearing weight had become an issue. He hoped that in the stirrup he would be all right. Pulling himself into the saddle was not a burden as he had anticipated. Sara removed the rope barricade and took a last look at the fire ring to be sure it was safe to leave. "Mount up!" At that, the dogs were there at attention awaiting departure. They seemed to know what those words meant, and they would not be left out of the ride! Sara swung her leg over Jazzy and settled into the saddle. She looked over to Sam and saw the faraway look in his eyes again. "Talking to God again? Might be a good thing if you were!" "Nope, just watching you mount that horse, my dear." She smiled.

Looking back at the barren cave, Sam reached for Sara. "You did good." He pulled her to him and kissed her. Those three small words to her were the biggest words she had ever heard. He was proud of her. She smiled.

It was good to feel the sun's warmth as they rode toward Anglin Pass. The snow was deep but light enough that maneuvering through it was not too hampering for the animals. The dogs were enjoying chasing the snowballs that flew from the hooves, and Jazzy and Roy had settled into a steady gait.

The pounding in Sam's chest was intensifying. He found himself short of breath with regularity. "We need to rest a minute, Sara." He was holding onto the saddlehorn, something Sara had never seen him do. To her, he was truly a cowboy in every sense and description. A memory from the rodeo at the Brandon Fair the summer after they married flashed in her mind. She smiled remembering that last Saddle Bronc ride when he won the competition. Eight seconds . . . ten . . . fifteen, and he finally dismounted Big Ben. The crowd stood up and cheered his ride. The announcer yelled into the microphone : "Now *that's* the way it is done, folks!"

"Sara? Sara . . . we need to rest." She knew that he meant *he* needed to rest; they had not been riding but for a couple hours. How could she agree with him and yet not wound his pride?

"Yes you are right. We don't want to tire Jazzy and Roy in the snow." She could see the relief in his eyes as he thought to himself that she was looking at the sense of a rest for the animals. She knew she had shielded her fears well. It was the second longest thirty minutes of her life, standing there seeing the pain on his face and in every slight movement his body made. She could not hold back the visions of his fall down the mountain . . .

"With the wind howling and the cold sinking in to my bones, I should think that I would not declare this a sight of greatness and yet it is . . . it really is!" They stopped at the edge of the North Grazing Lands. The ride through the Pass was slow, and fatigue was apparent for all. Sara reached over for Sam's hand and smiled. "We made it." "Yes, we did, Sara. And all because of you."

The snow was deep and the cattle were pawing the ground in hopes of finding grass. "They have been hungry a while, I hope they have the energy for the Drive home."

"Headcount time. You start on the left, I'll start on the right. We'll meet at the bunch with the 'bossy'cow standing there. Cows only . . . no calves right?" Sara pointed at the big black cow that seemed to be the boss now for several years. "Bossy Cow . . . still can't remember just why you named her that . . ." He was snickering as he spoke. "Count, Mr. Moore, count."

"Oh yeah, now I remember . . ." He squeezed her hand ever so slightly.

"One hundred ten," Sara stated. "One hundred twenty-five," Samuel added. They looked at each other and together wondered just how two riders and two dogs were going to get 235 head of cattle home. Cattle that were hungry and thirsty and not likely to be cooperative.

"We had 350 up here in the Spring. Not good, Sam, not good. Think it was wolves? Weather? Please don't say mountain lions. We have had more than our share of problems already."

"I tend to agree with the wolf and weather theory. We haven't had trouble with the cats for some time now."

Looking down at Rex and Bandit, Sam could see that they had been patiently waiting for their orders. "Look at these guys, would ya! Do they know their job or what!" Sara smiled. They could do this. These dogs were the best herd dogs in the county. Jazzy didn't have a lot of experience pushing cattle but she was starting to show promise, and this would be her greatest test. Roy, he could be a problem as he had never been charged by rogue runners or been in the thunder of hooves. He was always on the 'drag' line in the back with the other pack mules. "Well, here we go!"

"To the Draw, Mrs. Moore! To the Draw!"

"Rex! Bandit! Drive!" With command voiced, the dogs ran toward the herd, silently communicating with each other as they took positions on both sides. They approached the far end and separated, they slowed and lowered their stance. The riders approached slowly; the dogs held their lowered body poistion until the attention of the herd was definite. Sara looked at Sam and rode to Rex on the far side. The cattle were moving in circles as if trying to anticipate the moves of the humans. The bellers of the cows began, and Roy was a bit unnerved at the unfamiliarity of actually being among them. "You OK over there?" Sara yelled over the noise. "Oh yeah . . . just fine . . . no worries . . . he will settle." "You think she bought that, Roy?" he whispered to the mule. Roy flipped his ears several times as if to respond a very clear "no way." Sam reached down to pat his neck. "Time to be one of the big boys, Roy. Time to be one of the big boys."

The cattle moved slowly through the snow toward the draw at the southeast end of the mountain bowl[20]. Sara was pleased that the herd was staying together. A couple ran off at the start, but the dogs had turned them back and had kept a steady pace. Looking over at Sam on the other side, he appeared to be holding his own. "Please, Lord . . . keep your hands on him." She heard the cry of wolves in the distance. She sat up in the saddle knowing the cattle had heard the cries too. This could change the direction in a hurry and they needed to be ready.

"SARA . . .?"
"I heard it too!" The cattle began to run, scattering the herd. Rex and Bandit ran side line. Sam stayed to the drag, and Sara rode to the point. She had to circle around on each side a couple times to help the dogs. Jazzy sensed the urgency and came through for Sara. With the herd secured, Sara kept at the point through the Draw; the cattle followed obediently. Getting as far as the River Bed by night fall was their goal. She hoped there was still water there.

She heard the water before she could see it. She knew the animals were thirsty; the cattle rushed the River Bed in a frenzy. Sam and Sara stood back and watched over the herd. Jazzy and Roy waited as the cattle had their fill and then Sam and Sara pushed the herd up over the river bank. "OK, guys, your turn." Jazzy and Roy lowered their heads to the water to drink. "Well Sam, how do you think it is going so far?"
"We are at the River Bed. Next stop . . . HOME!"
"We've done all right for ourselves, that we have!" They leaned to each other and kissed.

---

[20] The 'bowl' is the area of open land between the foothills of mountains.

The herd had settled in for the night, appreciative of the grass under the snow. Rex and Bandit would work through the night keeping the cattle together. Sam had started a fire, and Sara was looking in the saddlebags for something that she could prepare for a meal. "Sam . . .?"

"Yes . . ."

"So I am trying to find something to eat, and I find wine glasses? Wine glasses! You are a clever one, that you are! Where the heck is the wine?"

"So much for my romantic surprise!"

"Oh, Sam . . ." He remembered the letter in the offside saddlebag. "Sara . . . my saddlebags . . . where are they?"

"They got pretty tore up in your jaunt down the mountain . . . I did manage to get the nearside and the cantle bag, but the offside was under Tonk. Oh! I found candles in your cantle bag! You are the best!" He could hear in her voice the rejuvenation of her spirits, and yet at the same time, he was downhearted knowing that the letter was forever lost with Tonk in the base of a ravine.

After a cold night of restless sleep, they woke to the rising of the sun. Rex and Bandit heard them wake; with wagging tails came to them in hopes of breakfast. "Good boys, that is what you are and you shall have some treats!" Sara bent down to pet them, hands filled with kibble. Bandit jumped on her and pushed her over all the while wagging his tail and trying to 'kiss' her. She began to laugh, Sam walked over to see what the commotion was about and received the same greetings from both dogs.

"Everybody likes your vittles darlin', everybody!" Sam laughed at the sight of the dogs and his wife on the ground all twirled together. "Um . . . how 'bout the man folk around here . . . do I get to eat?" "You feel up to setting grain for Jazzy and Roy?" Sara noticed his coloring was a bit off and his eyes looked almost hollowed. Hoping it was just from the cold night, she tried not to convey her concerns to him. "Sure do." Sam had just a slight hesitation in his response. The pain in his chest had not ceased. He could feel a heaviness not there yesterday. The ankle and the shoulder were no longer of concern. He had gotten used to the annoyance of those injuries. It was his heart and chest that caused him concern. Breathing was more labored, and he felt sluggish this morning. "I'll get the fire stoked and get coffee while you feed." "Good plan, my love, good plan" Sara could hear in Sam's voice that he too was aware of a difference in him.

Sara turned to the fire, reaching down for a stick. She could see from the corner of her eye Sam walking toward Jazzy. One faltering step, then another. Her attention now solely on her husband, Sara was locked in her stance as he clutched his chest and his knees buckled. He was down. "Sam!" Sara ran to him. He was on the ground staring up at her. She fell to her knees and cradled him to her. The dogs were there without her knowledge of their arrival. "No! No!" She began to cry as his eyes stared back at her. "No! please, God! No!" She held his head to her. Kissing him and crying, she could hear a slight moan. Raising her head so as to see his face, her tears fell on his cheeks, and she heard him softly whisper: "I love you. You have been the greatest love in my life. God has blessed me for eternity. Find love again, Sara. Find love. Do not forsake yourself for me. Michael . . ." his breath and voice fading . . . "Michael . . . tell him I love him and tell him how proud I am of him."

Shaking and through her tears, Sara held him to her again. "My love, my life." In that moment, she felt a heaviness in him. He was gone. She sat back from him just enough to see the death in his eyes. Slowly, she reached for him and closed the eyes of the man she loved. Closed them for the last time. She had looked into those eyes in love and in trust for so many years. She fell against Samuel and lay across his chest. Bandit and Rex lay beside her as she wept.

She did not know how long she had been there when she heard the cattle begin to shift. Bandit jumped to his feet and ran toward the herd followed closely by Rex. Sara had cried so hard and so long that her vision was altered. Was that a figure she saw approaching? She swept the tears from her face, and she was again trying to focus on the reason for the dogs to be barking. With the clearing of her vision, she could see a lone rider. Sara rewiped her eyes; the only plausible explanation was a mirage. Why would there be a rider out here now? She waited as the dogs approached the 'vision'. "It is a rider!" She was sure of that now. But how? Who? And what about Sam? She looked back at him. "Is this your doing? Is this God's doing? No one would be riding here this time of year unless with purpose. No one. Sam . . . oh, my Sam . . . have you sent him to me?" She cradled him to her. Rocking him so as to soothe herself, she could hear the stranger getting closer to her.

Riding past the herd assuring the dogs he was not a threat; they were at his side as he rode up to Sara. He could see a woman on her knees cradling a man in her arms. Looking at the scene of cattle, the horse and the mule, and only two dogs, he had many questions, none of which he thought the answers would be good.

She turned to him. He recognized the anguish on her face. It was the same as when he held his wife as she and their daughter died in childbirth. He turned away, the privacy of such a moment should not be disturbed. The woman murmored, "He was just walking over to feed Jazzy and Roy." The audibility of the words waning as she spoke them. His heart broke for her. He was at a loss for what to say. Fumbling through his thoughts, all he could seem to manage was: "Do you want me to feed them?" He knew his mistake as soon as he had spoken. Her tears let him know his blunder. "My husband is dead and that is all you have to say? Who are you and where did you come from? How did you know we were here?" Was she angry or thankful? He could not tell.

"Ma'am, my name is Russell. Russell Barnes. It seems as though we meet under poor circumstances. I am truly sorry for your loss." He had removed his hat as he introduced himself, he could see her expression change as he did so. "Well, Russell Barnes, my name is Sara Moore, and this here is my husband, Samuel."

"If it's no too painful for you ma'am, would you like to tell me what happened here?" Sara looked up at him; "Please, call me Sara. It won't due any other way."
"Then by all means, call me Russell".

"Would you help me with him? There is a blanket by the tent we can wrap him in and rope from the saddle. I suppose now is as good as any to get him readied for the ride home."
"Sara . . . you just sit there with him. I can do this for you. You should not have to." Russell walked his horse to the tie-line. "Give your horse some feed as well while you're over there. Looks like he could use a few pounds. You runnin' from somewhere or someone?"

Russell turned away from Sara as he tied his horse on the end of the line next to Jazzy. "Buck, just how am I gonna answer that? This woman has a situation here beyond her doing, she couldn't possibly care about the likes of a stranger and his horse." Checking his holster; he felt the handle of the gun his father had given him when he was fifteen years old. His father, Clint Barnes, the man that had evaded the law for so many years using false names working from ranch to ranch until just before the owners caught on to his game. He had secured many head of cattle through theft and had moved them to a ranch south of the state line. The Moore's ranch had fallen victim to his schemes as well. Though they did not know it, the cattle missing from this herd had not fallen to wolves or weather, they had been driven out by the Barnes's riders. Russell himself had been among the men on that Drive. He looked over at the woman on the ground, and for the first time in his adult life, he felt shame for what he had done.

"Guess you could sorta say both, I suppose." He did not know if he should elaborate or not. If she honored him as a man, she would wait for him to explain himself. If she was of the curious nature she would prod for more details. He thought it best to see what her response would be. He was relieved that she did not push for an explanation.

As they laid the blanket next to Sam and rolled him onto it, she began to tell Russell all that had happened on the ride to that point. He was awed by her bravery and her quick thinking. Never had he known a woman so strong yet so fragile at the same time. His mind was secured as to what he was to do; he would help her to get her husband and this herd home. No longer did he want to be part of his father's tretchery. He was his own man now, and starting today, he was going to prove it. Prove it by doing 'good', by being a better person. This woman before him in grief of her husband yet so strong-willed had changed him. The relief he felt in his heart caused him to smile and gave him conviction that he was at the right place and the right time for her as well as for himself.

"Will Roy be OK carrying a body. I know he is a pack mule, but this is different."

"He carried a calf once, does that count?"

"Let's hope so!"

Sara and Russell struggled to get the blanket roll over Roy's back. She should have been more help but was weakened by the days on the trail and the heartbreak of Sam's death. Russell secured the body and dallied the rope to his saddle horn. "Sara, if it would be all right with you, I will lead the mule. I can ride the dragline, and you and the dogs just do as you did yesterday."

"Thank you. But weren't you heading in the opposite direction? Were you going somewhere?"

"Plans changed, let's leave it at that, shall we?"

"Yes, I think we shall."

She held the reins and took a deep breath. This was going to be the hardest ride of her life. She bowed her head and thought of Michael . . . and John . . . and Mary . . . she would live the nightmare all over again and see the anguish in them. Dread was all she felt. She looked up to see Russell holding Buck's reins. Roy stood waiting patiently in the background behind him. Saying not a word, Russell nodded to her as if to tell her he understood her thoughts.

"Thank you, Russ. I don't know where you came from or where you were going when you got here, but I do know that with your help, the herd, what is left of it, will get home. The clouds are shifting, we best get a move on."

"Mount up!"

Russell watched as Rex and Bandit heeled Jazzy as the trio rode on to the herd. "Buck, those are some fine dogs she has there. You know, I think this is the first time that anyone has placed their trust in me like this. It feels good, Buck, it feels good." He looked back at the roll on the mule. "You were one lucky man, Samuel Moore, one lucky man."

******

"Michael?" Mary was working in the kitchen on a pie she was baking as a surprise for Sara and Sam's homecoming. She knew it had just been a couple of days since they had left, but for her, it was an eternity of waiting and worrying about them out there in the high country this time of year. A good meal and a pie was her 'fix' for just about every worry she could think of. "Michael . . . did you hear me?" "Yes, Gram, I heard you. Is the filling ready for 'quality control'? I've been waiting forever." He said the last few words with length and giggled as he entered the kitchen and came close to hug her. With a swoop of a spoon in the bowl, the smile on his face ensured the filling was just perfect. "You make the best pie, Gram! I bet Dad and Mom are already talking about it! They just gotta know you'll have one for them! They ought to be home today . . . right?" "Yes, they should be. Michael, are your chores done?" "Yup! The barn is all ready. I put extra bedding in the stalls so the horses and Roy can sleep real good. I moved my 'old boy' over to the end stall so Roy can have a bigger one for a couple nights." Mary looked at her grandson and smiled. "They will like that. I am sure they will be tired from the long ride."

"I hear them coming!" John ran into the house forgetting to stomp his boots. "I hear them coming!" Michael ran for the back entry to get his boots and coat on. Mary wiped her hands on her apron, grabbed her coat and hurried to meet up with John. "Thank you, Lord, for bringing them home!" Snow had started falling, masking a clear view of the homecoming. "Mary . . . get the binoculars . . . they are still so far off . . . " She ran to the hallway and retrieved them from the top shelf of the coat closet, nearly slipping on the melted snow from his boots when he announced they were in sight. "This is one time, John, I will not take you to task for not cleaning your boots . . . I hope you know that!" He was not there to hear her; she was so excited about their return she was talking to herself.

Putting the binoculars up to his eyes, John tried to get them in focus. Lowering them with a peculiar look on his face, he put them up again as to reaffirm what he had seen. He looked over at Mary. "What is it, John? What do you see?" "Well, I am not actually sure to be honest. I think that is Sara in the point position, but I don't see Sam or the dogs. There aren't near as many cattle as we had sent up there. Oh wait . . . I see the dogs. They are running the sides. I still don't see Sam." "Give me those things, my eyesight is better than yours . . ." She adjusted them for her sight and looked toward the herd. Moving from side to side of the horizon, she painfully searched for Sam. "They sure are moving slow . . . maybe it is just the snow that makes it seem that way."

Michael rode past them at a full gallop. He was heading toward Sara. "That little dickens had his horse all ready." Mary looked through the lenses to see Michael as he rode wide so as not to turn the herd. "He's at Sara. They have stopped. She is waving him on to point. By goodness, she is having him lead them home!" Mary lowered the binoculars and looked at John. They smiled at each other; not needing words, he moved in to stand beside her. Placing his arm around her, they stood there in silence. Both so pleased with the strength and goodness of their family.

"May I have a look?' As she handed him the binoculars, she kissed his cheek. "Thank you for our family, and thank you for our life together." He smiled and said, "We are pretty good, aren't we?"

Michael had opened the gates between the corrals earlier that day. Having anticipated close to 350 head of cows plus the additional calves, he knew they would need a lot of space. He wasn't quite sure what to do once they got in there, but Grandpa had told him to open the gates, so he did. Now he knew why. There was hesitation in the lead cows to go through the gates. Michael kept the cattle moving and the dogs directed them through the gates. Sara had stayed back, watching the precision of her son and the dogs as the last of the herd was in the corral.

Mary looked to John. "Something is wrong." It was a low tone that John had heard before. He knew his wife was worried. "What could possibly be wrong? The herd is home. They did it. They brought them home." "John, Sara is not coming in. I need those binoculars. NOW!" No sooner had he handed them to her, she had them on her eyes. He could see her start to tremble. Her legs were unsteady. He reached out to steady her . . .

"Mary, what is it? What do you see?"

"That's not Sam."

Three words that pierced through him like a knife. Her tone was now unreadable. He had never heard her speak like that before. She handed him the binoculars, and as he looked through the lenses, she placed her head behind him and, with both arms around his waist, began to cry.

John saw a man he did not recognize leading Roy. Where was Tonk? And then he saw the blanket roll draped over the mule's back. "Oh God! No!" He turned to Mary and held her to him as she wept.

"Michael . . ." she spoke softly. She stood back and spoke again. "Michael, where is he?"
"Still in the corral, Mary, still in the corral."
"We need to have him here with us, John . . . Please call for him." Not knowing just how he could shield his emotions as he called for his grandson, Mary took his hand and placed it on his heart. "Somehow, we have to be strong for him. Sara has no doubt been through a 'hell' of her own out there. I don't know how she has done it, but she has brought the herd and Samuel home. John, she must be exhausted as well as devastated. If ever there was a time that she will need our love and patience, it is now. Michael will need her, and she may not be able to handle that. It will be up to us. Oh, God . . . Please be with us as we try to keep this family together!"

John embraced his wife and held her tightly. A true matriarch. None better. If only she knew that it was her strength and convictions all these years that had made him into the man that stood before her, mezmerized by her courage and fortitude. "I love you, my darling, more than words could ever say."

"I love you too. Please, get Michael here. I need him to be with me when Sara rides in the gate." He let go of her and walked toward the corral.

"Oh, Sara . . . What happened out there? What did you live through? And who is the stranger riding in with you?" Standing as a statue against the wind and snow, Mary softly spoke her thoughts, all the while never taking her eyes off the riders now within a hundred yards of the gate. John and Michael came to stand beside her. She pulled Michael in front of her and placed her arms over his shoulders as if to hold him in.

"Gram, you're shaking, are you cold?"

"Maybe just a little, but you here with me is helping to warm me up!"

"I can't believe they are home! I can't believe they are home!" He tried to break free from Mary's hold and was alarmed at her strength in the pull to keep him to her. She knew he wanted to run to his mother. Mary knew Sara needed to do this her way. There would be so many questions and so many tears . . .

"Sara? How are you doing? What do you want me to do? How can I help you through this? Talk to me. Please." He thought of his favorite movie, *True Grit*. If ever there was anyone that had 'grit', it was Sara. Maybe not like in the movie but in real life she had more 'grit' than anyone he had ever known. "When we get there, would you help me down off my horsr Russell, I'm thinkin' that I won't be steady on my legs." "I can do that for you." They rode the rest of the way in silence.

"Gram? Who is that man? Where is Dad? Where is Tonk?"

"Well, Michael, I guess we will have to wait for your mother to answer those questions now, won't we?"

"Yes, ma'am." He was aware of the falter in his grandmother's voice and that caused alarm to him. He turned around and looked at her. "Grandma, something *is* wrong, isn't it?" She had never lied to him and was not going to now. But how do you prepare a child for this? What could she possibly say that would not break his heart. "Michael, I am sure your mother will tell us what we need to know." It was far from a satisfactory answer to him, and he pushed hard from her hold and was running to Sara before Mary could stop him.

"Let him go Mary, it will hurt no less or more . . ."

John started a slow pace toward Sara and the stranger. Mary was afraid that her legs would give way if she tried to move. It was all she could do to stay standing. Her son was in that blanket roll, she just knew it. Her beloved son was dead. She stood there in that wind and snow, and as the tears slowly fell on her cheeks, she could see the man with Sara helping her off the horse. John had reached them and was holding her. Michael fell to the ground. The unknown man reached to him to help him up; Michael tried to resist and then let him. The young boy went to his mother. John turned to Mary and walked toward her. Her sobs were uncontrolable, and John caught her as she started to fall to the ground. It was true. Samuel was gone.

Sara placed her arms around Michael. "I will tell you everything that happened after we get these horses to the barn. She placed her hand on Jazzy's neck. "Thank you, girl, thank you for getting us home. Time for you to get a good meal and a comfy stall." Sara's words were slow from the cold and her attempt at concealing the truths that she knew were soon to be told. How was she supposed to tell her son his father was gone? And Mary . . . a parent should never feel the pain of the loss of a child. Sara turned slowly to see John holding her as she wept. Sara had truly believed that she and Sam would be together into their elder years. They teased about growing old together. Her heart sank further as she knew now that was never to be. John and Mary stood as one in the wind and snow, holding each other.

"Mama?" Sara slowed her step and turned to Michael. "Yes, kiddo?" I see you looking at Gramp and Gram . . . do you want me to hold you too?" Sara burst into tears and tried to shake her head yes. She fell to her knees, and Michael put his arms around her, drawing her head to his shoulder. He took the reins from her and slowly stroked her hair and back. "Mama, I'm a man now, aren't I?" he asked in a near-whisper. She closed her eyes and held him tightly, thinking to herself this will be the last time that she holds him as a child.

"Mr. Moore, sir . . . um . . . what is it that you would have me do? I know the horses need tended to, and she needs to be with you all. If it would be all right with you, I would sure like to do that for her." John tried to smile at the man standing beside him. He was trying to do right by the situation, and John had no idea of who he was or why he was involved, but he knew Sara trusted him. "Mr. Barnes, I would be very much obliged if you would get the horses to the barn and settled into their stalls. The tack room is to the left of the ties. It doesn't matter which racks you use. I suppose with Tonk gone, you can set your horse up in his stall for now. There is plenty of hay and grain as well." "Thank you, Mr. Moore. Please, call me Russell. I'm kinda thinkin that the way in which we met kinda skips over the formalities."

"I do suppose you are right, son. 'Russell' it is." The name had familiarity about it that John could not arrive at while in the worry for the immediate situation.

Russell walked over to Sara and Michael and gently took the reins from Michael's hand. "I'll get her for you. You stay with your mom." Without a word, Michael let loose of the leather. "Jazzy . . ." Sara cried her name as the mare walked toward the barn. "Oh, Jazzy . . . you are a good girl."

Russell stalled the horses and then looked at the mule. He could in no way ask the grieving family to help him unpack the mule and untie Samuel. He was tired and sore, but the strength was found, and with a bit of strategy he managed to lay Samuel in the straw.

Cold, hungry and worn out, he knocked on the backdoor. "Come in, Mr. Barnes, Russell, come in." He looked at John. "Sir . . . what do we do now? Have you called the police or whoever you should to report the death? I am so sorry to ask . . ." "Before we do all that, we need to talk about what happened. We need to know how our son died. And where you fit into this whole thing." "You are right, we need to tell you everything." Sara had entered the kitchen as the men were talking.

With Michael on her right and Mary on her left, she reached out to them. Taking a hand from both in her own, she spoke slowly and precisely the events of the ride to the herd and the ride home. When she was finished, they were all silent.

Michael had lost his father in a horrific manner, and yet he saw the strength of his mother. He was proud of her.

Mary had lost her son so early in life, yet knowing that he was doing what he loved most with the woman he loved so dearly. How heartbreaking it must have been to hold him as he died, all alone out there. "Oh, Sara . . ." she whispered.

John looked at Russell. "Thank you. Thank you for being there or we might have lost them both."

The man was so stricken, Russ had never seen a man so deflated. When his mother had died, his father's reaction was not at all this intense. He knew that what he saw before him was a family that had honest love and commitment to one another. He himself felt a grief not only for the loss of Samuel's life but also for the family he had left behind—a family that Russ did not know, and yet he grieved for them.

Russ allowed himself a couple hours of sleep and then left in the middle of the night. As he rode out from the ranch, he stopped Buck and turned for a last look at the land and the family home of the finest people he knew. He really didn't want to leave in this manner; stealth was what he knew, it was 'his way'. "She deserves better than this Buck, they all do. I ought not leave without a goodbye. I just can't keep from feeling so bad." He tipped his hat toward the house, turned, and rode away.

The coroner arrived early the next morning. John and Mary were sitting at the kitchen table, trying to explain everything to him when Sara entered the room. "Did you sleep at all, dear?"
"A little, I suppose . . . just out of sheer exhaustion. Michael is still asleep. Is Russell up yet?" Michael had slept with Sara, and Russell set up in the bunkhouse. Mary had offered the guest room, but he felt the family needed privacy, and the bunkhouse was better accomodations than he had had in a long time.

PART 2

Thirteen

"Mom! Mom!" Michael was running from the backdoor nearly tripping over the threshold. "Easy there, young man, it may be your birthday but you still have to take off your boots when you come in!" Smiling, she moved in for a hug. "Have I wished you 'Happy Birthday' yet?"

"Yes, Mom, like a hundred times!" He pulled back from her. "Lasagna! Oh wow! You made lasagna! Can I invite Brent and Charles over? Please?"
"They are on their way."
"You already called them?"
"Of course, how could you have a birthday dinner without your best friends?"
"You're the greatest mom a kid, err ummmm, I mean a 'man' could have!"

"What was it that was so all fire important that you ran in here to tell me?" Sara questioned her son as he pulled his boots off. "You might want to sit down for this . . ."
"Ohhh . . ." She untied her apron, set it on the counter and reached for the captain's chair at the head of the kitchen table. She set herself in and looked up at her very grown thirteen-year-old son. "I'm ready . . . I think." She giggled. "I saw Russell Barnes in town today." Michael didn't know any other way to tell her than to just blurt it out; knowing her reaction to his news was going to open wounds in her heart no matter how he presented it. He thought the best thing to do was to just get to the point.

The smile left Sara's face.

"Mom . . . oh . . . Mom, I really didn't mean to upset you." He put his arms around her and could feel her trembling. "I saw him talking with the Sheriff. I don't know why he is here. Are you OK?" "Yes. I suppose I am at that." Taking a deep breath, Sara pulled herself up out of the chair and slowly walked back to the kitchen counter. Dazed, she picked up the bread knife and began slicing the fresh baked loaf on the cutting board. Michael walked over to her and gently held her hand. "I would like to do that for you if that would be all right?" "But it is your birthday, I will do it." "You are not going to handle a knife while you have that look on your face!" He could see that her thoughts were distracting her from the task at hand, and he was fearful she would cut herself. He smiled at her and tried to laugh just enough to let her know he wasn't really asking her if he could cut the bread; he intended to do so.

Brent and Charles arrived at six o'clock as planned. Sara was finishing the last details of the table when they got there. "Man, Michael you are a real lucky guy! Your mom is the best Lasagna cook around! There was no asking me twice if I wanted to come over!"

"Brent, you do have a charm about you!" Sara placed the pan on the table. "Michael, would you please tell your grandparents that dinner is ready."

"Don't you go eating it all before I get back!" He arm-tagged Charles on his way to the den. "You'd better hurry then!" Charles had his fork readied and tapped his with Brent's in the air. "Hurry up, birthday boy!"

While clearing the table of empty plates and the lasagna pan, Sara paused to look at her son and his friends. She noticed John pat Mary's hand. Sara's heart ached at the knowledge that Samuel was not there to see his son become a teenager.

"Happy Birthday, Michael!"
"Thanks, Mom, dinner was great!"
"I have something for you." He could see her eyes welling as she spoke. Was she still upset about him seeing Russell? He was not sure.

"Michael, it has come to our attention that you are now a bona-fide teenager. Just how that happened I am not sure. Seems like yesterday you were running and jumping into bed with Gram and Gramp! Now look at you! You are taller than I am and darn near as tall as your father. You took on resposibilities far beyond your years and have never let me, or your grandparents down. You have two very good friends in Brent and Charles, and with their help, you havehelped in the management of this ranch and kept our reputation in tact. I could not be more proud. It is time for you to have this."

He could see that she was holding back tears. Why was she always so stubborn about her emotions? She never was before his father died. Gramp told him she lost a part of her heart out there that day when Samuel died in her arms and now she hides the rest. He told him that women are complex, and soon enough, he would try to figure them out. Then Gramp had laughed and told him that he would not dare try to understand Gram; what fun would that be? Michael knew his mother to be a strong woman but wondered if she would ever again 'live' like she did when his dad was alive.

Gramp got up from the table and retrieved a large box from the pantry. "Help me with this boys would ya please!" Brent and Charles jumped up to help the elder. "This is heavy . . . What's in here?" Charles was pretending he was having difficulty moving it. Brent followed suit and together with their antics, they had everyone at the table laughing including Sara.

"Sara, honey, maybe you ought to sit back down." Gram noticed the difficulty that Sara was enduring through the presentation of the gift. Yes, it was the right time for it in terms of Michael, yet Gram wondered if the wounds could, or ever would heal enough for Sara. She watched as Sara slipped back to the chair. "You OK, Mom?" Michael too noticed the body language that told the truth of his mother's feelings. "I'm fine, silly. Open the box already!" She forced a smile. "Mom, don't ever play poker . . . promise me!" He gave her a quick kiss on the forehead and turned toward the box.

Michael stood over the box, stunned at the sight of his father's saddle. "Mom . . ." He turned to his mother and saw the tears she was trying to hold back. Gramp stood behind Sara holding her shoulders. He slowly bent down to whisper in her ear. "You are doing a really good thing here, Sara, a really good thing. And the 'right' thing too. I am proud of you." Sara let the tears cascade her cheeks. Her son was a man and needed a man's saddle, and the only one good enough for him was his father's. Michael walked to Sara, and kneeling beside her, knowing what this meant to her as well as to him, he held her in his arms and sobbed along with her. They were both feeling their reasons for the tears and could also know the reason behind each other's tears. This moment of embrace held mother and son together in their own thoughts of what the gift meant. "Mom . . . thank you." He pulled back away from her and looked into her eyes. "I love you."
"I love you too."

"Did someone say there was strawberry cake?"
"Yes, sirreeeeee! I saw it in the fridge earlier!" Brent and Charles pushed their way past Michael, running to the refrigerator to retrieve the cake. "Just look at those boys, would you! It's like you have three sons. You know that, don't you?" Mary smiled at Sara as the cake was placed on the table. "Yes I do, Mary. Yes, I do!"

Michael looked into the box many times while having his birthday cake; still amazed at the gesture of his mother. He reached to the skirting, knowing that there had been damage to it in the fall down the mountain.

Sara noticed him trying to hide what he was looking for. "They are still there. I had the saddle reconditioned, but I told Gus he had to leave the 'marks' as a reminder of the great man that once rode this saddle. It's all right Michael, you can look for them."

Now standing, he slowly moved his hands over the forks and the cantle, then down the fenders. He noticed the new stirrups. The originals were broken, and the replacements were safety stirrups like the ones his mother now had on her saddle. "Mom, I just don't know what to say . . ." "No need for words, Michael, I can see it in your face. You know you are looking more and more like him everyday." "That he is, that he is." Gramp put an arm around Michael's shoulder, and with a bit of a tug using his other arm, pulled him close. "We are all very proud of you." "Thanks, Gramp!" Michael turned back to his mother. "Can I go fit the saddle to Capp?" "Absolutely!" The boys were out of the kitchen and off to the barn as Sara began clearing the table.

Standing at the sink, Sara turned around to face the elder Moores. She wiped her hands on the towel and set it on the table. "I think I need to sit while I tell you something." Mary saw the concern on Sara's face and heard the change in her voice. "What is it dear?" "Michael saw Russell Barnes in town today." John stood up and walked to the window as if to appear to be checking on the boys out in the barn. Turning back to the women, he spoke bluntly. "I hope he stays the hell away from here! I'm going to the barn." He had his boots on and was out the door with a swiftness that startled both women.

"He didn't want to do it, Mary, I believe him."

"Maybe he didn't want to, but he was with his father when they stole so many from our herd and John just can't get past that."

"If it hadn't been for him, I could not have gotten the herd home, and he helped with . . . Samuel. Can't he keep that in mind?"

"Oh, Sara, of course, he knows that, and he thanks God every day that you were all right, but the rustling of the cattle is unforgiveable to a rancher. Russell's father betrayed a lot of men, many of whom are our close friends and caused a great more damage than just monetary. He broke trust. A true man never breaks trust." Mary knew that Sara understood, but she also knew that Sara was indebted to Russell for her own personal reasons, and for her, it was unthinkable to treat Russell as the villain when in fact the real villain was his father.

"Sara . . ." Mary put her arms around her and held her. "It's all right that you feel as you do. Just accept that John will never see the situation through your eyes and heart."

The women were still in the kitchen when they heard the horses running . . . Sara went to the backdoor just in time to see all three boys galloping out of the corral and out toward the main cattle lot. "He's grown up well." She smiled with pride as she watched Michael ride the lead., Sired by 'Captain', Capp was the fastest horse on the ranch. The day the colt was born, Michael knew him as his. The big colt was marked so much like his sire. Sara recalled the memory of Michael placing his ball cap on the colt's head and the nicker of acceptance. "His name is Capp! That's it!" And the young boy put his arms around the colt's neck and the bond was set.

Sara turned back toward Mary; "Remember when the colt was born?"
"Sure do, like it was yesterday. Four years sure goes by fast." Four years . . . It had been four years since Samuel's death. Four years since a true Christmas had been celebrated. Four seasons of ranch life without Sam. Four years of an empty bed beside her. Four years to Mary may have gone by fast, but to Sara it seemed and eternity. "Those two have been bonded from the day that randy colt was dropped." Mary had seen the somberness in Sara's face and tried to pull her back to the happiness of the 'now.' "That ole Captain sure could stamp his colts with his coloring. Do you ever regret gelding Capp? He would have made a fine stallion and would have carried on the line so well." "Not once. I look at Michael with that horse, and I know the right thing was done. Yes, he would have been the best relief stallion now that Captain is retired, but Michael had lost so much that year, and I just could not bear for him to not have the horse he loved so much be just for him. He may be young, but a rancher is what he is, and well, he grew up knowing the real bond of a man and his mount with Samuel and Tonk. I wanted that for him too."

Mary stood next to Sara; pushed her hair back from her cheek, and looked her in the eyes. "I love you Sara Moore, you are truly a fine woman, and I am so proud you are my daughter. I need to tell you something that may or may not be what you want to hear just now, but I am going to say it anyway. You need to start thinking about you. What do *you* want? You need to 'feel' again. Samuel loved you with all his heart, and you loved, and still do, love him. I overheard you one night as you lay alone in your bed talking to him. I heard you recall his words for you to find love again. I know you feel as if it would be wrong, but Sara, it would not . . . be wrong.

You are a very loving woman. The proof of that is in how deeply devoted to Samuel and Michael you are. Heck, John and I want you here with us for the rest of our lives and want you and Michael on this ranch for the rest of yours. Can you not see all that is here now you had a part in making? You are a strong woman with a strong will but you have a softer side too that has not been given the attention it needs, and I can see signs of it waning as the days and weeks pass. Don't think you ever have to leave here Sara. This is your home. This is Michael's home. If you were to find love again, he too will be welcome here. Look at me Sara . . . Please . . . even Michael has noticed, and let's be honest here, he is growing up and will soon be a man of his own, and who knows where that will take him. You don't want to be alone, do you? John and I are getting on and . . ."

"Stop it, Mary! Don't even go there . . . You and Dad are going to live forever . . . remember . . ."

"Sara, think about what I said, that is all I ask." "I just don't know how . . ." A tear fell from her right eye, Mary wiped it off. "Want an old lady to help? Of course, I'm not sure the men I know would be suitable, they're all past the 'romance-ability' stage."

"Mary!"

"Hey, I'm a 'hip' old woman! I can still remember . . ." As the women laughed together, John came through the backdoor. "Should I be concerned?" They looked at each other and laughed harder. "Women . . . never in a million years do I even want to try to figure them out! I'm going back to the barn!"

PART 3

Night Out

Sara was in the den with John when Mary called out to her. "Sara, honey, the phone is for you, it's Beverly." Sara slowly rose out of her chair and noticed the smile on John's face. "Sara, please, this time . . . please go out and have some fun. She is your best friend . . . she wants the Sara she has known for years to come out and 'play' a little again. It has been so long since you have, and I know how much you love to dance. We all know how much you love to dance."

Her thoughts took her back in time when she and Samuel would go out scootin' on Saturday nights. The trophies randomly placed on the bookshelves in the den were reminders that for years, there was no better duo on the dance floor at *The Holler*. Samuel only wanted to partner dance, saying that line dancing was for the 'single' people. She would jump from her seat everytime the band played for the line dancers, leaving Samuel there to watch her as if she was dancing just for him. Lost in thought, she was revived to reality as Mary called for her again.

"Coming . . ." Mary handed her the phone as Sara entered the kitchen; with her hand covering the receiver she said, "Go . . . you need to get out and have a little fun!" Handing the phone to Sara, she lipped again . . . "Go . . ." "Hey there, Beverly." Before Sara could say more, Beverly interrupted her. "I'm not taking 'No' for an answer tonight! I will be there in an hour to pick you up. That way you can't come up with any more excuses! One hour!" And the line was disconnected. Sara slowly returned the receiver to the cradle and turned to Mary. "I'll be leaving in an hour, it seems Beverly has taken matters into her own hands, and I have been given no choice." Mary noticed the slight elevation of spirit as Sara retreated from the kitchen and was on her way to her room to ready herself for the evening out.

"You look great, Sara! It's about time you prettied up this place!"
"Oh, Ron . . . quit . . ."
"Really, Sara, it has been way too long. We all miss you. I know it is hard to get past things, but we're your friends . . ."
Sara placed her hand on his mouth. "Enough talk like that . . . I do believe I hear *Cotton-Eyed Joe* and I am thinkin' that you sport a mean kick, so what do you say?" He took her hand in his and lead her to the dance floor. The crowd gave way to them, and all cheered as Sara and Ron danced. When the dance was completed, the lead singer in the band noticed it was Sara and played another verse just to be able to see her dance

a little longer. Sara laughed at the realization of what had happened; she was having fun for the first time in a very long while.

"May I cut in?" Sara recognized the voice of Paul Denton, the farrier for the ranch horses. Ron looked at Sara. She smiled and slowly he placed her hand in that of Paul. They two stepped to *Amarillo by Morning*. "It sure is good to see you out dancing again Sara. This place has really miised you." At the end of the song, he took her back to her table. "Take care of her girls, she just might remember how much she likes this!" He smiled at Sara and retreated back into the crowd.

Beverly had surprised Sara with having invited Cassie and Callie McGregor to join them. The twins were daughters to the ranchowner just to the east of the Moores. Cassie had married and divorced, and Callie caused a great stir when she had her daughter Katy out of wedlock. When Samuel and Sara married, the three girls became friends quickly. Sara hadn't realized that she had let that friendship wane in the years since Samuel's death. It was becoming apparent that she had let a lot of her 'life' go. Neither Cassie nor Callie would accept an apology for her behavior; they both said that they understood, and in her own time, 'Sara' would be back.

Sara noticed Callie staring toward the front door as if transfixed on someone or something. Waving her hand in front of Callie's face and with a bit of laughter in her voice, she said, "Hey there . . . yoo hoo . . . You in there?"
"He's here, he is actually here." Sara was certain she was referring to Nick Borden. Rumor had it that he was Katy's father. Sara knew only that Callie had loved him in her younger years, and when he left town, he had married Elizabeth Yern instead. Now that he and Elizabeth had divorced, she assumed that Callie would again be in pursuit.

"Callie, you OK?" Just as the words were spoken, Sara felt a hand placed on hers. "May I have this waltz?" The band was playing Don Williams' song *Amanda* as she turned to see the deep blue eyes of Russell Barnes.

She tried to speak, yet no words were audible. The instant flash of heat in her chest took her by surprise, and she had to catch her breath. The women at the table as well as the other people at tables around them were silenced instantly.

"I've been told you love to waltz" He effortlessly raised her from her chair. Still unable to speak, she followed him to the center of the dance floor; as if floating in a dream, they embraced for the waltz. He looked into her eyes, and the corners of his mouth were near to trembling. It was as if he wanted to speak, yet he too was unable. His eyes spoke all the words she needed to know. They danced as if they were the only two people in the room.

Unknowing of all the conversation among onlookers as to the pair on the dance floor, she would not have cared anyway. So long she had thought about what she would do or say when she saw him again. Would she dare confront him about why he left that night or why he had waited so long to contact her? His father's trial had been publicized heavily, and unbeknownst to Russell, she had been there to support him. She was so happy when she learned that he had been aquitted of the conspiracy charges against him. Sara was not surprised that Russell's father was sentenced to eight years in the state prison for having stolen so many cattle. She hadn't seen him since the day after the sentencing, and then, there had not been time for anything more than formalities, though she sensed more between them even then.

As the band was ending the last chorus, Russell lead her into a slow spin and then brought her back close to him. She felt the surging power of her awareness of his body so close to hers, touching her in a tenderness she had for so long been missing. A slight sigh was released as he drew her to him. She hoped he had not heard or felt it.

"Me too, Sara . . . me too." He placed his hand on her cheek to wipe away the small tear just ready to fall. "Oh, Russell . . ." was all she was able to say. She lowered her head and stepped back from him to start her return to her friends. As if the band knew the only way to keep them together was to lead right into another song, without a pause, *Hummingbird* was in full vocals. Russell swiftly caught her and without hesitation, began to swing dance.

"I see you can still 'Pretzel!'" He was leading her through all the moves of the step with ease. "I can shoulder 'cross-swing promenade' too!" She was maneuvering the motions, feeling the energy of the music as well as the beat of her heart. "You're pretty good at this" he said, as his arm was behind her turning her out for a spin. "You make me look good, Sara." She returned to him and smiled. Sara could feel while dancing with Russell a 'release' of the 'hold' that bound her to her sorrows. For so long, she had been just a shadow of herself; it was the first time in a very long while that she truly felt alive again.

The song ended and the couples dancing began to exit the floor. She realized that the fast pace of the dance had her heated, wiping her brow, she wondering if it was the exercise of the dancing or the man she was dancing with that had her in such a state of excitement.

"Sara . . . I want to see you again . . . soon. Would that be all right with you?"

Mamas Don't Let Your Babies Grow Up To Be Cowboys was playing on stage as they walked through the crowd toward her table. Midway there, Sara stopped, turned around and had to start over several times as she was hearing the words and truths written by Ed and Patsy Bruce. "OK," she said still slightly out of breath. "OK?" he asked her as if he needed her to repeat herself. "Yes, OK. But you know how John feels, and well, we will have to be careful. I . . . ah . . ."

"I understand, Sara. Will you be at the Rodeo this weekend? Perhaps we could 'run into each other' there." "Michael is Roping this year. He and Charles are Teaming, Michael is the heeler. Brent is going to try the Saddle Broncs. I am sure we will see you there."

He returned her to her seat, tipped his hat to the others at her table, picked up Sara's hand and gently kissed it. "Thank you Sara, for the dances. It has been a true pleasure. Your dancing reputation is well deserved." While still holding her hand to his lips, he raised his eyes to hers and smiled. She again felt the 'rush' of excitement. Her smile back to him let him know she reciprocated his thoughts. He released his hold on her hand, with his signature two steps back then a turn on his heels, he was lost in the crowd. Sara held her focus on the last moment of her sight of him; she was unaware of the stares her friends were giving her.

"Whoa . . . what just happened here?" Beverly was quick to ask even before Sara had fully turned back to them. "I have to go to the restroom." Sara was up and out of her chair before her friends had a chance to speak again. Her head lowered and pushing through the people standing in the area just before the rest rooms, Sara felt herself dazed.

"You looked good out there, Sara!"
"Nice to see you back on the floor girl!"

She heard many a comment directed at her, yet in the blur had no idea who was speaking to her. She reached the swinging doors, and as she pushed her way in, Linda Thomms was coming out.

"Holy shit, girl . . . Are you OK?. What's chasin' you?" Linda and Sara had been friends while the boys were young, but she had left Brent's father with no forewarning for a man in East Dale. Sara had asked Mark if he could get information. The only available information was that the man Linda was with seemed to have shown up one day and then vanished right after she moved there. Linda returned to Brandon and tried to pull the family back together. The 'pride of the cowboy' was too damaged and hurt for Ron to take her back. Brent stayed at the Moore Ranch while his parents finalized the divorce proceedings. It had been a source for much town gossip and speculation, most of which was untrue, and Linda had since 'fallen into the bottle' with a vengeance and had few friends other than the 'barflies' known to hang out at the Holler.

"I . . . ah . . . just . . ." Sara was through the swinging doors and into the santcuary of the restroom. She steadied herself on the first stall and after catching her breath, looked under all the doors. Relieved that she was alone, she turned to the mirror. Holding her abdomen with her left arm as she braced herself with her right."My God, woman! What are you doing?" she said to the reflection in the mirror, and then began to slowly laugh until she was consumed by the humor.

"Girl, you got a bit of explainin' to do!" The familiar voice of her friend behind her, Sara's eyes moved on the mirror to look at Beverly. "Oh, Bev . . ." "Here, drink this, you look like you need it! Heck, you look like a six-pack couldn't be enough! Talk to me!" Cassie and Callie burst through the doors. "We got Linda to sit at our table so no one would steal it. We just had to see what was going on." Callie looked at Beverly in hopes of information. Beverly took Sara's arm and swung her around to face them. "Well Sara, tell us, what is going on?"

Trying to find the words to explain herself proved more difficult than she thought. "I . . . ah . . . wow! Was that ever fun . . . dancing again . . . I still got the moves . . . yay-ah!" She knew they wanted to know about Russell. How could she explain it to them when she couldn't even explain it to herself? "Cut the bull, Sara . . ." Beverly took both Sara's hands in hers, lifted them, held them to her, and while still holding them, lowered them back down. "Do you need some air?"

"I think that would be a good idea . . . Oh man, what just happened?" "Come on . . . let's get outta here. Linda can have our table." The twins simultaneously said "Parker's Point!" Beverly looked at them . . . "What is it about that place that you two love so much?" Callie and Cassie shared a look of 'sisterhood' that neither Beverly nor Sara dared ask for the reason why.

Linda had been patiently waiting for them to return; hoping for inclusion into their group. She was disappointed when told that the table was hers, their night of dancing was finished. "Hold down the dance hall, Linda! Keep 'er here till next weekend!" Swooping up their purses, they were lost in the crowd. Linda motioned to a couple girls that she had the table, they came over and sat down. "'bout time they left! What took 'em so long?"
"Bitches."
"Yeah, well you may think that, but as for me, I miss them."
"They hung you out to dry, girl . . . did they ever look at you for you. Uh uh . . . just cast you aside . . . and you still want to be buddy buddy with them . . . uh uh . . ."
"That may be true, but they really aren't bitches. I do understand their reasonings."
"Girl, I just can't get a grip on the 'culture' as you call it around here. Where I come from, they would be bitches! Oh . . . they're line dancing! Lets go!" Linda did wonder just where her new friend Sancha hailed from. She had been a regular at the Holler for months, yet she knew very little about her. Linda had been so thankful to have someone to talk to that she had told Sancha the story of what had happened with Sara. She looked back at the crowd toward the door and again felt the remorse of having lost Sara as a dear friend. "You two go ahead, I'm going to head home" "Suit yourself." They rushed to the dance floor as Linda was heading out the door. Two men sat at the vacated table, Linda thought to herself . . . Perfect . . . those two will have fun all night, and I go home . . . alone . . . again . . .

Fumbling with her keys at her truck, Linda overheard Beverly ask Sara about Russell. She had her key ready for the door but pretended not to so she might get more information. Beverly looked in her direction and shielded Sara from sight to prevent Linda from hearing the conversation.
"Snoop," she said, as she placed herself in position. "Sometimes I feel bad that we all treated her like that, you know, we weren't in her boots at the time and certainly aren't now. Still, she was a friend to all of us, and we all but turned our backs on her." "Sara, your sense of loyalty is

wonderful." Beverly looked toward Linda as she was getting in her truck. "It really and truly is, and that, my girl, may just be the reason you are out here standing in the parking lot and not in there dancing! That man . . . Russell Barnes . . . Thank God he left . . . he is a distraction to you. A distraction because he was there with you at your most vulnerable moment. Like he was a hero or something. OK, maybe he kinda sorta was . . . but geez, girl . . . that was years ago. I know, we've been over your reasons for going to the courthouse when his family faced rustling charges, and still for the life of me, I don't get it, but tonight . . . dancing . . . there was an energy there that was charged to high voltage! What was up with that?"

Sara turned her back to the truck bed and leaned on it for support. Her upper body bending with hands on her knees, taking in several deep breaths, she began to relax and think with greater clarity. As she straightened her frame, she caught a glimpse of Russell's Jeep. Not wanting the other girls to know he was still there, she quickly cast her attention the other direction. She was glad to be able to disguise her reddened face in the beams of neon from the Holler's front sign.

"He's going to be at the Rodeo."

Beverly half-turned and then back again. "Are you serious? Is he entered? Or does he just want to see you in a public place? This is nuts, Sara, just nuts!" Sara looked Beverly in the eyes;

"I know. So why do I feel so drawn to him? Why when we were dancing did my blood race through my veins. Why did I want him to kiss me, but I wouldn't let him?" Turning so as to be facing the truck, she didn't want her friends to see her sobbing. Beverly put a hand on her shoulder. "He's really gotten to you, hasn't he? Well, then I suppose the right thing to do is to help you figure out what you are going to tell John Moore when he finds out about this."

Callie and Cassie leaned on the truck; one on each side of Sara, a glance of uncertainty between them. "We'll find out if he draws[21] at the Rodeo or if he's workin' it. Wouldn't mind seeing that 'wrangler butt' in action . . ." "Callie!" Cassie reached across Sara and slugged her sister in the arm. At that point, all the girls started to giggle and found themselves in a huddle, holding on to the side of the truck for balance.

---

[21]   To draw at a Rodeo means to enter one or more events.

The bar was closing and the parking lot was filling with people, many of whom saw Sara and she could hear the comments aimed toward her. "Looks like it's time to head home, girls. It's been a night, that it has. Whatever is the attraction at Parker's Point I'm just not up for it tonight." Sara got in her truck, and as she pulled out of the parking lot, glanced in the direction where Russell's Jeep had been; it was not there. The surge of dissappointment was unsettling to her, yet the knowledge that she could have the dissappointed feeling seemed to awaken a part of her long repressed. She drove home without the radio on.

PART 4

The Rodeo

"Good mornin', Mrs. Moore!" Charles and Brent were through the kitchen door and into Michael's room. Sara was clearing the breakfast dishes from the table. "Is there a fire or something? You boys are in an awful big hurry this morning!" She knew the excitement level of all three boys was peaked as today marked the start of the Rodeo. They had been 'tuning' their roping and riding skills as they called it; no cowboy would 'practice' . . . Sara grinned at the memory of that conversation with the teenagers. They were young men now, and she was very proud of all of them. "You boys have time for some warm apple fritters?" Before the sentence was complete, all three were back in the kitchen. "That's what I like . . . Good appetites!" She handed Brent and Charles a plate each, and they sat down to enjoy the "County Fair Prize-Winning" fritters that only Michael's mom could make.

"Mom, don't you be stuffin' my 'hands' so full they won't be able to work today!"

"Your 'hands'? . . . ha! We'll see about that!" They all began to laugh and as Sara looked at Michael, she could see how he resembled his father in more than appearance; he had his mannerisms and his sense of humor. Most of all, he had Samuel's heart and sensibilty. Seventeen years old, forced to be a man before his time—a son his father would be deeply proud of.

The boys finished their fritters and brought their plates to the sink; Brent on her left and Charles on the right of Sara. As the plates were lowered into the sink, they each turned to Sara and kissed her cheek. "You're the best second mom a guy could have!" Charles hugged her. "And I'm your best second son, right?" Brent stood proud and waited for her reply. He adored Sara and loved her for all she had done for him when his parents were troubled. "I love all of you! Now, are you ready for the rodeo?"

"Yup."

"Absolutely!"

"Where's my 'wild rag?'" Of course, it was Michael; that trait he got from her, seemingly misplacing things when actually they were right where they were supposed to be. "Check your back pocket, kiddo!"

"Oh yeah . . . I knew it all along!"

As the boys ran out the backdoor, Mary came into the kitchen. With an arm on Sara's to steady herself, she patted Sara's arm with her other hand. "You can can grow 'em up right and they still be kids! Good kids at that. I sure hope they can keep the light of youth lit a little longer. Manhood is just too close for them."

"And for us too, Mary, and for us too." The women watched as the boys loaded the horses in the trailer.

******

"You sure got Capp looking good! Benji here, well . . . we don't have all the fancy blankets and such that you have. He ain't a spoiled horse!" Brent was laughing while teasing Michael as he loaded Capp in the trailer. With the bigger gelding in, Brent threw the rope over Benji's neck and the horse went on his own up the ramp into the trailer. "That's the way it is done, boys! He loads himself!" Charles was leading his mare Lady to the trailer. "Make way all you gents, the princess is here for her coach ride!" When they were ready to leave, all three boys stood and looked at the matriarchs of the Moore family and bowed simultaneously. "See you from the chutes!" Michael waved an extra wave to his mother, and she could see his lips telling her he loved her.

"Ready Gramp?"

"Get in boys . . . it's time to get this rig on the road!"

John had told Mary how he was looking forward to a good day with the boys;'Man time' he called it. Just as long as the women remembered to bring the food later. Mary giggled as she had said, "Man time . . . Riiiiiiight! as long as the women are there for backup, you 'men' will have a good day!" They shared a good laugh and he embraced his wife.

"I love you, Mary Moore, I truly do!" He gave her a quick kiss on her cheek. "I remember Samuel's first ride as a 'man' at Rodeo." His voice began to falter. "Not now John, think not of Samuel, this is Michael's day. Be there for Michael, and whatever you do, you must never, and I mean it, not once shall you make comparison of father and son. You know what that will do to his concentration, let alone his knowing he has big boots to fill. Samuel's records still hold. The fact that his father is gone makes it that much harder on him." "I know, believe me. Michael is ready for this, I have been out of sight keeping tabs on his team practicing with Charles. Those calves have been worked well in the past few weeks, that is for sure. The boys look good, and their times have been improving. If it's enough to win . . . well, I don't know, but they sure have a good chance." "There's a cooler in the truck with goodies to hold you boys over until we get there."

She smiled at him as he turned away from her and headed for the truck. She turned toward the house to help Sara.

The drive to the Rodeo Grounds was full of excitement. "I know you have Jerry Jeff Walker and Chris Ledoux in the tape box . . . plug 'em in, Michael! We are off to the r-o-d-e-o!"

"Is it OK, Gramp? I know you really aren't a fan of the new style of country music."

"You had better find those tapes quick before your friends in the backseat burst out the windows!" John smiled at his grandson. He really did like the new style of music. He tried to keep it from Mary though; it was she that didn't take to it well. "Can you keep a secret, Michael?" John leaned his head slightly toward him and in a half–whisper said, "I do like your music, it's Gram that thinks it's changing too much." He sat back up straight, reached over to the tape player and turned the volume up. "Way to go, Gramps!" Brent reached forward and patted John on the shoulder, and then 'high-fived' with Charles and Michael. All four were soon singing and laughing. The time of travel passed quickly. Soon, they were waiting in line at the competitors' entrance gate.

"We're ridin' with the big boys today! No more kids' classes! Look out Brandon Rodeo, the 'new guys' are in town! We're gonna ride and slide and kick ass!"

"Watch your mouth, Michael. I know you are excited, but you must remember yourself at all times."

"Sorry, Gramps, it's just that . . ."

"I know . . . Now . . . get these horses unloaded and go kick that ass!" John embraced his grandson, and then with his arms motioned for the others, drawing them all to him. "I am so proud of all you. No matter what happens today, no matter how many rides you make, or falls you take, and by the looks of all of you, no matter how many hearts you break today, you must always remember who you are and what you believe. You must always retain the 'Cowboy Grace.' You all know it, you all live by it. Be respectful of it today, and you will have achieved the greatest accomplishment." Simultaneously, the three boys yelled, "Yes, sir." In their 'huddle' stance, they layered hands, then shouted, "Let's ride!"

They lead the horses to their assigned pens, noting the other cowboys that had arrived prior to them. "Oh man . . . Would you look at Tom

Bonner's new gelding! I heard he had a loud[22] Paint . . . That boy is gorgeous! Big too!" Charles knew the competition was going to be tough now that they were freshmen in the upper age group. He and Michael had won their previous division each year except their first. Tom Bonner had scored two points more at the last Rodeo and had taken the All-around[23] trophy. To say there was a rivalry would not be untrue, but more than that, there was respect for each other as they were all part of a lifestyle they lived and honored.

Tom could see the three young men as they passed his horse. "He is a bee-ute, ain't he!"

"Sure is, Tom. Where'd you find him?" Michael took great pride in their stock and was curious as to the lineage of Tom's horse. There was a resemblance to his father's horse, reminding him of how he longed to have his father with him. They should have been here together. They should be teaming. "Michael, you'll be happy to know that he is out of a mare sired by your father's stallion 'Captain' . . . got him from a girl over in East Dale, said she couldn't handle him."

"That explains why he looks a lot like Tonk." Charles could see the anguish on his friend's face as Michael ran his hand down the neck of Tom's horse. "Good luck to you, Tom."

"As well to you guys . . . ride safe!"

They waited in line at the entry booth with the other contestants. "How many girls do you think will be here to run Barrels?" Brent was laughing and pushing Charles aside. "Girls, you think about girls when we're signing up!" "Yup! You got that right! We're older, and that means they're older too!" Michael laughed at his friends' antics; from the corner of his eye, he spotted Katy McGregor over at the pen that Capp was in. He could see her looking all around as if seeking to find him. Tom, having heard the conversation, leaned forward from his position in line. "Looks like young Mr. Moore won't have to worry about that! There seems to be a rather pretty little filly over there looking for him!"

Brent and Charles pushed Michael aside. "You dog . . . And . . . Katy, of all girls . . . How did you ever get her to be a lookin' for your sorry butt anyway?" "She knows cowboy class when she sees it!" Michael put his thumbs on his belt, pushed out his chest and while rocking back on his

---

[22]   A color pattern of the hair that has a greater amount of either the base color or white to the other color in the pattern.

[23]   Trophy won by the competitor that scored the most points in combined events

heels, grinned at his friends. "Next . . ." The woman in the entry booth was not patiently waiting as the three boys made their way to the table.

"Well, well . . . It's the 'Three Amigos' . . . Here for a run at the big boys this year?"

"Yes, ma'am." Michael was the first to find his voice. All three removed their hats, placed them on their chests and smiled curtly. Mrs. Harrison handed them each an entry form and a pencil, then she placed the number cards on the table. "Who wants which number? You'll have it throughout this age group, so take care of it. Michael chose 601; Brent, 602; and Charles picked up the last card, 603.

"At least it's the low 600s . . . if you get my drift!" He noticed the grimace on Mrs. Harrison's face. "603 . . . that's the number for me!" Trying to replace a smile for the frown, it didn't work. "Yes, ma'am . . . I'll fill out my entry card now."

They were heading back to the horses when Katy caught up to them. She skipped herself to Michael's side, slid her arm in his, and put her head on his upper arm due to his being nearly a foot taller than her. "I'm runnin' Barrels today . . . you gonna watch me?" She tightened her arm on his. Blushing; as he could see the facial expressions of Brent and Charles as they too were in anticipation of his answer, Michael asked, "What time do you ride?" Though his friends were trying to silently tease him about the forward approach she had taken, he was impressed and relieved that she came to him so he would not have to make the 'first move'. Girls were just starting to be of importance to him and he was naïve as to how to handle them.

"We run after the Bronc Riding; I drew third go." Katy kept her hold of Michael's arm. "He can watch you after we pick Brent's butt up in the Saddle Broncs!" Charles interupted the stare between Michael and Katy with his jestful remark. "He's riding broncs this year? Does he know the string that is here?" Brent turned his attention to her with interest. "Ain't they the same as last year? And the year before that and the year before that. They always bring the Bowman string[24]." She looked worriedly at Michael and then turned back to Brent. "Old man Bowman died over the winter, and his son thinks he can make more money at the bigger Rodeos.

---

[24]   The 'string' refers to the livestock used in the Rodeo events supplied by the Rodeo.

He don't want bothered with our 'little fair' any more. Got a new string this year owned by Russell Barnes." All three boys fell silent, unable to speak.

"Did you say Russell Barnes?"

"Yes, why?" Katy was taken back by the consternation in Michael's voice. Michael looked at Charles; "That's why he's been in town lately." "Do you think your mom knows?" Trying to hide his concern, Brent placed his hand on Michael's shoulder. "No way. No way she would hold that from me." He looked at his friends and in a continuance of Brent's gesture, placed a hand on each of their shoulders forming a triangle. Katy, feeling left out wiggled into the center. "Gonna let the girl know what this powwow is about. Oh goodness! Russell Barnes . . . Oh, Michael, it just hit me, he's the guy that helped when . . ." Her voice faded as she saw the drop of his face as the memory flashed in his eyes. "Shit! You know we gotta tell her . . ." Brent was the first to pull back from the triangle.

Michael turned toward Katy. She knew what he was about to ask her. She really liked him and wanted him to like her, but was not sure if she could do what he wanted. "Katy, you need to help me. I mean it. I can deal with him being here, I actually kinda like the guy, I mean think about what he did for total strangers . . . He really ought not have left in the middle of the night, but that was his way of stepping back out of a matter that really wasn't his. Mom was hurt more because she wanted to thank him and send him off proper for all he had done for us. She was not able to do that for him. She got mad at him in her grief, but in truth she has always admired him for what he did for us. I know this because when you mention his name to her she tries to hide interest but it is clearly there."

"Michael, I . . ." she was cut short. "She and Gram will be here for the Saddle Broncs. She still loves to watch the cowboys *try* to beat Dad's score. That's why before you ride, could you maybe do what you girls do and sit with her and somehow get in the conversation about this being his string? Katy, Please! I just don't know if I could handle her reaction, and frankly, the distraction to my concentration could really affect my rides." He was grasping at any plausible reasoning to convince her. She swished her head back and forth, and after a slight moan, looked at him and felt the heat increase as her heart beat faster when she placed her hand in his. "OK. I'll put on my 'big girl boots' and do this. How bad can it be anyway?" Brent and Charles turned to walk away; they knew it was time to let them be alone.

"Thank you." She heard the relief in his voice. "This means a lot to you, doesn't it?" She was seeing a more personal side of him; not just the fun riding, always joking around, 'slam-his- locker' guy known as "Mountain Man Michael" for his height and muscle mass. She liked knowing that he could be sensitive too. "One condition . . ."

"Uh oh . . . what is it?"

"I want first and last dance tonight." She quickly hugged him and darted off toward the grandstand so he would not have time to back out with a lame excuse for not being at the dance. She knew this way he would have to be there; for no other reason than respect for what she agreed to do for him that he could not do himself, even though he really should have. She knew him well enough to know she was going to have the first and last dance and hopefully many in between. Katy's infatuation with Michael had been born in kindergarten and grown as the years passed. She patiently waited for an opportunity like this to get him to realize he should like her too.

Michael found his friends at the pens grooming their horses. Anticipating their reaction, he approached slowly. To his surprise, there was no ribbing as to having a girl do his 'dirty work. Instead, Charles stopped currying Lady and walked to him. "You OK?" "What, no smart remarks? You guys are dissapointing me!" Michael feigned a joking attitude. Benji grunted as Brent joined Charles. "Hey man, we're 'brothers', and as much as this is like great, and I do mean great . . . fodder for jokes, this is your mom, our mom too . . . and that Katy is really stepping up for you."

"She wants to dance tonight."

"Oh, hmm . . . *that* will be good material! Mr. Dancing is for sissies. Can't wait to see this!" Charles knuckled Brent and began to laugh. "It is the least you can do for her!" Brent had joined Charles in poking fun at Michael.

"Attention on the grounds!" The loudspeaker was close to their stalls; the volume startled the boys out of their conversation. "All constestants, please go to the 'truck in' chutes to help move the horses and cattle." Mrs. Harrison's tone to her voice had not improved since they were at the sign up table. "Well, boys! That's the whistle! The Rodeo is o-fish-ill-ee started! Head 'em up and move 'em out!"

Brent and Charles increased their pace toward the cattle hauling trucks. Charles looked back at Michael and Katy, "He better be on his game today, this is like our enterance into notoriety here. Between that girl and the Barnes fellow, I'm a thinking I may have to be a gettin' a bit on the worried side." "You're worried about Michael? Don't be. There is more to that 'mountain' than muscle and height." "Nice try Brent, but you're not the one countin' on him to loop the heels!" "He'll be just fine, besides, he'll be wanting to show off for Katy so he sure don't want to miss!"

They both had to catch themselves as they nearly tripped while laughing.

Though Michael was following closely, his focus was on the grandstands. The family habitually sat on the fourth bleacher row in the center section. He studied the crowd until he located Gram. Relief came over him. They had made it on time. To her left was his mother arranging the coolers and stadium chairs. Looking deeper into the crowd he could see Katy approaching on the right. He could tell she was calculating how to rearrange her arrival to be on the left. He thought to himself how he should be doing this and how Katy had been gracious to oblige. There she was . . . seated next to his mother . . . He smiled. Charles grabbed his arm . . . "Get the lead out, would ya . . . don't want 'em to wait on us. We gotta make a good impression!" Michael released his attention on Katy, and the boys took to a race for the chutes.

"Mrs. Moore?" Two women said "yes", and all three laughed. Gram had a smirk on her face as she leaned in to Sara. "She most likely means you seein's as she be the right age for an interest in a certain young cowboy we both know." Sara's heart skipped. It was true. Michael had grown so handsome and tall that the girls were sure to start vying for his attentions. He was well-liked in school and had proven to the town that he was as much an asset as his father despite his young age. There standing in front of her was Katy McGregor, granddaughter and heir to the second largest ranch in the county. "Don't get ahead of yourself Sara!" She silently scolded her thoughts.

"Hi! My name is Katy McGregor." Sara saw confidence and poise in the young girl and was appreciative of her respectfulness. A strong woman would be what Michael should have in his life . . . when the time comes; again the silent scolding.

"Yes . . . Katy, I haven't seen you in a long time! You have grown up well. How are you getting on after the death of your grandfather? I still feel just awful that we could not make the funeral."

"The tree you had delivered has grown in strength as a remembrance of the true patriarch Grand Pop was. May I sit with you to watch the

Bull Riding?" Gram leaned toward Sara; "So polite this girl is, wow, I'm impressed!" She winked at Katy and smiled. That small gesture of Gram's helped ease the pressure of what Katy knew would be pensive moments as she carried out Michael's request of her.

"Certainly Katy, please . . . sit here next to me. Have you seen Michael and the boys yet? Are you runnin' the barrels today? Get up a minute Gram, I need to open the blanket for Katy to sit on . . . Sorry, I only brought two chairs, hope the blanket will be OK."

"The blanket is fine, thank you. And yes, I am running today; I drew third go. I did see the guys heading over to the loading chutes to help out." Gram again smiled and winked at Katy. "Good boys they are! They are going to be fine young men."

With a blush Katy smiled and said, "They already are, Gram Moore, they already are!" At that Sara smiled as well, looking at Katy as a mother deciding for her son if the girl was worthy in her pursuit. "Katy McGregor, you are blushing!" She leaned over to her and whispered in Katy's ear. "I know that blush well, it may have been a great many years ago, but I will never forget how I felt when I thought about Samuel . . ." It was as if Katy could see the memory of it in Sara's eyes. Katy's heart ached for her.

As young girls do, she dreamed of her wedding and husband. She and her mom had managed well, though she knew the loneliness her mother endured feeling condemned to a life without a husband and a father for Katy. It was known well, the marriage of Samuel and Sara Moore. Katy wanted to emulate as best as possible the true romance they shared, less the tragic ending. The look on Sara's face and the way she spoke of him, Katy realized that even now, she still loved Samuel Moore.

"Attention in the grandstands!" Mrs. Harrison's voice was again crackling out of the speakers tied onto the poles at each corner of the arena. "All contestants to the arena for the Opening Ceremony. Ceremony will start in five minutes." Katy stood up, turning to Sara. "I'll be back after the opening ceremony, if that is OK . . ." Sara patted the blanket where Katy had sat. "We look forward to it! See you soon . . . and hey, if you see the boys, tell them I remembered the brownies! That will give them a reason to find us!"

"Will do, see you soon!"

As she descended the bleacher rows, she was thinking of how Sara had said she was looking forward to her return. If she only knew. And of course, Michael was going to grill her as to his mother's reaction. Katy nearly tripped over the last step; finding herself in Michael's arms as he caught her before she fell. "Whoa there, cowgirl! You don't want to be a hurtin' yourself before your winning ride!" His smile erased all doubt she may have had in her pursuit of him. "That would have been bad, huh!" "Let's get to the ceremony. Did you talk with my mom yet? I feel like I should do it, but I don't know how . . . I love my mom so much and, well, I . . ." "It's OK, I can do this. Haven't yet, but I will. I am going back after the Anthem and will work it in then."

"Thank you, Katy. Really. I mean it." He drew her to him and hugged her at the bottom of the bleachers. If ever there was a hug that she never wanted to end, this was the one.

"You seeing what I'm seeing?" Gram asked Sara. "That would be a yes there Gram. A big yes." Her mind flashed to Michael as a baby, then kindergarten, then the middle years and through Samuel's death and now into High School. Her beloved son was growing up. As she was reliving all the proud moments all the while fearing the time when his departure from her would lead him on in his life. "When did he do it? When did he grow up?" The two women put arms around the other and held together. "You did good Sara, you did good." Sara thought to herself, "that's what Sam said to me in the cave . . ."

"All rise!" The speakers were again screeching. Sara and Gram stood with the other spectators in the bleachers. Below them in the arena, she searched for Michael, Brent and Charles. She found them, and with Michael stood Katy. Gram laughed as she stated, "She's marked her territory. Does he realize that!" "He's too busy with a newfound 'enthusiasm' to see the 'Cow*girl* Code' happening before him. He'll learn all too well and all too soon enough!" As both women were laughing, Sara felt a hand on her shoulder. She turned around to find the nearest other person too far from her to have done so. Placing her hand on the same shoulder, she closed her eyes.

In her thoughts she knew it was a touch from Samuel.

The Pledge of Allegiance was recited, the Star Spangled Banner sung, and the Prayer for the Cowboys and Cowgirls was the grandest in all the years Sara had been in attendance. Katy had returned to her seat next to Sara.

"The bulls have always scared me." Katy was the first to speak. "Thank goodness the Clowns this year are all former Bull Riders. I heard they have their own 'school' now. It is over in Hardenton." "That so? I didn't know, guess I have been away from the arena life longer than I thought. They still using the Bowman string, or has that changed too?" Sara's question to Katy relieved her of figuring out just how to broach the subject of Russell Barnes. "No, actually, Mr. Bowman died and his son is only leasing out to the sanctioned Rodeos now." After taking in a deep breath, Katy continued, "Mrs. Moore, the new string is owned by Russell Barnes."

Katy waited for Sara's reaction. Gram began to choke, and Sara was patting her on the back. "You OK, Gram? Katy, be a dear and get a water out of the cooler." Sara returned her attention to Gram as if she had not heard a word Katy had told her. Gram drank the water and as she recovered her breath, she gazed at Sara. "Thank you, dear. I don't know what came over me. Oh wait, yes, I do!" she had a grimace on her face. "New string this year and the name Russell Barnes . . . yup! That would do it!"

Sara looked back at Katy. "The boys are expecting the same horses and cattle. They are used to them. What do you know of this new lot?" Her look of concern alarmed Katy; did she not think they would be safe out there today? "Don't really know, sorry. But you don't have to worry about Michael or Charles and Brent. They are really good riders, they will be fine." She wasn't sure who she was trying to convince; Sara or herself. "You're right Katy, they have been working hard and are ready for a good challenge. Can't keep on the same stock and improve yourself now can you?" Not understanding the vagueness of Sara's reaction, Katy questioned the reaction of Michael, Brent, and Charles when they learned the owner of the stock.

With the bulls loaded in the chutes, the Cowboys donned their chaps and began working their gloves. Anxious and ready to buck, the massive beasts snorted and pawed in anticipation of the gate opening. The first rider was set. The gate opened, and it was then proven that these bulls were fresh and it was not going to be the same Rodeo as in the past. Sara heard someone behind her remark, "Good bulls this year! It's about time!"

The young cowboy was on the ground before the buzzer, and the clowns were heading the bull to the return pen. The rest of the event was much the same. Tom Bonner's older brother Dan won with a score of 91. There were only six rides that made the eight seconds. As the last bull returned to the pen, the crowd stood and cheered. They cheered for there having been no serious injuries to the cowboys, and they cheered at the renewed spirit of competition regained through the new stock and excitement of the sport.

The next event was the Saddle Bronc riding. Sara watched as the horses were loaded in the chutes. This had been Samuel's claim to Rodeo fame as he would describe it. His score of 93 had put him in the state record books; he was never given the chance to challenge his own score and it was yet to be done, though many were trying. After his death, the Rodeo Committee had placed a plaque of recognition on the third chute where he and Big Ben had bucked out in remembrance of Samuel and his exceptional score. Gram reached over and placed her hand on Sara's. No words were exchanged between them, yet what they were saying to each other was understood.

"Brent drew a horse named Big Bopper . . . he was told that he comes out of Idaho. I think he has chute 3 too. That's a good thing right?" Katy spoke to Sara yet looked straight forward at the line up of horses in the arena. The pick-up riders were in position and the first horse was out of the chute. A score of 68 for the first cowboy. "What's up with that horse in 2?" Gram had a worried tone to her voice. "Big Paint in there, bet that guy is wishin' the old horses were here!" He didn't even make five seconds. The big horse was a spinner and too much for the young rider.

"Brent's up." Sara loved him as a son and the worry would not go away until his ride was complete. Big Bopper was aptly named. He wasn't a big horse, but he sure was rearing and fussing in the chute. She could see Brent settling in the saddle, he tipped his hat, and the gate was opened! His shoulder mark was perfect! He had a rhythm with the horse that was not usually achieved so soon in a career. "Folks, the cowboy is Brent Thomms, and he is a ridin' that 'belly full of bedsprings' today like he wants to chase the record!" The eight-second buzzer blared and Brent was still riding the gelding. John Mann knew his job as pick-up rider and was there waiting for him.
"Climb on son, that was a great ride!"
"Thanks, sure am glad it's over!" John reached his arm out and smiled at Brent as he crawled on behind and waited for the right time to dismount after the bucking horse was turned toward the return pen gate. The crowd cheered; he picked up his hat and waved it to Sara. A mark of honor to the woman he respected and loved and also for Samuel. "Score of 79 for the young cowboy, Brent Thomms!" As he approached the chutes, the other competitors congratulated him. Charles ran to him and hugged

him, picking him off the ground. Michael grabbed him from behind; "You better polish your dancin' shoes, buddy . . . after that ride the girls will be a flockin' after you!"

When the last rider had been scored, Brent was awarded the winning belt buckle.

Sara again felt the hand on her shoulder.

"I need to get to the practice ring, there aren't very many bareback riders so I will be running soon.' "Ride smart, Katy." Sara held Katy's hand and with a slight squeeze, let Katy know she approved of her interest in Michael. "Thank you, Mrs. Moore, I gotta stay safe so as I am ready for the dance tonight! I'm plannin' on teaching a certain cowboy some moves on the dance floor!" Sara smiled at the young woman as she walked away. "She has no idea that Michael can dance, does she?" "No, Gram, I would suppose not. He doesn't advertise his 'twinkly toes' much." "You did right by him makin' sure he can dance. Even if it was only in the kitchen. And for all his fussin' about it, he's gonna find out tonight why you did and just how much all his grumblin' was worth it! That little lady is about to be added to the list of us swept off our feet by the Moore men!" Both women were the object of many stares as they laughed. Marilyn Bonner was walking down the bleachers and stopped at Sara and Gram.

"Good to see you here Sara. I sure hope you brought your apple fritters. The concession stand has been very lacking without them!" Sara reached into their basket and retrieved a wrapped fritter. "Special for you, Marilyn." Marilyn sat down beside her, bowed her head, and after accepting the fritter she held her hands in her lap. "Sara, I should have called on you. I am truly sorry." Sara hesitated before speaking. "At a time like that was, to be honest, I myself would not know what to say to someone. Even now that I have been through it, I still wouldn't know. Please, do not feel bad. There is no need to apologize. Just knowing that you didn't know what to say, actually says it best." She reached over, and the women hugged each other. A sigh from Marilyn audible only to Sara instilled once again the bond of friendship. Marilyn stood up, and as she turned to continue her walk down the bleachers, she looked back at Sara. "They look cute together, Michael and Katy. Maybe they will be like you and Samuel and be the 'high school sweethearts' everyone else wishes they could be." She let go of Sara's hand and merged into the crowd of people decending the steps.

"There you are! We were wondering when you would get ready for your run."

"Where is the 'we' Michael? All I see is you!" Michael turned toward the pen Katy's horse was in. "I'll help you tack up." He reached for the saddle pads as she took the dandy brush over Chance for a final touch up. "You ready, boy? This is it . . . we ride with the big girls now . . . no more sixteen seconds will do." She leaned into his neck softly whispering. Michael came around from the offside. "You will knock 'em out! You have this horse so fine- tuned that these girls won't know what hit 'em until they realize they are now the 'has-beens' and you are the contender!" Katy smiled. "And just to make sure you know it . . ." He drew her to him and placed his hands on her waist, lifting her to the brush box, they shared their first kiss. Katy thought time stood still. She had longed for this moment, trying in her mind to picture how it would be. Though not as she had thought; this was perfect.

"Come up for air, would ya!" Charles had been looking for Michael, when he saw the kissing, he paused long enough to let him have his moment. "Sure glad I found you . . . The second rider scratched. Katy, you need to get to the arena." She stepped off the brush box and they finished tacking up Chance. As she was about to mount the horse, Michael placed his hand on her arm. "Need a leg up, lil lady?" Katy bent her left leg at the knee, and he lifted her to the saddle. They smiled at each other, not needing words, they each knew the thoughts were of the kiss.

"I'll be waiting at the gate for you!" He withdrew his hand from her thigh, she reined the horse back and with a tight spin on the haunches, she was off to the warm up pen. He stood motionless; watching her, amazed at how a kiss could 'change' him.

"Hey, lover boy! Let's get a move on . . ." Charles had broken the trance Michael seemed to have been in. "Charles . . ."

"Yea?"

"Have you kissed a girl like that yet?"

"What! Me? Uhhhhh."

"It's like nothing you could ever imagine!"

"Do not, and I repeat, do not go gettin' all mushy on me here . . . We have a lot of riding to do today, and you need the head on your shoulders doin' your thinking today!"

"I'm good . . . just askin' that's all."

"Truth . . . no I haven't. Not like that anyway." Charles fisted Michael's arm. "You are one lucky guy, Michael Moore . . . she is crazy cute!"

"I guess I kinda am, aren't I?"

They got to the arena just as Katy was entering; unlike most of the riders, she rode a courtesy circle before the time line. She had an interest in learning to jump and having read many books and watched a great many demonstrations, she saw the importance of the circle and how it was beneficial in the 'mindset' for the Barrel run. Katy and Chance's times were indicative of her reasoning. As she was coming out of the circle, she saw Michael; she flashed a smile his way and set the horse for the run. Katy heard Michael shout "Showtime!"

"In the arena now is Katy McGregor and 'Happen-Chance,' their first run in this division. Let's give the young cowgirl encouragement!" She knew he was speaking, she heard the cheering of the spectators, all she saw was the barrel ahead of her . . . "Let's do this, big guy! Yahhhhh!"

The first turn was flawless; as she headed toward the second turn, Chance slid out on his shoulder, losing his tightness to the barrel. She knew that could cost a second or two and they would have to make it up at the third turn and the run home. Approaching the third barrel, she could hear the roars from the crowd. "Go, Katy, Go!" She heard Michael's voice. The last turn complete and the run for home was all that remained of this ride. She smooched at Chance, and as he dug his hooves and turned, she braced herself for the thrust of speed. "Go!" She leaned forward, and in a flash was past the time line and in the commencing courtesy circle. As they walked out of the arena, she turned to check her time on the clock: 14.036 seconds. "Did you see that folks! Wow! What a debut for the freshman rider! Hope you other ladies are ready to ride! That will be tough to beat!"

Waiting at the gate, Michael caught up with her as she and the next rider exchanged places in the 'alley'[25]. He had heard the comments from the other competitors while she was in the arena. This feeling of wanting to be with her to tell her how proud he was of her was new to him, and though he really didn't understand it, he smiled. "Katy . . . Wait up!" She reined Chance to a halt and let Michael catch up to her. The rider after Katy had completed her run: 15.001 seconds. Michael placed a hand on Katy's thigh. "You're gonna be tough to beat there, Miss McGregor! That was some awesome run!" "He had a slip on the second turn but did recover

---

[25] The alley is the enterance in and out of the arena; on the short side—or end—for the runners to enter and to exit.

well." She patted the horse's neck. "Ann Potts hasn't run yet . . . she drew eighth. I really want to see her."

"It's 15.22."

The third rider was back through the gate. "What was the first rider's time? Do you know?"

"Over 15." Katy smiled at Michael. "My, oh my! You are actually paying attention to the Barrels aren't you?" "Not the Barrels, Katy, to you." They both blushed. Mrs. Harrison announced that two more riders had scratched.

"Hear that . . . They know they can't beat you."

"It's Ann . . . she up!"

They turned back and faced the arena. Ann Potts had won the silver belt buckle and the trophy four years in a row. Last year, she set a time record of 14.021 seconds. Katy knew she had to run that again this year to make it five buckles. Part of her wanted Ann to win as it was her last year in the division, and she would be the first ever to win it every year of competing. The other 'part' of her wanted that buckle so much . . . If she could get it, not only would that be indicative of her abilites and Chance's and would earn them both points for year-end awards, but it would also be impressive to Michael. She had dismounted and was standing next to Michael and holding the reins. He had his arm around her shoulder as Ann entered the arena; he could feel her tensing.

"You got this one!"

"I am not that confident . . . Yet"

They could hear the murmurs of the others watching. "She's running hot today folks! Gonna have to if she wants to take the top spot!" Ann's horse was turning the last barrel and heading for home.

"That's 14.101. Wow! What a ride! That is our second place time so far! Two more to go!" The voice was still speaking as Katy and Michael turned to each other and smiled. He pulled her into a quick kiss.

At the completion of the final run, the placings were set. Katy, Ann and the others rode to the center of the arena in the order of their ribbons. When Katy and Ann were the final two in the arena, Katy dismounted and let the reins drop in a 'ground tie' and walked over to Ann. The crowd fell silent. Ann dismounted, dropped her reins as well and the two girls embraced. "Cowgirl Code, Ann."

"Cowgirl Code, Katy."

Only they could hear what was spoken between them. Walking to the ring steward together, Ann received her red ribbon and Katy was presented the blue and the buckle. They returned to their horses, mounted, then rode out side by side. The crowd cheered for Ann in respect and honor of her years winning and for Katy who had proven she was an up-and-coming star in the Barrel class. They smiled at each other as they exited the arena.

"Ya know, Sara, that McGregor girl is an awful lot like you."

Sara turned to Mary. "And just what makes you say that?" Sara beamed a smile at the woman that she had had to prove herself to in her own youth. Mary leaned forward to her and with a hand on Sara's thigh, said "She's cute, she can ride a horse, she caught a young Moore's eye, and best of all, she 'understands' . . . meaning she has respect. Just don't see that as much anymore in the young people. What she just did out there is a reflection of her upbringing and her values. Yup, she is sure a young 'you'." Sara looked at Mary with a small tear in the corner of her eye. "Mary, I don't know what to say. I did not know you thought that of me. I tried so hard to please you and John." "Stop right there Sara, you were my pick from day one of all the girls after Samuel and you have never once caused me to doubt that. What we have to do now is focus on Katy for Michael. She gets my vote." "She gets mine too." Both women returned their attention to the arena. The clowns were performing their intermission show.

Katy had Chance back in his stall sponging the sweat from him when she felt a tap on her shoulder. She had not heard the approach of whom it was, her heart skipped a beat at the hopes that she would see Michael standing there. To her surprise Russell Barnes was smiling at her.

"That was a very impressive ride, young lady! You have a fine horse here." He stood at Chance's flank and ran his hand over the croup and down his leg. Chance stepped sideways at the touch of an unfamiliar hand on him. "Good gaskin muscling. Is he a young horse? Has he worked any cattle?" "Just stop right there, Mr. Barnes. If you are hoping he's for sale, you will be dissappointed. I raised him from a colt and would never think of letting him go." She had a hand on the horse's neck and leaned into him.

"A man can hope can't he? Don't know until you ask. I certainly did not mean to offend you, Miss McGregor. By the way, have you seen Brent Thomms? I want to congratulate him on his ride earlier. Not too many a cowboy has heard the whistle while still riding Big Bopper. I'm impressed!" "He's over with Michael and Charles, they will be Roping soon." Katy waved in the direction of the cattle pens. "Thanks. And if you change your mind . . ."

"Nope!" Her answer was swift and curt. Russell knew it would not change. He backed away from her, spun on his heels, and was on his way to the cattle pens.

Katy asked herself, "Hmmmm I wonder about that man, what is he *really* up to?" She soaked the sponge and continued to work on her horse.

"There you boys are!" Russell was out of breath as he neared the pens. Michael glanced at his direction and then looked at Charles with the familiar 'unspoken' language that as young boys all three had developed. Charles leaned toward Michael and said, "Don't have a clue!" Trying to keep an eye on Russell as he approached; Michael asked Charles, "Where's Brent?"

"Getting lunch I hope! I'm starved! Can't make a winning run on an empty gutt!" They both turned as Russell came close to address him.

"Mr. Barnes . . ."

"Please, call me Russell."

"Can't do that, sir, not here at the Rodeo. Wouldn't be right, you owning the stock and all." Michael had no intention of letting on to the other competitors there was any connection between them other than professional. He had every intent to prove himself, his horse and his 'team' with Charles as honest and forthright. He did not want to compromise that integrity now or ever.

"What can we do for you, Mr. Barnes?" Charles decided it was a better idea that he speak with Russell than Michael, given the history Russell had had with Sara.

"I'm looking for Brent Thomms. He had a helluva ride on Bopper, wanted to congratulate him. Know where I can find him?"

"At the concessions probably."

"Thanks." Russell turned to leave and then stepped back to Michael. "Don't worry, I'll keep my distance."

"I'm sorry, Mr. Barnes, I didn't mean to be rude. It's just . . ."

"I know, son. Sometimes, you find yourself in awkward places. I'm in one right now." He could see Michael's questioning look. "I got the contract for your Rodeo last minute. I should have turned it down, but frankly I need the money. Starting a string of this quality is a big investment. I vowed to do it right. I want to regain the trust my father shattered in this county, heck, in the state. And . . . I want to see your mother."

Michael stood still, unable to speak for what seemed minutes when in fact had just been moments. "Hotdogs! Get your steamy mustard-laden hotdogs!" Brent was at a run as he approched his friends, breaking the silence between Michael and Russell.

"I . . . ahhhhh . . ."

"Not now, Michael. I'll find you later. You just keep this to yourself. OK. I have honest intentions as far as your mother and would not dare to risk what little ground I gained the other night at the 'Holler' . . ."

"Ahhh, at the 'Holler.' You were there?"

"Yes, I was, and I danced with her and . . ."

"OK. OK . . . I get it! Really, I do, seems I have just recently come into an understanding about that sort of thing myself . . . I have always believed you to be a good man for what you did for us. I'll get the word to my mom you would like to see her. But right now, I am starved, and if I don't get to those dogs soon, there won't be any left!"

"Talk with you later."

"Yeah . . . OK."

"Hey . . . Mr. Thomms . . . Great ride this morning! You did good kid!" With that said, he backed and, turning on his heels, walked away from the three boys he had a hunch would soon play an important role in his life.

As Russell was leaving the pens, Sara was on her way to see Michael before his ride. They saw each other simultaneously. Feeling her heart race and noticing the instant heat on the back of her neck, she tried to look away but could not make her eyes leave the lock with his. He stood there frozen in place as their eyes met. He was so wanting to see her, to speak to her, to take in the fragrance of her perfume . . . He could feel the increase in his heart rate and noticed the sweat on his palms. To himself he said, "You are a grown man, Russell Barnes, and you are acting like a school boy!" He did not know that at the same time she was in a similar self-conversation.

He was there standing with her, having never broken eye contact as he approached. A smile, if she would smile for him, he would have the reassurance he desperately sought.

"Hello, Russell . . . so good to see you. I understand this is your string." She chastised herself for being so casual with him. "It is good to have the challenge of new stock. I did not know that you had invested . . ." He took her hand, and her words fell short of what she had wanted to say. Was that heat from her or from him? She could not determine. What she did know was that he set her 'whole being' on fire.

———

97

"Sara, I want not to place you in an awkward position. We shouldn't talk here, but . . . Please . . . later at the dance, may I seek you?"

"Yes, I, ah, would like that." She tried to mask her desire as well as the look on her face that clearly illustrated her thoughts as she recalled his embrace as they danced. "I will find you, I promise." He smiled, backed two steps, turned on his heels and walked toward the Crow's Nest[26]. She did not realize that she had kept her attention on him.

"Was that the Barnes fellow? I've been looking all over this dag blame place for him, he's still got a bunch of papers to sign!" Mrs. Harrison had ended Sara's trance. "He's on his way to the announcer's booth, you can catch him there, I would think." "Looks to me like you already 'caught' him!" She was quickly too far from Sara for a reply. Sara set back on her left heel and placed her hand on her hip. She smiled, and in a low tone to herself said "No, Sara . . . don't go there! There is too much history you just don't want to drag up again. But . . . but . . ." He roused her. She had been so long without this type of emotion in her life. She'd had a few dates over the years; all very good men, yet none of them had this affect on her. "What am I going to do?"

"Mom! Look out!"

Sara turned just in time to see the frenzied horse running toward her. A bronc from the string had managed to get loose and was in a panic. Instinctively, Sara put one arm up and had one hand ready for the halter. There was much chaos among the onlookers that only fueled the 'flight mode' of the horse. "Easy there. Come on . . ." She was not convincing to the horse as it rushed toward her. "Mom! Get outta there! Let him go! We'll get him in the arena!" She stepped back just as the horse raced through the footprints she had left in the dirt. Russell was there at her side without her noticing his approach.

"Are you all right? Are you hurt at all? Why would you even think to step in front of a raged horse? You could have been killed! I would never forgive myself if anything happened to you. Sara . . ." "I'm OK . . . really . . . and for your information, Mr. Barnes, I've had my fair share of experience with rodeo horses so you can thank me for trying to help one of yours!"

---

[26]   The Crow's Nest is the name given to the elevated announcer's booth.

"Sara, I'm sorry!" His expression clearly indicated the truth in his words. "Well, all right then, that is settled. They have that randy gelding in the arena cornered . . . Think I would like to know it has been caught . . ."

Sara ran to the pipe fence and saw Charles leading the horse toward the gate. Brent could be heard above the cheer of the crowd; "Just ain't a good Rodeo if ain't something don't get loose!" More cheers from the stands were felt as well as heard as the boys lead the horse out of the arena. Charles handed the lead rope to Russell and smiled at Sara. She could feel the heat rise to her cheeks and was certain that Charles had interpretted the reasoning correctly.

"Thank you, Charles, and you too, Brent and Michael, good 'cowboyin'." The boys stepped away as Russell began to lead the horse back to the pens. "See you tonight, Sara . . . See you tonight." Sara turned around and there stood Michael, with his hands on his hips, smiling. "Maaaaahm . . . You wanna explain all that?"
"Nope!" she said with a giggle. "Isn't it time you get ready for the Team Roping, young man?" "You're not off the hook, Mom . . . not in the least!" He was laughing as he rolled his brow to her in jest. To herself she muttered, "Not off one, but definitely on another . . ."

Michael had caught up to Brent and Charles as they were knuckle-punching each other in the shoulders for their heroics with the bronc. He turned back to smile at his mother and mouth the words "I love you" in her direction.

The screech of the loudspeakers as Mrs. Harrison announced the Team Roping event had people rushing for their seats in the grandstands. Gram had returned before Sara and was cooling off with a cold ice tea. "You look frazzled, Sara . . ."
"I could use one of those teas please. Too bad they aren't from Long Island!" Mary chose not to inquire as to the reasoning of Sara's statement, knowing it most likely had something to do with Russell Barnes. Sara was unaware that she had seen the commotion in the arena and that Russell was there with Sara. Sara sat beside Mary, drank the tea quickly, and fell silent as the first team entered the chutes.

"Michael and Charles are the fourth team. I took a look at the cattle and seems as though Russell knows his stock, most are Corriente." "He's got good horses too, I think he really is trying to make a go of a good

Rodeo. Seems he's being his own man now and a good one at that." Mary smiled at Sara as if to tell her that she needed to look forward and not to the past when it came to Russell Barnes.

"OHHHHHHHHHHHHHHHHHhhh!" The crowd was loud as the first heeler missed his loop. The header had been quick to rope both horns and dally back. At the last second, the steer kicked his heel up and the hoof that had been caught slipped out of the rope. The heeler threw his second loop, again catching one hoof. "Tough luck for these cowboys today folks, a ride of 14.8 with a five second penalty for only one leg caught; total time 19.8"

Our second team is the reigning champs from last year, Bill and Bob Thorne from East Dale. Will they keep their title?" Bill threw a 'half-head'[27], and with the precision that had earned them the buckles last year, he turned the steer. Bob then looped both hind legs and had the stretch in 10.2 seconds. "There you have it folks! Our time to beat has been set!"

"Mary . . . Do you see the third team. Who are they? They are both girls! Yeeeeesssssss! It's about time we show the men we can rope too!" Sara noticed that many of the spectators were just realizing that the team was female and were soon on their feet voicing "You go, girls!" Mary opened the program and soon had the names of the girls now vying for the buckles. "Says here they are Marge Pelton and Mary Shanks. They're from over by Carnon. Hmmm, this could put an interesting twist on things!"

"You ready, Marge?"
"Ready as ever! Sure am glad they have an electric barrier and not a rope!" The chute opened, and the steer was out. The horns caught and a good loop for both hinds.

In the holding area, Michael and Charles were speechless as the girls were in the arena and the time of 10.45 seconds was announced. "Are we winnin' this thing?" Michael looked at Charles. "Oh yeah . . . We're winnin' this thing all right! We sure as heck ain't gettin' beat by girls! That is for sure!" Michael felt a punch to his right thigh; it was Katy . . . "What's that about girls?" She smiled at Michael . . . "Come here, cowboy . . ." She motioned for him to bend to her, and when he did, she kissed him for good luck. Charles laughed at him and then remarked, "I gotta get me

---

[27] Roping only one horn is known as a half head.

one of those . . . A girl . . . that likes to kiss that is . . . Maybe one of those Ropers . . . what do you think?"

The boys were laughing as Marge and Mary rode toward the gate; tipping their hats to them, the girls smiled back. After they passed, Michael looked at Charles . . . "Good luck with that . . . 'stuuuuuud.'" Katy noticed the looks between the girls as they rode past Michael and Charles . . . To herself she remarked, "They could be trouble . . ."

Michael backed Capp into the box. "Easy there, big boy . . ."
"What's up with Capp?" Just as Charles was asking Michael, the gelding bolted from the box in a frenzy of bucking and snorting. Caught off guard, Michael's seat was not balanced and he was nearly thrown. The crowd was silenced in concern for the young cowboy. Michael knew that he was in trouble, he put a hand on the forks of the saddle searching for the leather scars left behind from the day of his father's accident. To himself he said, "Dad, help me! Please!" At that very moment as Sara was watching in disbelief the behavior of the big horse, she felt a hand on her shoulder; she knew it was Samuel. "Help him, Samuel, please!" She reached up to touch her shoulder.

The gelding settled slowly, and Michael soon had him under control.

Returning to the box, Capp refused to go in. Katy ran to the box rail and noticed an arching wire on the ground near where Capp would have been standing. "Wire! UH . . . wire on the ground . . . there . . ." she pointed to the right corner of the panels. "Holy Crap! I'm outta here!" Charles spurred Lady forward to prevent chancing her getting shocked. Facing the boxes, the two boys waited for the Stewards to assess the situation. Sara was now at Katy's side.
"What happened?"
"Loose wire . . . something must be wrong with the 'eye'." She looked toward Michael, "I'm fine mom, really!" Sara put her arm around Katy; simultaneously they said to each other, "They're fine."

"Pull the 'eye,' gonna have to use the rope. You OK with that, boys?"
"Yes, sir!"
"Well, OK then, I suppose we have to check the rule book . . ."
A Flagger was pulling a rule book out of his pocket as the men were removing the wires. "Can't find nothin' against it . . ."
"Get the Judge."

"Yes, sir." He was off and soon returned with Mr. Dewain, a former Roping champion from Idaho.

"What have we got here, boys? We fussin' over something big or are we wasting my time?"

"Michael?" Charles leaned over to speak softly. "Yeah . . ." "He is a big man . . . Kinda scary too . . ."

"Yup. Sit up and don't look so worried. We're making an impression here. How am I doin' at faking it?" They both laughed. Mr. Dewain glanced at them, and in an instant, they were silenced.

"Set 'em up . . . let's get this moving . . . we're burning daylight." The electronic eye had been removed, Walt Sanderson took his position on top of the chute to push the calf forward, and the rope barrier was set. Capp had settled and was willing to back into the box; "Ready, Charles?"
"Ready."

Michael looked at Walt and with a tip of his head, he made his 'call for the steer'. When the barrier released, he was out of the chute and had a perfect loop over the horns. Capp's timing was right on, and as Michael dallied and turned to the left, Charles was ready with his throw. Effortlessly, his loop was around both hind legs; when his dally was complete, they stretched the steer. "Folks, that is true team roping there! Fine work, boys! Let's hear the time, Judge . . ."
"8.92."

They released the steer, and as they rode out of the arena they 'high-fived' each other. Sara, Katy, and Brent were waiting for them at the gate. "Holy crap! Did we really just do that?"

"Yes, you did . . . wow!" Michael dismounted and hugged his mother and then received a congratulatory hug from Katy. Brent started to lean in to him. "Ahhhh, womenfolk only there big boy! Oh, what the heck! That was awesome wasn't it!" The two young men slapped each other's backs as they kept their distance yet still embraced. "Mom . . . where's Gramp?"

As he asked the question he could see John approaching. Handing the reins to Brent, Michael walked to meet his grandfather. The elder Moore put his strong arms around his grandson and with the strength of his years as a rancher nearly picked Michael up off the ground with his exhuberance. "Did you see us Gramp? Did you see?" "Yes, I did! You two were . . . how do you kids say it? . . . you were 'awwwwwesome!'" When

Charles walked over, John embraced him as well. Brent gave the reins to Katy. "Here . . . s'pose you ought to get used to this . . ." He winked at her and joined the men.

John stood back and gazed upon the three young men. "I am so proud of you all. Brent, you had a great ride today, one to remember always. You two boys just kicked butt in the Roping. And looking over there with your mother, I see young Katy McGregor. I'm thinkin' she's gonna be joinin' in a few more of these with you guys . . . her Barrel run was impressive. I do believe that you all have made your first 'mark'!"

Sara took the reins from Katy and nudged her to join the circle. As she approached the men, she hesitated just a bit and then John smiled at her. "Come here, girl . . . you're 'in'!" Katy slipped inbetween Michael and Charles. They all held out an arm and with hands atop each other, heads leaned in close, as one voice whooped, "A–M–I–G– O–S . . . amigos all the way!"

Meanwhile, as the celebration in the holding area was happening, the remaining four teams had competed. The announcement of times had been given of 9.13 for Henry Little and Howard Beele plus a five-second penalty for roping only one hindleg, 11.0 for Ben Carter and John Houseman, and Wes Grant and Joe Hinder were disqualified due to the 'three refusals' rule of a horse not entering the box. In true cowboy way, Joe accepted his young horse's fright of the crowds and graciously exited the arena. Wes was not as accepting of the situation. He threw his hat when they were out of the arena, much to the surprise of the spectators. The last team to compete finished in 10.9 with an additional 10 seconds for a broken barrier.

Mrs. Harrison's voice was again on the loudspeakers, and she was announcing the placings. The crowd cheered for the young men as they received their trophy buckles. "Looks like there's new competition in town fellas! These boys have shown us that they are serious Team Ropers!"

While Michael and Charles were receiving their winnings, in the holding pens a group of men had gathered; surrounding an angry Wes Grant. "Where the hell is Barnes?" He was encircled by contestants as well as staff and handlers of the Rodeo. "I want another go at it . . . Gimme another partner!" He swung around flailing his arms; a half-empty whiskey bottle he had grasped in his right fist let loose and shattered on the ground.

Michael wanted to go see what was happening. "Stay here, do not get yourself involved in that . . . He is drunk and nothing good will come of this. You are young, and involvement in a situation like that now will haunt you a very long time. What you are not a part of you cannot be blamed for." Gramp had a firm grip on Michael's arm. As Michael stepped back, he could see the security officers leading Wes off the Rodeo Grounds. "This ain't over, Barnes!"

"Keep your voice down . . . you're sorry ass is outta here! You got a good grip on him, Nate, sure is squirrly for a drunk dude!" Two officers led Wes Grant to the exit gate.

"Time to load up and get home, boys! I do believe you kicked that ass you spoke of this mornin'!" Sara threw a glare at John and then smiled.

PART 5

The Dance

"Mom . . .?" Sara was in her room looking at the photo of Samuel and Tonk, now complete with the tuft of forelock. She had placed the frame with the others around the mirror of family photographs on the wall above the clothes bureau. Hearing Michael calling for her, she answered back "You all spiffy and got your dancin' boots on?"

"One more time through *Cotton-Eyed Joe* . . . Pleeeeeease?" He reached for her hand as she entered the kitchen. Sara noticed that the table and chairs had already been positioned against the wall to accommodate the space needed to practice the dance. Passing the phone stand, Michael pressed 'play' on the cassette player.

"Whew, I must be getting old! That's a lot of work!"
"Mom, you will never be old! You'll always be the prettiest 'belle at the ball!' You sure can dance the best, that is for sure!" Sara turned to her son, and looking up at his strong stature, she was taken back to Samuel as a young man. Returning her thoughts to the present day, she smiled at Michael. "She has no idea does she?" "Nope! Not even the guys know. Gram told me a long time ago to keep this 'hidden under my hat and in my boots' until the right moment, and I would know when that moment would be. It's been hard, but Gram insisted . . . and well, when Gram insists about something, I sure as heck don't want to question why!"

Mother and son began to laugh. John and Mary looked at each other in their chairs by the fireplace in the family room and simultaneously rose to see the source of the commotion. When they got to the kitchen, they were already holding hands and began a swing step to the music. The four dancers completed two more songs.

"Mary, I need to sit the next one out! I'm not . . ." "Me too, dear. That sure was fun, but . . . this old gray mare ain't what she used to be!" The exuberance of the dancing faded quickly for elder Moores. Michael looked over to his grandmother sitting with her hand on Gramp's arm. "This is it, Gram! This is it!" John looked at Mary. "This is what?" "Oh . . . just something between a grandmother and her favorite grandson!" Mary smiled. "Mary Moore! You just keep me guessing as to the logics of a woman! You know that don't you!" "John Moore, there are just some things you just leave up to me!" "Yes ma'am."

Mary treached up and held Michael's right hand between both of hers. "Knock her off her feet! You two are going to remember this night for always. Just like I remember the first dance that I had with your grandfather at the Huntston Rodeo in '38. He wore a blue plaid shirt and had the buckle he had won Calf Roping secure on his belt. I think it was the first time he had those boots on because he kept complaining they were still tight and that was the reason he kept missing steps of the dance. I fell in love with him that night and have loved him every day since and will love him through all eternity." She turned to John, and they embraced. Sara smiled at Michael trying to hide the haunting of her heart at knowing she would never have with Samuel what his parents shared. He was taken from her too soon . . . Michael read his mother's thoughts in her facial expression and held her close. "I know Mom, I know."

"I believe your ride is here!" Charles had use of his father's ranch truck for the night and had boasted that he would be the 'big shot' because he had the 'wheels'. As Charles and Brent approached the backdoor, the Moores separated from each other so as to not let on what they were doing. They were quickly trying to get the table and chairs reset when the boys flew through the backdoor.

"You're not serious, are you? Were you getting pointers from your grandparents on dancing? No offense there, Gram and Gramp . . . But seriously? They like dance to the 'oldies'! Again, no offense meant, you know I love you." Brent tried not to laugh at his friend. Charles could not hold back and had turned away from the conversation to hide his laughter. "Come on, twinkle toes . . . Miss Katy McGregor has no idea what she is in for tonight! Hope she can handle your two left feet!"

"You think those roping girls will be there tonight? I saw one of them smile at me . . . maybe I got a chance! Ya think?" "Charles, you best remember her name if you want a chance." Michael fisted Charles's shoulder. "Name . . . yeah . . . that would be a good thing to know, wouldn't it?"

"Marge Pelton and Mary Shanks. Who is who, is up to you!"
"Thanks, Momma Moore. I love you!" Charles kissed Sara on her cheek. "You boys have fun! Be good! No racing on the road, that truck is held together with duct tape! Be home on time!" As the three young men passed Sara, each kissed her cheek. "My boys . . . Oh my goodness, look out girls, they are a comin' to town!" She turned to Mary. "So what were you two watching on TV? Care if I join you?" Sara followed Mary and John as they returned to the den. Sara tried not to think about her promise

to Russell. She just couldn't convince herself to go as much as she seemed to want his attention earlier. Those thoughts had escaped her heart and entered her fears; she couldn't go. Not yet. But . . . she wanted to.

The old truck pulled into the parking area at the fairgrounds set up especially for the dance. The Dance Committee for the Rodeo had worked hard all day setting up the lights and balloons strung between poles to act as the outlining of the dance floor and constructing the stage for the band. There was a punch bowl and food table set up to the left of the music band's platform.

Charles found a good place to back in so as to have the tailgate and bed of the truck for seating in view of the dance floor. He didn't want too close to the food table and have a crowd around his dad's truck. He did manage a spot close enough to enable himself and Brent to see all the girls as they walked by. The steady line of trucks arriving continued the pattern of backing in.

"Man, we got here just in time! You got us the 'good seats' Charles! We gonna be right up with all the action! Which also means we gotta stay to the end 'cuz we ain't gettin' back out!"

"Nope . . . We are here for the duration! And we got the bench seat from the old truck out behind the barn for comfort as we watch Mr. Twinkle Toes there make a fool of himself with Miss Katy McGregor!"

Charles had climbed into the bed of the truck, and with a slow throw of himself, he was sitting with his back against the cab on the bench seat. "Boys! This is livin'!" He put his hands behind his head and looked to the sky. "Don't look now Charles, the roper girls just got here and have parked two trucks over to the right behind us." Brent was standing in the bed of the truck taking in the entrances and the parking positions of their friends and fellow competitors.

"Oh . . . This is gonna be gooooood!"

"What's gonna be good? What have I missed already?"

"The two roper girls are over there . . ." He pointed to their truck. "Holy Shit! That rig is brand new! Either they got rich daddies or they are toooooooo old for you Charles! Whooo eee . . . look at all that chrome!" Michael fisted Charles in the arm while trying not to laugh. "Have you figured out who's who yet lover boy?" "I was kinda hopin' to employ your new girlfriend for that . . . oh, look here she comes now!"

Michael turned just as Katy was approaching the tailgate. He stood speechless as he looked into the eyes of the 'girl' that had kissed him earlier today and then saw the 'woman' standing before him. She had on skin-tight jeans tucked into her twenty-inch hole pull Tony Lama[28] boots complete with underslung heel, her belt held the buckle she had won in the Barrel Racing, and her halter top was pink and green. She wasn't particularily well 'formed' yet but that was OK to him. Michael leaned on the tailgate, mezmerized by Katy's appearance topped off with her straw Stetson[29]. Smiling his approval to her, he thought to himself, "She is 'cowgirl perfection' and she likes *me!*" Michael stood up, set back on his heels and put his thumbs in his pockets. With a sideways glance to his friends, he puffed his chest. "Boys, I got something I need to tell ya . . ."

"Yeah, we see her . . . and well . . . I guess we'll see *you* after the dance." Brent had a somber tone to his voice. "No . . . you don't understand . . . that's not it . . ." Michael was cut off by the wail of the speakers as the Dusty Boots Band was warming up and checking their instruments. He had wanted to tell them he actually had learned to dance and was going to surprise Katy; but he was not given the chance. He thought maybe it was better this way, just surprise everyone at the same time, they would not have believed him anyway.

Katy reached Michael; she could see in his eyes that he liked what she had chosen to wear. In her slow approach, she had made quite sure that he saw every detail. Reaching out to her, he then drew her close. "Wow! I am not sure where you have been hiding all this, but I am glad that you have . . . I'm gonna be fighting off a lot guys tonight, I can see that!" "The only one that matters to me is you, Michael. I may dance with others, but you are the one for me!" He lifted her so she was standing on the small cooler and pulled her to him, and without hesitation, found himself lost in a deep, sensual kiss.

"I like that." She smiled at him. The kisses they had shared earlier were playful and teasing . . . this one had truly taken her breath away. "I really like you." "I really like you too, Michael. Kiss me again . . ."

******

---

[28]   Tony Lama is a brand name for a line of western boots.

[29]   Stetson is a brand name for a line of Western hats.

"Sara, do you need to talk? You sure have been quiet. This is your favorite movie, and you haven't said hardly a word." *Big Country* was on the television; her favorite part when Gregory Peck tries to ride the horse in the corral and gets thrown time and time again had just begun. "Mary, do you think the boys are OK?" Sara was not actually worried about Michael, she just didn't want to talk about what had happened with Russell earlier at the Rodeo.

"The boys? Come on, Sara, you can't fool me! I saw you talking with Russell Barnes today. That is what this solemn mood is all about isn't it?"

"Barnes? You were with Barnes today?" John's attention from the movie was redirected to Sara. "What the hell for?"

"John!"

"Sorry dear, shouldn't have cussed. What on earth would you need to speak to him about?" Sara knew she was cornered. "He owns the stock that was used today. I was over at the chutes . . ."

"Mary, I would like to watch the movie. If you two want to talk about Barnes, take it in the kitchen." He turned away from Sara. His irritation with her was apparent, fueling her apprehension of chastisement from Mary. "Sara, I think it best we talk away from John." Mary looked at John with a shake of her head. Why couldn't he accept that Russell Barnes was not his father? He was his own man and trying hard to prove that. The subject of Russell Barnes was one of the few times John's bold stubborness angered her.

Sara sat at the kitchen table with her hands in her lap. "Would you like a cup of tea dear?"

"Yes, thank you Mary." Retrieving a mug from the cupboard, Mary kept her eye on Sara. The 'pained' look in her eyes and the nearly nondistinguishable quiver of her lips as she spoke greatly concerned Mary. Sara glanced toward the den and with a sigh, turned back to her tea. "He's never going to change, is he?" She slowly lifted the cup to take a sip.

"He's a Moore . . . stubborn as a blind mule. You know that. He won't come around on his own, dear, that is up to you to get him to see that Russell is not the man that John needs put the blame on. To be truthful, I think deep down he knows that. It's just after all this time, to admit he may have misjudged the man . . . Well, that will take an effort that he is not ready to concede to. Will he ever? That I cannot say. What 'makes each man' is for that man and that man only to truly know. All we, as women, can hope for is to have the heart of a man trust us enough to be a part of 'who the man is'. John Moore is a man that takes very seriously the tradition of family and trust. His heritage is of struggle and sacrifice. It is that heritage that sets him steadfast in his beliefs. He loves you, Sara. He loves you deeply. I think he fears losing you. It would break his heart all over again." "I love him too." Sara began to cry. Mary leaned toward her and placed her arm around her. "He knows you do . . ." Sara put her head on Mary's shoulder.

"I'm so torn apart. I feel like I am betraying Samuel with feelings for Russell. Or am I just transferring lonliness to the person that showed me a kindness at a time when I was most vulnerable? I don't know if what I feel is real or not. If it is real, how do I face John? And what about Michael? If it isn't real, then how do I make myself stop feeling this way?" Sara looked at her matriarch for what seemed minutes. Mary spoke no words as she let Sara's thoughts seemingly hang in the air between them.

Taking Sara's hands in hers, Mary then took one hand and lifted Sara's chin. She used her mother's handkerchief that she kept with her always to dab the tears cascading Sara's cheeks.

"My dear, Sara . . . do not feel as though you are betraying Samuel. He, of all people, knows the way you love and need you have for love. I know my son enough to be able to tell you for him, it's all right for you to love again, even marry again . . . Neither John nor I want you to ever leave, but we cannot be the reason why you stay. We are old, and you have so many years still . . . The ranch is yours and Michael's when we 'pass on' and that will never change. No matter where you are in your life or who you are with. Michael will be on his own in just a few short years . . . Have you thought about that? Where do you want to be and how do you want to be there when that time comes?

"We were so fortunate that Samuel stayed on here, and I know Michael will too, in time. But I do know he will have to find his own way in life as the kids these days have far more options and choices for themselves than we did or even you for that matter. Sara, think about it, please. You are a kind and generous soul that longs to not be alone. Your choice, now, well, that may take time to get accustomed to, but we will, if he is really to be for you. John will come around . . . have you not noticed that I am an expert on turning his opinions my way and yet he still thinks he has not altered?" She put her arms around Sara. "Thank you, Mary . . . And yes, I have noticed your knack of persuasion." Together, they laughed as John entered the room.

"Girl stuff?"

"Yup! Girl stuff!"

"What's in that Tea. I think I need some!"

"How's the movie?"

"It would be a lot better if my bride was sitting with me!" Sara looked at Mary. "You're right, I need to think . . . I'm going for a drive . . . maybe help clear my head a bit. It's too late to ride so the truck will just have to do!"

Mary gave a concerned look to Sara. "No, don't worry . . . I am not going to the Rodeo Grounds; Michael would never forgive me if I showed up there and embarrassed him. That dance is for them."

She had told Russell she would be there. She had told him it was OK to find her. Why had she said that? She was sitting in her truck, both hands on the steering wheel with her head on the center horn push. She lifted her head, staring through the windshield. "What am I going to do. How do I fix this?" She had spoken aloud as John approached the truck without her being aware he had followed her outside. "You're going to 'live' again Sara . . . That is what you are going to do! You have spent far too long in the shadow of yesterday. When the sun rises tomorrow, you need to open your eyes . . . you go on your drive now . . . You do your 'thinking' . . . You get settled with the reality of today and tomorrow . . . Let yourself 'live' again. See you at breakfast." He turned and was walking toward the house before she could utter any response. That was his 'way'.

"I love you, John Moore!"

"I love you too!" She had no idea he would hear her, but he did.

She put the truck in gear and was heading to the end of the driveway. Her eyes moist with tears, she focused on the archway standing as a sentry above the entrance to the ranch. The iron silhouettes of cattle and horses surrounding the Moore brand—so many times she had looked at it while passing underneath, each time a feeling of great pride would overcome her. Now, she almost felt shame. Shame of herself. Samuel was gone, Michael was heir to the ranch . . . And she, she had thoughts of another man. A man that had a history both good and bad with the very people and ranch she loved so much. Her heart pounded as she wept. Unknowing, she turned right at the main road.

Mary was waiting for him when he came in the door. "Things may just be different now, Mary, just may be different. I think she is ready, finally.

We can only hope. Sure wish it had been someone other than Barnes, but if that is what has to be, then that is what has to be."

"Have you told her that? She is so afraid of letting you down . . . She loves you so much."

"She knows I love her."

"Men! Just have to be stubborn with emotion . . ." John took Mary in his arms and kissed her deeply. "How's that for emotion?" Taken by surprise at the ferocity of his embrace, she gasped for breath. "John! I don't know where that came from, but I like it!"

"Let's skip the end of the movie . . . we've seen it already anyway . . ." He took her hand and lead her to their bedroom.

****

Sara had been driving the back roads with the tape deck blaring *Marshall Tucker*, *Pure Prairie League*, and *Alabama*. There was just something about overly loud music that comforted her in her contemplative mood. *Fire on the Mountain* was coming to a close as she found herself stationary in front of the enterance to the Rodeo Grounds.

She was startled out of her trance by the yelling of the driver behind her. Regaining herself, she pulled forward into the parking lot and managed to stay out of the lighted areas, settling in the back corner behind the grandstands. Turning off the ignition, she looked toward the dance floor, and hearing the sounds of the band playing, her mind slipped back to the dances with Samuel.

"I have to stop this! John is right, I have to be thankful for the past and cherish it always, but this is 'now' . . . And 'now' needs me to 'let go' . . . *I* need me to 'let go' . . ." She spoke to herself as she took in all the 'life' that was around her. The enthusiasm of youth . . . had she really lost it? Could she ever find it again? She lay her head on the steering wheel and grasped it tightly. Moments later, she straightened her back and knew she had to find Russell.

The band was into the second set. Brent and Charles were sitting on the bench seat and Michael leaned on the tailgate observing the dancers on the floor. Michael had held his word and danced the first dance with Katy. As she was 'teaching' him a swing step, he politely followed her and did not let on that he knew the steps and even a few more. He wanted to give this to her as a "thank you" for all she had done earlier in the day for him. She and her friends had had a good laugh at his expense; he was about to change their minds.

"Think I'll find my lil gal for another spin on the dance floor!"

"What? That first dance wasn't enough humiliation for you?" Charles punched Michael's shoulder. "Easy there, I just might need that arm for swingin' her and maybe a 'dip' or two." Brent and Charles looked at each other and simultaneously spit out their pop in laughter. Charles nearly choked. "Easy there, you OK?" He looked at Michael. "See what you did to him!" He was still laughing himself. "Hold on, boys! You are in for the surprise of the night!"

He set his drink on the tail gate and searched for Katy. She was over at the roper girls' truck. "I see Katy is talking with your 'ropers' . . . guess you conned her into finding out 'who is who' after all!" "She's a good one that Katy . . . Yupp that she is!" Charles's cheeks were red from embarrassment. Michael thought to himself, "We'll see just how good she is when I get her out on the dance floor!" "The rest is up to you guys . . . I'm getting her for a dance. Good luck with that Master Charles!" Michael hustled away toward Katy.

He walked up behind her and tapped her shoulder. He had no idea that she was actually there to make sure the girls knew that Michael was not to be pursued by them. She had noticed the looks they gave him, and she was setting the territorial lines—Cowgirl Code. She made sure that Marge and Mary were made aware that Charles and Brent were unattached. It was clear that they had both had hopes for Michael, and Katy knew that she was going to have pay close attention to these girls. They weren't 'local' and she was not going to allow them to influence Michael. Feeling the tap on her shoulder, she turned to see Michael. Flashing a smile at him and then a warning smile to the girls, she put her arm in his.

A slight tug on his arm and he bent to kiss her. With thoughts that this was intended for Marge and Mary, he thought it best to play along and pulled her close to him as they kissed. Setting her back down, he looked at the other girls. He tipped his hat to them and put out his hand. "Hi! I'm Michael Moore." "I'm Marge Pelton, good to meet you. You had a great run today." Mary stepped toward Michael as if to set Marge back. "I'm Mary Shanks, Katy here has told us all about you." Girls. Territory.

Gramp was right, understanding women was a complexity he didn't know if he would ever figure out.

Michael pointed toward their truck. "Nice rig . . . noticed it coming in." Marge, wanting to take advantage of Michael being impressed by her father's birthday gift to her, stepped toward him. Katy held tighter to his arm. "Daddy wanted me to have it for my birthday. Mary is my stepsister, she'll probably get one next year when she turns eighteen." Katy looked at Michael to see his reaction. His face told her that he thought Marge was boastful, not a trait in a woman many cowboys want. "Have you met my friends Charles and Brent yet?" Michael wanted to change the topic of conversation quickly and find a good 'exit point' for Katy and him to go to the dance floor. Pointing to Charles' truck, he saw the girls smile at each other.

"Well, maybe we just ought to go over there and introduce ourselves. Any friend of yours should be a friend of ours!" Arm in arm, they were heading toward Brent and Charles. Katy looked at Michael, he could see the thoughts she had in the expression on her face. "Katy, don't worry, I only have eyes for you. Those girls could never be you." He heard her sigh of relief.

"Would you care to dance again?" He took his hat off and bowed to her as he asked her. She curtsied in jest at his antics and replied, "Why, yes, I would be honored to partake in another jaunt on the floor for dance." Taking her hand, he led her toward the other dancers. As they passed Brent and Charles, he waved his arm to them. "We got a front-row seat to watch you make a fool of yourself again! Thanks for the entertainment!" Katy stopped long enough to tell Charles that Marge was wearing the blue boots and hat.

Sara had kept herself concealed behind the parked trucks as she made her way toward the back of the grandstands. Her heart racing in fear of him being there as well as him not being there. She slipped under the wooden structure and had a good view of the dance floor. To her right, she could see Michael holding Katy's hand as they walked through the lights. Sara put her hands up to her mouth to silence herself. "This is it . . . he's going to do this . . . I have to see him . . ." She backed under a seat brace out of any light. "Oh, Michael, our lives are changing tonight. In different ways, but they are changing." A slow tear made its way down her cheek, she wiped it away and smiled as she watched her son two-step and swing. The crowd around them separated to watch in amazement the skill of 'Mountain Man'. She could hear the cheering of the onlookers and soon many joined them. "Dip her! Come on, Michael . . . just like I taught you . . . yes . . . just like that . . . good boy . . . You have her now . . ." Katy and Michael stood still in the middle of the floor, and he kissed her as their friends cheered.

Noticing the importance of what was happening on the floor, the lead singer of the band turned to his musicians. "Boys, this calls for a waltz!" He motioned to the back stage area for a woman to join them. "Lizzie . . . quick . . . you're up!" She hesitated and was pushed by a fellow crew member onto the floor. Her husband handed her the microphone. "Sing 'Anne', Lizzie . . . sing 'Anne' . . ." She held the microphone in her hands and looked out to the dancers on the floor. As Michael released his embrace of Katy, she began to sing *Can I Have This Dance*. Her voice was so similar to *Anne Murray* that many stopped to make sure that she was not the famous singer.

Michael placed Katy's hand in his and waltzed with absolute precision around the dance floor. He swung her out, drew her in, spun her, and held her. She was awestruck by his precise execution of the steps and how he flowed so lightly; he literally swept her off her feet. At the completion of the song, Katy was without words, she looked into Michael's eyes searching . . . She wasn't sure what for, but she could not take her attention from him.

"My mom taught me." He could see she needed answers to questions she did not know how to ask. "Gram told me not to let on until the time was right and with the right girl." Katy could not speak, she jumped up, Michael caught her. She wrapped her legs around him, and with her arms crossed behind his back, she kissed him. He held her under her buttocks and twirled around. Neither noticed the rest of the people surrounding them.

Sara leaned back on the beam behind her. That had been a very private 'mom moment', and she would cherish it forever.

"Holy crap! Dude! That was like totally righteous! Where did that come from anyway? You been holdin' out on us or what?" Charles met Michael at the edge of the dance floor. Brent was soon there pushing Michael's shoulders. "Wow! I guess Mr. Twinkle Toes here is all sorta full of suprises!" Katy was still at his side when Marge and Mary arrived at the truck. "Think you could teach these 'yahoos' here a little of that footwork?" Marge pointed to Brent and Charles. Michael hid his face from the girls, lifting his eyebrows, he mouthed to them: "You scoring here?" Both his friends smiled back to him as if to affirm the answer to his question. While Michael was turned, Marge reached to Katy and tapped her arm. "No worries, little girl, no worries." Katy wasn't pleased at the 'little girl' reference; the assurance from them that they would not be a threat outweighed any irritation from their words.

****

Russell parked his truck over by the Crow's Nest. He had never really understood why the announcer's booth was named as such until he heard the squelch of Mrs. Harrison's voice over the loudspeakers earlier that day. Climbing the stairs, trying not to be noticed, he sat back to be out of sight should anyone happen to look in that direction. "Atta boy Michael!" he softly spoke as he watched Michael and Katy on the dance floor. 'If only I could dance with your mother . . ." he hung his head and with a slow brush sideways, sighed. When he looked up, he saw Sara moving out from under the grandstands. He would not have seen her had he not been in the 'Nest. "Oh, Sara . . . you are here . . ." He bent forward to keep hidden as he descended the stairs. Pausing to hold his chest, his heart was beating wildly and his breathing had quickened. He held the post at the bottom of the staircase while looking toward where he had seen her . . . where could she have slipped off to? The movement of the dancers and the socialization of those surrounding the dance floor made it difficult to get a sight of her again. "Screw this! Get a grip man . . . Go find her!" He stepped out from under the 'Nest.

Sara had managed to keep herself secret in her traverse across the parking lot behind the cattle chutes and holding pens. Just at what point in time she had made the decision to go to the Crow's Nest, she did not know. She felt as if she was following someone else's lead; her legs carried her to where her head said not to go. Standing at the corner of the bull pen, she saw movement in the darkness. An overwhelming uneasiness swept over her. Remaining as still as she could, she waited to assure herself that whoever or whatever was over there had either moved on or would not know she was there.

Movement again. This time over by the footers of the 'Nest. Her heart still pounding from the first intrusion of her delicate frame of mind, she now felt the need to hide within the pens. Looking around her in the darkness, a sudden panic of entrapment came over her. Her back slid down the gate panel until her knees were bent and she had her arms around them, head tucked in. She did not realize that as she slid into this fetal position, her jeans had caught on a barb in the panel tearing the pocket.

Voices . . . She was aware of voices. Rising slowly so as to not alert anyone of her presense, she turned to their origin. "Oh my God! Russell," she said to herself as she realized it was him under the 'Nest. Another person rushed him from behind and pushed him to the ground. A fight ensued; she could barely make out the words lashed out to each other. Russell kept telling the man "Stop, it wasn't his fault" to no avail. Russell, still on the ground, broke free of his assailant, turned to face him and with a rock he had found on the ground while pinned, he gave one last blow to the other man's head. The man crumbled to the ground. Russell then stood over him, and when there was no more movement from the man on the ground, he fell to his knees.

She slid back down, holding on to the rungs of the panel, head between her arms . . . "Nooooooooooooo. Oh, Lord, no . . ." She took a deep breath, pulling herself up she regained her balance, brushed off her jeans and quickly walked toward Russell. She was still in the labrynth of pens when the security officers arrived at him. She sould see him being handcuffed, and as he turned with the two men, their eyes met.

They stared at each other in consternation, neither knowing what to do. He did not want the officers to see her, yet he knew not how to keep her in hiding—without drawing attention to her. She wanted to run to him, she wanted an explanation for herself and for the officers. With the pain of uncertainty in her eyes, she tried to smile at him; she could not. He hung his head and looked away from her, hoping she would retreat to the darkness.

Her attention turned to the motionless figure on the ground, the sounds of emergency sirens filled the air. In a haze, she could see commotion on the dance floor as many of the party-goers were in pursuit of the ambulance. Sara knew she had to leave, she could not risk being seen. She turned, and in the blur of urgency, she felt lost in the puzzle of so many corral panels. She turned around slowly until she found a way to the other side. Her stride was hastened each time she heard nearby voices. Out of breath, she realized she was leaning on the back of the supply room under the grandstand. She had no recall of her journey there; she was just relieved that she escaped to safety without being seen. A quick glance to Charles's truck and to her relief, she saw Michael and Katy sitting on the bench seat.

Having caught her breath and relieved at Michael's noninvolvement, she retreated to her truck. Once inside, she inspected the pain in her left knee from the slip in a puddle that she had tried to jump on her way to the truck. She noticed blood on her hand and reached to her back pocket for her grandmother's hankie . . . It was not there. Searching frantically through the truck for the small cloth that had been hand-stiched, the tears were for the loss of the memento more so than for the injury of her knee.

"Look later . . . gotta get outa here . . ." One last glance toward Michael and Sara had the truck in reverse, a slight hesitation before shifting to drive and she was slowly making her way to the exit. She had no idea that just moments after she pulled away, Michael and Katy had stood up in the truck bed and taken in the panoramic view of the fair grounds.

"People must be starting to leave." Katy had noticed tail lights leaving through the gates. Michael glanced over to the exit just as the lights were out of sight. "Don't see anyone else leaving, wonder who that was?"

"Hey . . . did you see the truck that just left? Looked like your mom's!"
"Naaaaa, couldn't a been . . . sure did look like it though!" Charles had not been noticed as he approached the tailgate.

****

"Michael! Breakfast is ready!" Gram was placing the bacon and eggs alongside the biscuits on a plate when Michael opened the mud room door. "Do I have perfect timing or what?" He hung his ball cap on the hook and stood at the sink in the mud room to wash his hands. "Do I smell biscuits?" He peered around the corner as he folded and placed the towel on the counter. She stood at the table; a firm grip on the plate she held out for him . . . he reached for it, and she pulled it back. She smiled at her grandson as he tried several times to get a hold on the plate.

"How was the dance last night? How was your surprise for Katy? You gonna tell your Gram all about it?" "I'm kinda thinking if I want my breakfast, I am gonna have to . . . huh!"

"You know your grandmother . . ." John peered out from behind the morning newspaper. "It's another one of those 'girl things' . . . just go with it, son . . . Just go with it . . . Your eggs are getting cold!"

"Gram, can I ask you something?" Michael had a spoon in the jam jar, he stopped his effort to spoon the berries for his biscuit and looked at his grandmother. Mary turned from the stove, wiped her hands on her apron and sat in the chair next to him. "Anything, Michael . . . you just ask your Gram whatever you want to"

"Where was Mom last night?" Mary had thought for sure he was going to ask about girls or what he felt for Katy; she was not prepared for what he did ask. John set the paper down, he too wanted to hear the answer. After a slight pause to gather her thoughts, she said "Well, we were watching *Big Country*, and your mother deemed it neccesary to go for a drive. Said she needed to 'think.' She has been a bit distracted lately."

"Was *Marshall Tucker* on high volume?" John let out a near-snort when Michael revealed his knowledge of her 'thinking mode'. "You know about that, do you?" "Yeah, it's really bad if she plays *Restless Heart*." There was laughter all around the table as Sara entered the kitchen.

"Smells great, Mary. What have I missed?" On her way past Michael, she put a hand on his shoulder. "How was the dance last night . . . Did you knock their boots off?" She was adding a biscuit to her plate and pouring a cup of coffee.

"Mom . . . get your coffee and sit . . . I will tell you all . . . all about it . . ."
"More coffee, anyone?" Sara filled John's mug and set the pot back in the brewer. Settling in her chair, Michael passed her the jam.

He told them of the dancing and how Katy and everyone had been amazed at his hidden talent. He told them how Brent and Charles had somehow managed to convince Marge and Mary . . . known as the 'roper girls' to dance and join in with them. Sara listened as her son spoke of how it felt to really be impressed by a girl. She smiled as he confessed how he likes kissing her and holding her even though he is so much taller than she is. As he described how she looked at him, the adults at the table knew for certain he was smitten with Katy McGregor.

Upon completion of his account of the previous night, Gram rose from the table to continue with the dishes. "We've heard the fun that Michael had, now what about you Sara? How was your drive?" Before she could respond, John slammed the newspaper on the table. "Barnes got himself in trouble again!"

Mary dropped the forks and spoons she held in her hand, Sara set her coffee mug on the table and Michael sipped his milk slowly so as to not be able to respond until an adult had the opportunity. "Happened at the dance last night . . . seems he made out better than the guy in the hospital! Not sure of the motive yet, the police are going to have a full investigation. Got himself in a fight. Man's old enough to know better . . . Michael . . . what do you know of this?"

"Not much, I knew there was a fight, didn't know it was Mr. Barnes though. You said not to get involved in matters that weren't mine, and well, I had all that mattered to me with me so I figured I best keep away from it. There was an ambulance there and the cops were swarming the place, asking everyone questions. They had the guy in the cop car, we couldn't see him. I stayed at the truck mostly until we left which wasn't long after the band finished the last set. Had to dazzle them with *Cotton-Eyed Joe* just like you taught me, Mom . . . Mom. You OK?"

Sara was staring at her plate, hands in her lap. "Think I'll take that ride today. If you don't mind, I will excuse myself and head out to the barn."

A last swallow of coffee and as she stood, Mary held out her hands for Sara's mug and plate. "I'll get that for you dear, you have a good ride. Would it be all right to add some of your clothes to the laundry today? I need to complete a load." "Yeah, sure, whatever you want." She was in the mud room, pulling on her boots and reaching for a denim jacket. "Here, boy! Want to go for a ride?" Rex lifted his head as if to ask her if she meant it. "Come on . . . I know it won't be the same without Bandit, but you haven't been on a ride since he died, and it will do you good. Me too, to have you with me." Rex leaped to his feet, and the pair was out the door.

"That's not a good sign! She has more on her mind this morning than she did last night!"

"Gram, you don't think she was at the dance last night, do you?"

"She said she wan't going to go there. Didn't want to embarrass you." Mary was walking back through the kitchen with an armload of Sara's clothes on her way to the laundry room. "I take it breakfast is done?" John pushed back from the table. "Even when he's not here, that Barnes fellow causes a stir! I'm heading over to the McGregor Ranch today to see their new bull, want to join me, young man? You might catch one of those kisses you like so much!"

"Gramp, easy there, you laugh much harder and we'll be picking you up off the floor! I shall be turning down your invite . . . Katy isn't going to be there today, she is going to East Dale with the Marge and Mary. Seems we have a couple new additions to the 'Amigos'." "Suit yourself . . . Mary, get your man a couple biscuits for the road." Having securely encased the fresh biscuits in a satchel, he kissed his wife and was through the door.

PART 6

The Letter

"I'm going to follow her Gram, just so you know. Please don't try to stop me."

"Wouldn't think of it. Hmmm . . . this is interesting . . ."

"What?"

"The pocket of her jeans is ripped off, and there is blood on the left knee. These are the jeans she had on last night." They looked at each other both with the same thought, neither able to voice a doubt in a woman they both love. Mary quickly put the jeans in the washing machine, poured in the detergent and slammed the lid down. She looked at Michael as if to tell him to not let anyone else, meaning his grandfather know of this.

"I understand, Gram . . . My lips are sealed. If you don't need me anymore, I have to get ready, preparing for 'stealth mode' is going to be challenging." He walked to her, and with a gentleness not easily attained by a physique such as his, he embraced his grandmother. He felt a slight tremble from her. "It's going to be OK, Gram, she has a perfectly good explanation . . . come on . . . this is Mom . . ." "You're right . . . You just have to be. Ride safely today, something tells me she is headed for the Ridge." "My thoughts exactly. Hey, the news about last night is on . . ."

They listened to the radio as the newscaster spoke of the events at the dance. " . . . The ongoing investigation has taken a new turn, the victim, now identified as Wes Grant, has died from a head trauma. It appears as if he suffered a blow from a blunt object. There was a large rock recovered from the scene with his blood on it. Russell Barnes has admitted to hitting Grant in self-defense after Grant allegedly attacked him from behind. Barnes, being held in the County Jail stands by his statement. The police are seeking witnesses to the fight to verify Barnes' statement. The County Prosecutor's office is not releasing the extent of charges against Barnes at this time. Persons with information that may assist in the investigation should contact the Brandon Detectives' department. And now, today's weather . . ."

"Gram, does that mean that if he can't prove 'self-defense' that he could be charged with murder?"

"I suppose he could at that."

"I gotta tell Mom!"

"You better hurry . . . there she goes heading for the Red Pasture gate." As he rushed to the doorway, she reached out for him. He stopped and then turned back to her; she took his hands in hers and said, "Be careful what you say to her out there, it is a long ride back."

"I love you, Gram." She smiled to him, and he was out the door.

Capp was at the gate interested in Jazzy's departure. "Time to ride my friend! I know I promised you the day off, but things have changed." The horse nickered to him as if in agreement and understanding. Michael saddled the horse quickly and just as he was ready to mount, Gram stood in the doorway with an insulated bag. "You're going to get hungry as is your mother. She left out with no provisions. There is enough for you both here. Best use the large packs." Michael retrieved the large saddlebags from the tack room and laced them to the tie rings on the back of his saddle. "Thanks, Gram! You're the best!" He placed the lunch bag in the nearside pouch and as she handed him a canteen and jacket she said "Here, put these on the offside to balance out. Is the blanket still in the cantle bag?" "Yup, thanks. Time to go, Gram . . . I love you." "I love you too."

She stood in the barnyard and watched him ride toward his mother. Her memories of the day Sara and Samuel rode out to the herd came rushing to her. Wrapping her arms around herself, she could feel the slight tremble to her balance. Her thoughts turned to Sara and Russell's return with Samuel's body draped over the mule. "Be with them, Lord. They each need you in their own way. Please, bring them both home to us." She stood there until there was no sight of Michael. In the distance, she saw a hawk in flight above the Red Pasture.

The trio of woman, horse and dog approached the fence line with a slight hesitance. "Whoa there, girl, I know it has been a long while since we were up this far. I just couldn't do it, I could not re live that day. And you, little miss, glad you are a bit better behaved today." She reached down to pat Jazzy's neck. Rex was at the latch of the gate barking. He hadn't been up this far since the drive two years back when Bandit died in a stampede. "Well, I guess we both have tough memories to get through today, don't we . . ." Sara patted her knee, Rex was on his hindlegs with forelegs on her calf. "We're a hell of a team, big boy, a hell of a team. I hope we are ready to face this." A quick bark and he was down on the ground and waiting at the gate. Sara reached down on the offside and unlatched the gate.

"See, Samuel, I did teach her to do this!" He had taken great pride in Tonk's abilities as a ranch horse and teased her that Jazzy was a 'fancy girl' and didn't think she needed to do such things as gate opening when Samuel would always open them for Sara. The mare had been reluctant at first in her training, but the end-result of which was that she became proficient at more than gate opening; she had done well in the sorting of the cows and calves in the pens when the Drives got home. Sara had not gone out with the ranch hands for any of the seasons since Samuel's death.

Michael had kept himself hidden in the trees along the trail; stopping, he watched his mother reluctantly passing through the gate. "Easy there Capp, I know you want to run, not this time, buddy, not this time. We have an important job today. Next time, I'll let you run again . . . next time." Capp snorted, stomped a hoof and then lowered his head. "You really do understand me, don't you! Gramp wanted you for a breeding stallion, I am so happy Mom won that one!" He heard the clang of the gate latch as it closed.

Sara began to tense in the saddle and Jazzy could sense her anxiety; she quickened her step and began to snort. "Oh Jazzy, I am so sorry. I just want to cry right now. I still love him so much. Those days were so horrific. I just can't seem to let go of the pain. I have known nothing but for so long now. He was my heart, when he died it is like I died too. Oh look, there is the place where we saw the wolf prints . . . Oh Jazzy, my life has not been whole since that day. I want to feel whole again. I want to teach Michael that 'loss' doesn't mean a final end. I have to show him the strength of prevailing in the toughest of situations. I have to let him know that it is OK to love and to not fear the loss of that love. Oh, listen to me, I sound so good now when there is no one here . . . Rex, buddy, back over here. We're taking the trail to Tonk's Ridge." She reined Jazzy to the right and was soon enveloped by the tree boughs. Still unaware that Micahel was behind her, when she had called Rex back to her, he had actually caught a scent on the wind of Capp's manure and was turning back to investigate. Obediently, he returned to Sara with a sense of security that they were not alone.

"That was close . . . huh Capp . . . She is heading for the Ridge . . . I wonder if she knows how much I love her, and for all these years, she has been dad and mom . . . She thinks she is weak . . . Far from it! What she did that day out so far away from the ranch, she is the strongest woman I have ever known. That John Wayne movie about *True Grit,* if ever a woman had 'grit,' it's her. Now if I can just keep her safe . . ." He heard Rex bark. "Pick it up, boy . . . she must be moving out, and Rex is letting us know . . . Hahhhhhh!" Greatly relieved that he was asked to speed his pace, Capp galloped through the tall grass toward the trail head.

There was an eerie silence in the woods as Sara walked the mare along the same trail they had taken in the snowstorm. It was as if the forest and the living residents were all silenced in respect of her as she entered again after so long a time had passed. Sara wanted to hear birds, she wanted to see deer, she wanted the woods to be filled with the 'life' that Samuel so loved. "Whoa up there a minute, girl . . . This is the tree. Sure got here a lot faster when not fighting a freezing wind!" The mare stopped, with a trembling hand, Sara reached for the tree she had carved the heart on for a location marker.

The tears cascading her cheeks blurred her vision but not her recollection of the day she carved the heart. As her fingers traced the scarring on the tree, a lone hawk flew just overhead. Sara looked up and smiled at the soaring wings of the red-tailed bird of prey. Samuel had said that a hawk was good fortune; by keeping the small predators at bay, in a sense the hawk protected the ranch. "Of course, it would be a hawk . . . a lone soul . . . are you here, Samuel?" Jazzy tensed as the silent wingspan shadowed her. "I think we ought to go down there, what do you think?" The horse started to seek footing over the edge of the trail. "Yeah, that's kinda my thought too . . . you're going this time. I don't want to climb up again, and you don't want left behind."

Halting Capp and placing his hand on the marker 'Tonk's Ridge' that Paul Denton had wood- burned into a board and then volunteered to set on the trail for Tonk and his father, Michael looked ahead to his mother. He sighed as she placed her hand on the tree. His mother, she knew so much about survival out in the 'wild', and yet she could not save Samuel. It tormented her heart, made her question herself for all these years. He could see in her movements how feeling that marker was a reminder of her inabilty to prevent the inevitable. "Oh, Mom, you did all you could, you did more than any other person would have or could have . . . My God, you got him out of the ravine . . . What are you doing? Are you heading down the side of the Ridge? Get ready Capp, I had no idea she would go down there. I was thinking that just being here at the top . . . oh man . . . there she goes." He recentered the horn bag and the cantle bag, checked the strings on the side pouches and leaned over to check the cinch. "All set, Gram, I sure hope you're sittin' at the table praying for us!" Capp stepped off the trail and began the descent down the side of the Ridge. "Here's to hoping she thinks we are deer in the distance . . ."

"Rex . . . here, boy! You're going to have to help me . . . we need to find the ravine." Rex slowed his pace and then stopped and turn to her as she spoke to him. He yipped as he lunged to the left, jumping over a downed tree. "Slow down there boy, Jazzy here has to go around the trees!" Sara maneuvered the horse through the forest of Pines, Aspen, and Junipers. As the pair moved further into the denseness of the trees and rocks, it became apparent to Sara that she was unsure of where she was. Remembering she had tied the flashlight to the mule 'then' she was aware she had no beacon now to help her get back to the trail.

There was a stir off to the right that caught the attention of the trio. Jazzy snarked to the left in a surprise movement that nearly unseated Sara. "Easy, girl . . . Geeze . . . you have heard deer before . . ." As she pet the neck of the mare, she heard Rex growl. "Ahh . . . that's not good . . . Rex . . . heel!" She checked her gun; John had mentioned there had been sightings of a mountain lion on the next ridge, it would be possible for it to have wondered into this area. Not taking any chances, she set the gun across the forks of her saddle and readied it.

That same stir in the woods had startled Capp as well. Michael was peering through the trees, trying to keep sight of Sara when Capp stumbled. In his effort to regain his stance, a rock slid out from under his front left hoof; the hole left behind tripped him again, and this time, recovery was not possible. Capp fell to his knees, a hind leg losing hold and slipping. With ease, Michael pushed himself out of the stirrups and dismounted the horse; he was standing uphill from Capp, holding the reins when they both heard the rustle in the underbrush again. "You had better be OK there, big guy . . . Gramp mentioned something about mountain lions . . ."

Awkwardly standing on the hillside, the horse was becoming impatient as Michael began his inspection of Capp's tendons, knees, and hocks[30]. He would have liked to have checked his hooves too, but the gelding had taken on a nervousness that Michael had never seen before.

"OK, you win . . . lame or not, we're outta here! Oh man! I lost sight of Mom!" Mounting from the offside as he sat in the seat, the horse was already in motion. Michael reached for the rifle scabbard and unsnapped the holding strap. He had thought to just have it ready to pull when he heard the mountain lion growling off to his right. "Where are you, kitty? Me, pick me, leave my mother alone!" He had the rifle in position should he need it in a hurry.

---

[30]   The hock is the center large joint on the hind leg.

Rex barked at a level that Sara had not known that he had. Jazzy began spinning and was not listenening to Sara's commands. She knew the mountain lion must be very near. She called to Rex to heel, yet she feared his closeness to the frenzied horse. As the horse spun, Sara looked for the wild cat. "Where the hell are you? Oh, God, please help us!"

The commotion caught the attention of Capp; he and Michael sped their pace toward Sara. Michael had let the reins down on Capp's neck and was able to steer him with his legs and seat. Dodging trees, downed logs and maneuvering through rocks; they were closing the distance when he heard the attack growl. Michael kicked the horse and with a lunge forward, he could see Sara and Rex . . . and the mountain lion just above them. She had her gun aimed . . . Michael brought Capp to a halt . . . Sara should not have taken her attention away from the lion; as she did, he leaped from his stance and was in the air toward her. Seeing that she would not have time to shoot as the lion started his leap, Michael aimed the rifle and pulled the trigger. The lion fell to the ground in front of the mare.

Breathless, Sara looked at the lifeless body on the ground and then turned her eyes to her son. Unable to use her voice, in an almost squeak, she managed to utter "Ahhhh . . . lion! Big one! I don't know whatever prompted you to come out here, but you just saved all of our lives!" He could see she was trembling, he rode to her, dismounted, and was at her side. "Guess I know now why there are no birds and animals about in the woods . . . they are all hiding . . . I should have known the hawk had a warning for me. My God, Michael, that was close. Oh no . . . look at Capp . . . he's bleeding!"

Michael turned to his horse and began to laugh. "What are you laughing at? He's bleeding!" "It's OK Mom, he stumbled a ways back on the trail, not a very graceful act, I may add. He gets through that without harm, he plays 'hero horse' and can't seem to stay out of the berries. It's not blood." Capp lifted his head at the sound of the human laughing. "You know, he almost looks like he has that 'kid in the cookie jar' look on his face." Mother and son embraced each other as Rex jumped up with his paws on Michael as if to thank him too.

Sara stepped back from Michael; she started to walk toward Jazzy to gather up the reins. Before she got to the mare, she turned back to her son. "You truly are your father's son, you know that ? . . . he knew when I needed rescued whether I knew it or not. Just why is it that you are here?

Does Gram know you are out chasing your foolish mother on the Ridge? What do you mean Capp stumbled? . . ." She was asking more questions before Michael could even answer a one.

"Mom . . . stop . . . Yes, Gram knows I am here, and yes, Capp fell, rock slid out, and he fell to his knees . . . but most of all, I am here . . . for you. I had not intended for you to know I was tailing you . . . I just wanted to make sure you are safe. You have been kinda strange lately. Don't look at me like that. I'm your son, I know when you have a burdened mind. I think it has something to do with Russell Barnes . . . and with Dad. I had a feeling you would be riding to the Ridge today . . . You haven't been here since Dad died. I had no intention of breaking your privacy, and I am sorry that it turned out that way. Really, I am."

"You know what . . . I am not sorry . . . no, really I'm not. I am relieved to have had your protection from the mountain lion, that is for sure, but . . . I think I would like you to be with me and I think your father would be . . . is . . . in agreement with me on this. Michael, something is pulling me to where Tonk died, and I am not sure I can find it again after all these years, let alone get us back to the trail. I just know I need to go there." She stepped back and picked up the reins still hanging over the tree branch and then with a turn back to her son, she smiled. "Mount up! The Moores have a ride to finish!"

Michael swayed his head and stroked Capp's neck; he then grabbed the saddlehorn and swung himself into the saddle in one motion. "Capp, that is one 'good woman' and one great Mom!" Nudging Capp forward, they were soon riding behind her with Rex barking as if letting the humans know that *now* 'things' were as they should be. He settled into line behind Michael as they worked their way down the hill side. "Good to have you back there Rex, but I am kinda thinkin' you need to run point as you are the one to lead us to Tonk!" Sara motioned her hand for the dog to come forward. Michael pulled off to the left and let Rex go ahead of him, "Keep going boy . . . out front with you! I do say, he knows what we tell him!"
"That he does, Mom. That he does."

The forest animals had returned to their normal liveliness in the absence of the threat posed by the mountain lion. The trees and sky again with bird activity, Sara and Michael rode in silence. He knew his mother had a deep sorrow she was facing, and he respected her need to handle it her way; she would talk when ready. Michael felt a touch on his right shoulder, he reached up with his left hand. "Dad, is that you?" He spoke low so she would not hear him. "Help me, Dad . . . Help her . . ." The red-tailed hawk flew through the trees on the right of them. "Let's follow the hawk, Mom, what do you think?"

She had not realized her son was aware of 'signs' such as the hawk. Pleased that he could acknowledge a 'bridge to heaven' and the existence of angels in those 'signs', she could ride easy, knowing he knew that his father was with them. The hawk swooped down and remained just ahead of them. "Yes, I think we'll follow the hawk."

"Why are you stopping Mom?" Michael rode up beside Sara. She was staring ahead at the hawk alit in a tree overlooking a ravine. Without a change in her attention, she slowly dismounted. "We're here" Two small words spoken that Michael knew to be of great emotional power. He quickly dismounted, tied Capp to a tree, and then held out his hand for her to hand him Jazzy's reins. When both horses were secured, he returned to his mother.

"Mom. You OK?" he put a hand on her shoulder; she reached up and took his hand in hers.
"Yes, I am. I really am. The horses OK?"
"As long as that was the only lion, then yes, they are fine."
"Let's do this . . . Rex! Here, boy!" Side by side, they walked toward the ravine, simultaneously quickening the pace as they drew closer.

As she approached the edge, she stopped, put her hands over her face and turned away. "You look first . . . Is Tonk . . ." her words faded as she turned away from the resting place of Samuel's horse and, in that, a part of his heart too. She could see him as he removed the bridle . . . Falling to her knees, Michael knew there were memories flashing in her mind she could not escape from; he knelt and held her as she cried. "Are you sure you want to do this?"
"Is Tonk still there?"
"The scavengers have done their job, there is no trace of flesh and very few bones. Mom . . . I think there is a saddlebag down there!"

"A saddlebag? Your father kept asking about a saddlebag, I could only get one, the other was under Tonk. He had such a sad look when I told him I had just the one. Suppose we ought to retrieve it now. Maybe the mystery of its importance will come to light." "You stay here, I'll get it." Sara took

Michael's hand. "Thank you." He smiled at her and started his way down the hill that his father and the great horse had taken together years ago.

It was not a far distance, yet each step he took was weighted. As he made his way through the logs and rocks, he wondered if his father had been injured by any one or ones of the same as he was stepping over them. Almost to the bottom, he saw a piece of torn cloth. Michael recognized it as part of his father's neckerchief. Reaching for it, he too had memories flash . . . The first time his father had set him in a saddle on that ornery pony Ranchero, the camping trip with Gramp when Michael was eight, the science fair . . .

"Oh, Dad, why did you have to leave us? Why did God need you more than we do? I have missed you so much. I have tried to be the 'man of the house' for Mom and for Gram and Gramp . . . they miss you too. It has been so hard . . . You would be so proud of Mom, she really has been strong. Maybe a little too strong. She holds it in, you know, like she doesn't want anyone to know . . . She won't let anyone get close to that part of her anymore. I love her so much, but in truth, I sure miss how she smiled and laughed and 'played' when you were still alive. She just has a saddened heart."

He had retrieved the cloth and was walking toward the saddlebag as he continued to talk with his father . . . "I think she may finally have a reason to open up a little . . . I think she likes Russell Barnes. I know he likes her, but I am afraid she thinks it is a betrayal to you if she pursues her feelings. Dad, you just have to let her know it is OK . . . you have to help her to see the good in it for her and for all of us. I know I am young, I know I probably really don't know what I am talking about, but if you really are here and have heard me at all, please, help her let go only just enough to see ahead and hold the past in her heart but not live in it." He reached the saddlebag held fast by a large limb.

"You have it yet, Michael?"
"Pulling the limb off it now, Mom. Be right there." Moving the limb with his right hand, he picked up the saddlebag with his left, the right hand moving to the leather. The years had dried the stitching, and there were cracks in the leather walls of the bag. He paused his hand on the buckle of the flap.

Sara placed her right hand on his left shoulder. Startled, Michael turned to her. "Mom!"

"I changed my mind, I wanted to come down here, don't know just why, but I got a feeling . . ."

Michael knew his father had heard him and in his way had spoken to his mother. "Here, you open it. Whatever is in there was for you, so you should be the one to open it." He raised his hands to help her as she knelt beside him. She slowly took the worn leather bag from him. Still holding it away from her body, she stopped, staring at it in an almost fearful gesture. Moments passed in silence. She then drew it to her bosom and held it as if she were holding an infant. She stroked it as she did Samuel's head as he lay in her lap weeping for his lost friend. "Oh, Samuel . . . my Samuel . . . hush there, you're going to be all right. We are going to get you out of here . . ."

Michael sat back and pulled his knees to his chin . . . thinking to himself . . . "My God, she is reliving that day . . ." He had never seen so deep an agony in her eyes or heard it in her voice. He now could understand the depth of their love and the intensity of what had happened in the very place they were now at. He thought a son should do something . . . *He should do something* . . . He leaned forward and kissed her cheek. As he did, she dropped the bag and let him hold her.

The hawk flew from his perch, swooping down to the mother and son on the ground. Sara saw the talons out as if the bird was going to pick its prey. Her eyes followed the path to them and it was apparent to her that the bird was after the saddlebag. She got the saddlebag firmly in her grasp just as the bird was near clutching it. The closeness of the wingspan pushed both people backwards. "Wow . . . that was close! Why would that hawk want this bag?" Michael now understood what was in that bag might very well inhibit her from the healing she so needed. What was in that bag would remand her back to the past again. His father did not want that for her. He looked to the where the hawk had flown, to himself he thought "You tried, Dad . . . I know you tried . . ." The hawk was gone.

Sara rose to her feet. "I need a log to sit on, these aging bones can't stay cramped that long." Michael got up and followed her to a downed tree just behind where they had been on the ground. "Mom . . ." He was reluctant to tell her he had found a piece of the neckerchief. "Mom, I found this on the way down the hill." He opened his hand and showed her the torn cloth. A slow tear came to her right eye. Her lips trembled in recognition of it. She closed his hand with hers and looked him in the eyes. "You keep that. You'll have a piece of him with you always."

She placed her right hand on the saddlebag; with shaking fingers she undid the buckle. Carefully lifting the flap so she did not put too much strain on the fragile stitching, she opened the bag. "Hmm, just what is left of a rolled-up blanket. I can't imagine what the fuss was about." She put her hand inside and felt around the blanket. "Nope, nothing else . . . Let's see what's left of this blanket . . ." She raised the frayed plaid blanket from the hold of the leather. Standing up while she opened the folds, the letter Samuel had written to give to her on the cattle drive fell to the ground. Mother and son looked at each other and then at the letter on the ground.

Sara hurriedly folded the blanket while sitting back down on the log. Michael reached for the letter and handed it to her. She looked to the sky. "So this is what you were wanting . . . this is why you were so sad I could not free the off saddlebag . . ." Her fingers traced her name on the envelope. "Your writing . . . So well-scripted for a man . . . It always impressed me . . . your fine penmanship" Turning the letter over, she hesitated as she placed her fingers in position to carefully open the aged seal so as to not damage the envelope.

My Dearest Sara:

Tonight as we are together in yet another adventure as you call it, I want to let you know how much I love you and why I love you so much.

From the very first time I saw you at the Auction, I knew you were the one for me. I had found the love of my life and vowed then that I would be the love of your life.

You have taught me patience in myself as well as in others. You have taught me a new kindness to people and to animals. You have taught me how to smile with my heart.

From you, I learned the importance of a rainbow. Do you remember the 'triple' we saw that afternoon we rode out in the rain . . . you laughed at my insistence . . . we stood on top of the hill, and there it was. You told me how a rainbow can make a person truly know God's power of the true 'awesome'. You are right Sara, so many times I had neglected to stop and take in His Love. I have known a love with you that only He could have created. I think maybe I don't always let you know that when I and look at you, I do know His love through you.

You have taught me how to love a woman, how to love you.

Sara, I so hope that I have taught you to trust a man's heart. You were torn and broken for so long, I try every day to heal the wounds you had endured. I want to have taught you that the heartache from loss need not impede your chance of happiness from love. I do truly know that you have learned to forgive the causes of your pains. I will be forever in love with you and want only for you to always be loved.

I have taught you, my dear Sara, how to love a man, how to love me. Our love has brought to us a strength and bond shared only in a trueness of one heart. The joy of you as my wife is a wonder that so few men will ever know and experience. You are a woman of faith, fortitude, and fearlessness.

I love you for every moment we have shared together and for every moment yet to be. I love you for the mother you are to our son and the daughter you are to my parents. I love you for your daring to correct me when I am wrong and your willingness to accept correction from me.

You have brought a true 'life' to this cowboy that I know would not have been so fulfilled without you.

You are a woman that needs to love a man and have a man love you in return. For my lifetime, I will be that man.

I love you Sara, you do not hold your love inside you . . . your heart is so deep and you thrive the highest when you share all that you are. Never hold that back, for all those around you are bettered by you . . . myself, most of all.

I love you my wife

Forever our hearts are one

Samuel

He wasn't sure just at what moment she had finished reading the letter; her hands shook until the tattered paper fell to the ground. She seemed as if to not even know it had left her hands; with her fingers still in a position of 'hold' and her eyes focused on where the letter had been held in her hand . . . "Mom? . . . I don't know what to do or say here . . . Mom?" There was no response from her.

The passing of mere minutes seemed as though hours had escaped them. Michael reached to her, taking her hands in his and closing them in her lap. No response. He embraced her. No response. He reached for the letter. No response. He sat back and thought the letter too personal for him to read it. Those words from his father to her had struck her hard. He knew he had to wait for her.

"Where are you hawk? Why did you not take this from me?" Michael was startled by the sudden plea from her. He could see her trying not to cry. "You can cry Mom, it's more than OK considering the circumstances. Maybe you need to cry. I will go check the horses and leave you be for a while." As he stood, she touched his thigh; he reached down and placed his hand on hers, bent over and kissed the top of her head. "I love you, Mom. I'll be at the horses. Here Rex, you're with me . . ."

Picking up the letter, her thoughts bounced from the morning she and Samuel left for the cattle drive, to his fall and then to holding him as he died. She could see Russell Barnes leading the mule home . . . Samuel's funeral . . . Michael's birthday . . . Her tears flowed as she reread the words of his heart. "Stop it woman! Enough! This is not what he would want . . . he wrote this to make me happy. Not to fall me farther into sorrow." She held the letter to her heart. "I miss you so much!"

Retrieving the blanket, she returned it and the letter to the saddlebag. Pausing to take a last look at what remained of Tonk's resting place she said "Tonk, you were a great horse, he was a great man. I know you are together, riding bareback as Michael has your saddle. Oh, Samuel, your son, he is so like you. He has your true heart. He has your strength. He has your love for this ranch and lifestyle. You are two of one man. I am so proud of him. I know you are too.

"I can only hope you are proud of me as well. I have never stopped loving you Samuel, it is not possible. These words you wrote, that only now I have knowledge of, these words are all true. We taught each other the importance of what love is and can be. We learned to love another and ourselves too. You are right when you say I am a woman that needs to love and be loved. Without you with me I am not whole . . . I miss so much being held at night, making love to you and listening to you sleep. "The years of my 'aloneness' have been marked in so many ways and have affected more than just myself. It took a while for me to realize that. I miss you, you knew what you wanted as for your 'lifetime', you and I were as one. But . . . I live on . . . I need to know you are OK with . . . me . . . Oh, Samuel, I will never replace you, I couldn't. I don't want to. All who I am is because of our life together. I just . . . sometimes . . . I don't know . . ."

In her difficulty to say the words of her thoughts that she was wanting to act on her emotions and perhaps find love in her life again, her attention was diverted from the few remaining bones on the ground to the large rock just beyond. There, she saw the hawk. The massive bird opened and closed its wings three times before taking flight. Sara turned round and round as the bird circled her. He swooped down to her. As he passed her, he lifted just his head and turned his eyes to her, seemingly looking right at her. She stood as still as she could, barely breathing. One last squawk and he was gone.

She found herself smiling as she held the saddlebag to her heart. Not only had she finally been in receipt of his words of love while he had been alive, she had also been in receipt of his act of love in death. There was a 'peace' in her that she had longed to feel. Clutching the bag tighter she closed her eyes, looked to where the hawk had flown and whispered "thank you."

Michael watched her as she stood facing away from him; he recognized the body language of a woman as she wept. Was she relieved to read the words of her beloved or was she pulled farther into her sorrow at the loss of him? His heart ached for his mother; either way, he sensed this 'find' was going to be a turning point for her and he needed to be prepared for either reaction.

Still facing the sky where last the hawk had flown, she said, "Michael . . ."
"Yes, Mom . . . I am here." He soon stood behind her and placed his left hand on her shoulder; he felt the trembling ease, and soon it was ended. Sara slowly turned to him, she looked at him as he embraced her. "Mom?" "I'm OK, Michael, I'm OK. Wasn't sure at first, but I am OK." He released his hold of her, she stepped back. "This ride has been long needed, but I am sure it was not to be until the time was right. Do you believe that?" "Yes I do, Mom, yes I do." "Me too. I love your father and always will, I think

now I can hold that love in my heart, never to lose it. I feel as though he has pushed me to accept that and let myself be open to the possibility of love again. Oh, listen to me, talking to my son about a man other than his father . . . it seems so inappropriate."

"Mom, listen to me . . . maybe you don't want to admit it, but I have seen the way you are around Russell Barnes. Heck, everyone has seen it, even Gram. The two of you have a history that you cannot deny and seem to act on when ever you are within a hundred yards of each other. I followed you today because I thought that you were coming out here to sort your thoughts about him. You sure left the table in a hurry when Gramp mentioned the newspaper article. I know this is hard for you, and well, I didn't want you to be alone way out here."

"You sound like you approve."

"Yes, Mom, I do. And Dad must also if he brought you to this place today."

"You think the hawk was him, don't you?"

"Yup, sure do!"

"And the lion?"

"Just a mountain lion Mom, just a lion." Together they laughed as the wind swirled around them.

"Shall we head home?"

"Mount up!" Rex was at Jazzy's side before Sara; he was trying to untie the rope from the tree, as if wanting to get it for her. His low barking seemed to be his approval of their departure.

Sara placed Sam's saddlebag in the nearside pack, patting the leather when closed. Watching her son mount the same way his father did, to herself she smiled. "You will always be with me, Sam . . . all I have to do is look at our son." She put the rope in the cantle bag and reset the reins to the bit. "Time to find that trail up the top of this ridge . . . good thing I'm riding a 'homing pigeon!'"

PART 7

The Storm

"There seems to be a storm brewing out there" John came in the backdoor to the kitchen. Mary had a pot of water on the stove waiting for it to boil; she was preparing spaghetti and meatballs for dinner. "Spag tonight, huh?" As he stood behind her, he reached around her to hold her to him. "It will hold until they get back" "Hope their getting back is soon, I heard rumbling from the north. Last thing she needs is another storm when up on that ridge. Have you seen Michael? He's been hiding all day" "He went out to keep an eye on Sara. Please don't be angry John, he just wanted to stay close enough to know she is all right." "He sure loves his mother, and he is so much like Sam. Remember when he followed me to the graveyard after Pop died . . ." Mary turned and before he could finish his sentence, she placed her fingers on his lips to stop him talking. The thunder of the storm seemed to be intesifying and there was lightning in the distance. "Just pray they are home soon. Now, get me the bag of noodles over there, please."

"Yes, dear . . . love your spaghetti . . . if they knew it was for dinner, they would already be here!"

"Mom . . ."

"Yeah, I heard it . . . got home just in time. Let's get these horses settled in the barn and see what Gram has for dinner!" Both horses nickered at the others in the barn as Sara and Michael removed the tack and quickly brushed them. Rex came in the barn, barking as if to inform them the storm was getting closer. "Good boy, Rex . . . You did a fine job today. Sure bet you are tired, you haven't been out in a long time. Go ahead, get to the house, then they will know we are home." With a wave of her hand the dog understood her command and was out through the carriage doors and on his way to the back porch of the ranch house; his bark at the kitchen door was audible in the barn.

"Sure is tough seeing him get older . . ."

"Don't go there, Mom . . . Just don't go there. Here, let me get your saddle for you . . ." Michael easily lifted the saddle to the rack and placed the bridle on the front hook. "A little hay for the horses and we're outta here!" Stepping carefully on the straight wooden ladder to the barn loft, Sara pulled herself to the hay mow. "Incoming!" Michael stepped out of the way of the falling bale of timothy, alfalfa and mixed grasses. "Don't forget the cow in the end stall . . ." "Listen to her, how could I?" Mother and son laughed as the beller of the old cow filled the barn.

Mary stood at the stove deep in thought of all that may have happened on the Ridge. She was concerned for Sara as the emotional strain of returning there after so many years . . . she knew that Sara was physically strong enough for the ride, but how was she going to handle being *there* again . . . The sound of Rex's bark at the door jolted Mary from her trance. "John! John! They are home! Rex is at the door and I see lights in the barn! Oh! Thank you, Lord! Thank You for bringing them home before the storm hits!" "Well . . . let the poor dog in, Mary . . . he has to be exhausted!" As she opened the door for the dog, she saw Sara and Michael in a race to the house.

Behind them on the horizon, she had the first glimpseof the storm forming and had view of the lightning from cloud to cloud. The winds were gaining strength, and she could see the trees yielding to their power. "Hurry up, I think this is going to be a doozy!" Mary had her arms out for Sara as she skipped the steps by twos to be on the porch. Nearly tripping on the top step, Sara fell into Mary's arms. Mary could sense the relief of being home in Sara as she felt her relax during the embrace. She knew the ride went well. Before letting go of her, Mary softly whisperd in Sara's ear, "Yet another time your courage amazes me . . . you are a brave one, Sara Moore . . . That you are." Sara smiled and released the embrace. Stepping back, she took Mary's hand in hers and looked in Mary's eyes. "I learned my strength from you Mary. Thank you." They shared a mother—daughter moment of recognition, love, and respect.

Michael had stood back as the women greeted each other. John had been standing in the doorway taking it in. He motioned to Michael to come in the house. As he passed his mother and grandmother, he hesitated at them as they were hand in hand . . . "Strength . . . yes, cooking . . . well . . . ah . . . sorry, Mom but that would be a 'no' . . . ahh . . . except for your lasagna, oh and your apple fritters . . . those are great! What's cookin', Gram? I'm starved!" John pulled Michael close to him; "Boy, you've got some learnin' to do when it comes to saving yourself . . ." "Pig's knuckles and sour kraut!" Mary replied as she was still looking at Sara. Both women tried with little success to hold in laughter as Michael stopped abruptly. "Whaaaat?" Gramp stood in the doorway holding his midsection as his boisterous laughter had him nearly off balance. Reaching for Michael, Gram regained her composure. "Spaghetti, we are having spaghetti and meatballs, Michael. You sure thought it might be knuckles though . . . You should have seen your face!"

Set between the women, Michael put his arms around his mother and grandmother as they walked to the doorway. Gramp put his hand on

Michael's shoulder as the women entered the doorway before him. Smiling at his grandson, he motioned for Michael to go ahead of him. Shaking his head, the elder Moore was still in a chuckle as he removed his boots and made his way to the kitchen table.

As the family ate Sara and Michael told of the events of the day's ride.

The mountain lion recount was particularily of interest to John. "Going to have to get the men together and scout the area. Best let the other ranches know too. Mary, looks like it's time to organize one of those 'women things' . . . We haven't had an all-out git-together in quite a while . . . seems like a good time . . . don't you think?" Mary looked at Sara; it had been a long while. Not since Samuel's funeral had there been a gathering at the ranch. Years prior had seen a great many galas hosted by the Moores. The finality of the funeral seemed the end of reasons to continue the tradition. Sara set her fork on her plate, patted her napkin to her lips, placed her hands in her lap and looked first at Mary and then at John. "I think that is a fine idea. We should start on the preparations right away." John, somewhat surprised yet relieved, raised his glass of milk in a toast. The others followed. "To the Moore Ranch . . . finest family around!"
"Yee haw!"

The crack of thunder silenced the jovial mood at the table. John looked at Michael. "Best get to securing this old 'stead for a storm."
"Yes, sir."
"Mary, you and Sara . . . you OK in here?"
"Yes, get to the barn. We'll get the insides ready." Storms were not uncommon in their area, and as with most ranches and ranch families, there was a 'storm plan'. Each person had specific duties to get the house, barns, and livestock secured.

"I think that is record time!" John looked at his watch. "Fifteen minutes and we are all back here again. What's for dessert?" Sara placed the chocolate bundt cake before him and flipped the knife handle to him. "Would you like to do the honors?" As he took the knife from her, thunder shook the house, and lightning flashed with such intensity that the yard light went out.

"She's here . . ." He set the knife down. Mary picked it up and secured it in the covered tub in the sink. "No need to have a potential weapon in the air . . . just in case." They heard the oak tree at the fence gate split as the next bolt of lightning struck the massive trunk. They were looking out the window into the darkness, waiting for the next flash to light the yard for a visual of the damage. When next there was illumination, all four people gasped at the sight of the huge tree smoldering on the ground.

"We can't let it ignite, Gramp! We learned in science how a smoldering tree like that can just burst into flames! It might catch the house if the wind blows just right! I'm going out there!"

"Michael . . . stop, it is too dangerous, you have no way of keeping safe from more lightning!" Sara was frightened for her son. John looked at both women. "He's right, we have to contain that tree. And he has to be the one to do it, I can't run fast enough with water buckets."

"John! No . . . he's just a boy!"

"Mary, he is a young man and willing to do 'man' things . . . we need him to do this. I will be out there with him filling the buckets . . . the hose won't reach the tree. Together, we will get it done and be back in before you know it. If it would actually start to rain, then we can get back sooner." They were out the door before either of the women had a chance to protest further.

Holding each other, the women stood at the window watching as son and husband methodically filled buckets and doused the tree. Sara wanted to be there with them but knew that Mary needed her there with her. Each crack of thunder shook them as well as the old frame of the home. A lightning bolt illuminated the sky, resulting in the barn and the shed being silouetted in an eerie manner. They held to each other with greater strength. As Mary began to weep, Sara turned to her. "They will be all right . . . They have to be . . . They are Moores . . . They are strong and strong- willed. Let us get the towels ready for them, theycould be wet when they get in." She knew she had to redirect Mary's attention away from the window. "You are right, if ever there were two men . . ." Before she could finish her sentence, the sound of rain pelting the roof was both a relief and a worry. They looked out to see what they thought had been rain was actually hail.

The women turned to each other, and as if in one voice said: "Tornado!" As they pulled back from each other Michael and John were quickly entering the backdoor. They could see the women and read the facial expressions. "Not going to happen! Not on my ranch!" John embraced Mary. While still holding her tightly, he said "The cloud is up there, we saw it . . . it won't touch down here . . . Mary, it's OK . . ." It was only moments and the hail ceased and the rain began. "Michael . . ." "I'm OK, Mom. The good news is we got the tree taken care of and the rain will help keep it that way." "Time to start praying for whereever it does touch down." Sara was relieved for her family, yet the worry for others now concerned her. Michael looked at his grandfather; they had seen the direction the cloud was heading—it was over the McGregor Ranch.

With flashlights in hand, Michael and John went to the barn to check for storm damage. Mary and Sara stood in the doorway taking in the sight of the sunrise shadows beside them. "Sara . . ."

"Yes?"

"Now that we are alone, do you want to really talk about what happened on the Ridge yesterday? I just know there is more to it than what you said at dinner last night. I could tell you were holding back. Most likely because of John. You can tell me, dear, you know I love you and will not judge you." She looked at Sara with a smile, reached in her pocket for the hankie she always had ready and put it to the slow tear on Sara's cheek. "I don't know where to start."

"When you do, I'm here. Always know that." Sara leaned to Mary, and the women embraced.

"See that Michael . . . that's family. Those two ladies are like one person sometimes. Just can't figure out how the female nature is so entwined with each other. We men have a tough job . . . we have to untangle them at times and then be willing to accept that we just can't keep them from tangling back up!"

"I'm finding girls have a lot of 'secrets', Gramp . . . don't know if I can figure it out."

"Don't even try son, don't even try . . . just go with it, believe me you'll be much better off!" They were laughing as they returned to the porch. "All is well in the barn. Other than no electric yet and having to haul water from the old pump for the livestock, we came through the night just fine. What's for breakfast?"

"I need to go to the McGregor's to make sure they are all right. Is it OK to ride over there this morning?" "Michael, that is a good idea, that cloud was heading their way. But how 'bout we take the truck and some tools just in case."

"Thanks, Gramp."

"Meet me at the truck in fifteen minutes. Mary, love, could you maybe please pack us a bit to eat and some drinks? No telling what we might find over there and how long we will be. Something tells me young Michael here has plans of his own at the McGregor's!"

"Ahhh, Gramp!"

"We'll put together some food for you and some for them too"

"You're a good woman, Mary Moore, a good woman!"

Standing beside the truck, Sara lifted the basket to Michael. "Be careful. When phone service returns please call and let us know how things are over there."

"Yes, Mom, will do."

"I love you!"

"Love you too!" The men drove through the gates and turned left. Without breaking her focus on the end of the ranch driveway, Sara gripped Mary's hand a little harder. "If we don't hear anything by noon, we're going over there."

"You got that right!"

Pulling in the McGregor driveway, they could see the barn had suffered the worst of the damage. Michael was out of the truck before John had it actually parked. Running toward the barn, he repeatedly called Katy's name.

"In here . . . we are in the barn!" Michael got to the doorway and could see Katy, Callie and Cassie trying to reset the supports to the back left corner. John entered the aisleway. "Michael, get that beam over there . . ."

The five struggled as the barn resisted the bracing; several failed attempts to get the beam in place had dampened the hopes of success. Finally, with an impelling last effort, the beam was placed upright. The creak of the old wood seemed a 'thank you.' Huddled together and leaning over with arms on knees, they all sighed their relief. Uprighting herself slowly, Callie tappedJohn's shoulder enticing him to nudge Michael. "Timing is everything! Thank you, Mr. Moore and young Michael, you two have just saved this barn!" She was exhausted, and although her words were broken, the meaning was received as intended. John pulled both the women to him. "You girls have a strength together that is amazing, don't you ever forget that! I am glad we got here when we did. Any other damage you need help with?"

They heard a whinney from the horse pen behind the barn. Michael turned to Katy . . . "Chance!" His voice faltered as he spoke the gelding's name . . . not only in fear of the possible injury the horse may have endured, but also that if he had been hurt, Katy would be devastated. He knew how much the horse meant to her. Her dedication to him and commitment to his care far exceeded the term 'horseowner'. She and Chance had a true bond. Michael prayed to himself that the horse was all right.

Katy looked to her mother for permission to leave the barn. "Go on you two . . . go check on that darn plug mule out there!" Callie McGregor smiled as she watched Katy and Michael race out the doorway to the horse pen. "Quite a pair there, Mr. Moore . . . what do you think?"

"I'm thinking our families are going to be seeing a lot of each other! Let's go check that horse!" John had his hands on his hips, and with elbows extended, Callie took his right and Cassie held to his left. The three approached the barn door, and in a simultaneous halt of motion, looked to the pen just as Michael leaned over to kiss Katy. Just as they had stopped, as if in one motion, all three stepped back in retreat to the aisle of the barn.

"Think they saw us?"

"How could they?"

"Shhhhh . . . Let them be . . ."

"We could use a little help behind the house . . . do you mind?"

"Not at all, my dears . . . lead on!"

Michael and Katy were unaware of the laughter in the barn.

While walking to the porch behind the ranch house, John recognized the sound of Sara's truck even before it came into view. "Seems like a few more recruits have come to join us!"

"We can use all the hands we can get. Mr. Moore, you haven't seen the rest of the damage." Cassie turned to him and held a hand to his chest. "I just can't begin to let you know how thankful we are that you are here." "My girl Sara, just seems to know when and where she is needed. I will let her know that we are behind the shed. Do we need tools?" "Chainsaw would be handy if you have one, it's the big oak . . . fell on the shed and got a corner of the house."

"Your mom is here." Katy stepped to the side of Michael and in a single motion, placed her hands around Chance's left forearm, massaging the heavy muscles that helped to give the horse the strength and speed in the turns around the barrels. Michael smiled at the rising blush on Katy's cheeks. "Why, Miss McGregor, I believe you are . . ." Before he could finish his sentence, Katy gasped and fell to her knees, hands still on the horse's leg. "What is it? What's wrong?" He could see the rise and fall of her shoulders as she tried to hold back the tears she could not contain. In a low murmur that he had difficulty understanding, she stared at Chance's leg.

"I think the radial carpal extensor and the digital extensor muscles are torn."

"English please . . . I haven't been studying up on all the veterinary terminology like you have." He regretted his words the moment he spoke them. "I'm so sorry, Katy . . . I didn't mean it like that. I'm just not as smart as you about the medical stuff and horses." He waited until she smiled at him, and he was sure she had accepted his apology. "So, Doc McGregor, care to explain to a cowboy just what it is you see with this horse?"

Katy reached for Michael's hands. "Here, put your fingertips under mine, I will move them over the muscles of his foreleg." She slowly moved his hand, enabling him to feel the swelling and sense the tenderness as he relocated his touch. "Can you feel the differences?" "Wow, it is like different muscles in the same place. I have never felt that before, it is sorta creepy, Katy . . . just not right at all . . ." She could sense his concern and questioning simultaneously as his voice faltered when he spoke.

"No, it is not. Not at all. I had hoped it was just bruising from when the beam that fell . . ." Michael knew at that moment that Chance had been in the barn during the storm. Recalling the condition of the beams when he and his grandfather arrived, he pictured in his mind the trauma the horse had to have sustained as the structure collapsed around him. "Oh geez, Katy . . . Chance was in the barn?" Katy understood his interruption to have been through fear for the horse; she reached for him and stood back from Chance. "Yes, he was in the barn. We found him in the corner pinned by the beam. It took all three of us to get the beam moved enough for him to get up and out from underneath it. I have no idea how long he had been there, but he sure was happy to see us. He even helped with his hindlegs to move the one end. Tt had to have hurt like hell . . . he groaned so intensly as we worked to free him. It was awful. I thought he was going to die." Michael pulled her to him and held her. "He didn't. He wouldn't. He is too strong-willed, Katy, that is what gives him his determination running barrels, that is what drove him to survive this too." He could feel her sobbing again. "Just put the idea that he may not recover from this and won't compete again right out of your head . . . If anyone can get him through this, it is you. I know you can and he knows you can." "Oh, Michael . . ." He lifted her chin with his fingertips; looking in her swollen eyes, he smiled. "I want to kiss you, Katy McGregor." He leaned to her and gently placed his lips on hers.

John was reaching into the bed of his truck when Sara pulled in to park next him. Quickly at his side, she put her arm over his shoulder. "How bad is it? When you weren't back and hadn't called, I put together a few more tools and came over to help. Where is Michael? He should be here getting this for you." She removed her arm from John's shoulder and climbed into the bed of the truck to help unload the tools. Standing up at new height, she could see Michael and Katy in the pen, and she could see Chance holding his leg up.

"John . . ." Seeing the direction of her sight, he knew what she was about to ask. "He was in the barn when it collapsed. A beam had him pinned. The twins didn't go into much detail other than that. Katy is real tore up about it. I haven't pressed Michael for too much help as he is trying to keep Katy from losing it. She is trying to stay 'strong' for him so if that's what it takes . . ."
"Well, I'm here now. Where do you need me?"
"Fetch the big chainsaw, the oak fell on the house out back." Mary had hold of a basket of bedding she had put together. She knew an invitation for the McGregors to stay anywhere else would be declined. Ranchers 'stayed on' no matter the dire circumstances. "John . . ." He smiled at her. "Oh, Mary . . . we were spared this time . . . " He shook his head. "They need us here. The house is safe structurally, you can go on in. We are working out back where the tree fell."

Michael could see his mother and grandparents walking toward the house. "Katy, I really need to help them. If you want I can ask my mom to stay with you." "I could use the help with the dressing. I would like your mother to help me, that would be great."

Michael turned, and in his approach to his mother he could see her looking toward the horse pen and then back to him. "So how bad is it?" "Mom, she thinks the muscles are torn. I can tell by her voice that she is really worried. I don't know what to say. I don't know horse anatomy stuff like she does. She wants to be a veterinarian even though there aren't many women admitted to the Vet schools yet. Will you help her? She is trying to be tough, but well, that 'Cowgirl Code' you all try so hard to maintain does at times need to be let down, and she sure as heck is not going to do that with me."

Sara smiled at her son as he spoke to her. In her mind, she was imagining him trying to feign understanding of Katy's emotions. "You have learned a lot about 'girls' in a short time, haven't you?" "Mommmmmm . . ." Sara put her right hand on his left arm. "Go help your grandfather. I got this . . . and take this chainsaw. They are behind the house." "Thanks, I owe ya!" He picked up the chainsaw and paused to smile at his mother. With a wave of her hand as if pushing him away, Sara promted Michael to help his grandfather. "Go, would you . . . I got this, really!"

"Katy? Can I help you? What is your opinion on Chance's leg?" Katy wiped the tears from her cheeks as she stood up to talk with Sara. "Wow! You want to know what I think . . . You don't push what to do on me . . . Thank you." Sara brought Katy to her for an embrace. "Young lady, you have been studying the horse since you learned to read. I have every confidence that you know what you are looking at and have a pretty good idea as to what treatment is needed. Michael says you want to go to Vet school. I know your mom is limited in funds . . . Don't look at me like that . . . I have been friends with your family long enough to know things like that. I would never bring that knowledge to anyone else, please believe me. But . . . if going to Vet school is what you want to do, then you can start applying as soon as you need to. You have the Moore Ranch financially backing you all the way." Katy could not hold back her tears of appreciation and astonishment at the same time. "One stipulation . . . We are your first client so you best learn about cattle too!" Sara was nearly knocked off her feet as Katy threw her arms around her. "Ah . . . the horse, Katy . . . let's get to work on the horse!" "Thank you so much! I will make you proud of me, I promise!" "Katy, I have been proud of you since the day you were born! I am your godmother and have loved you as a daughter since the moment you looked at me when the nurse brought you into your mother's room for your first feeding. Don't you ever forget that. Now, let's get your horse taken care of so we can help the others."

"I gave him 'bute'[31] this morning when we found him and hosed the leg for nearly a half hour, then rubbed a little 'Tuttles Elixer'[32] on him to

---

[31]   Common reference to Phenylbutazone, a nonsteroidial anti-inflamatory drug for short-term treatment of pain and inflamation

[32]   Tuttle's Elixer is a leg and body wash for soothing muscles and stimulating blood flow. It holds a registerd trademark and patent of the Tuttles Corporation.

help with the soreness while we worked on the barn. I really need to assess more completely, thank you for being here, this is going to painful for him."

"What would we do without Tuttles? I swear that has been around for as long as I can recall! Even my parents used it!" Sara rubbed Chance's neck. "You're in the best hands here, big fella, we gotta get you all healed up." While attending to Chance's leg, Sara could hear trucks approaching from the direction of the driveway. "You've got company, here, let me finish wrapping that for you . . ." Katy looked at Sara and then to the driveway. "Go, they have come to help you, I'll finish up here and meet you behind the house." "Thank you, Mrs. Moore." Katy hugged Sara, handed her the bandaging and was on her way to see who had arrived.

"Reinforcments are here!" Charles announced his and Brent's arrival as they unloaded tools from the bed of his truck. "Cowgirl power too!" Marge and Mary waved their arms in the air above their heads as they came around the back side of Charles' truck. Katy stopped, astounded that they had put aside work on their own ranches to help the McGregors.
"Thank you . . . really . . . thanks. I can't believe you are here!" Charles put an arm over Katy's shoulder. "Brent Boy and yours truly went to 'Twinkle's' house and Gram said that she and Michael's mom were getting ready to come over here. We stopped at the 7-Eleven and saw the lovely 'roper girls' and invited them to an afternoon of thrills here at your ranch . . . actually, we thought you could use the 'girl support', and then they said they had tools and would help . . . I'm thinkin' these girls are gonna fit right in . . . And they are cute too!" "Good thing you learned who was who! Huh?" "Shhh about that . . . OK?" "Our secret" Turning to Brent, Marge and Mary, Katy swayed her head and smiled at her friends. Charles had taken his arm off her shoulder and returned to help Marge carry a chainsaw. To herself she said "Friends, true friends. I am so Blessed."

The work of supporting the porch and clearing the tree seemed effortless as they worked into the early evening. Cassie and Callie retreated to the kitchen to prepare a meal for the entire 'crew'. The addition of teenagers meant a much larger fare, and they wanted to let everyone know their appreciation.

As the meal was enjoyed, Cassie stood back from the table with her camera setting up the delay. As she ran back to her seat next to Callie . . . "Say cheese!" The red light blinked just seconds before the flash bulb indicated the photo had been completed. John raised his hands up in the air. "Newfangled things, what will they come up with next?" "Who's ready for dessert?" Their attention was diverted from John's exclamation to Callie's setting a plate of cookies on the table.

Sara removed herself from the table and walked to the bench nestled between the wisteria trellises, sitting down slowly so as not to upset her plate of cookies. Sara took in the scene of friends all together for a common cause of more than the work, but for the love of each other . . . she found herself smiling, a 'knowing' in her heart that this is 'family'—this is what is important. "My dear sweet daughter, I can see in your eyes that you understand the blessing that is here." Startled, Sara looked up at Mary. "Yes, yes I do. I truly do." "Come on . . . help me with the bedding for the girls. Michael . . . you help Katy with the dishes. Callie and Cassie deserve a break after serving such a wonderful meal." "We'll help in the kitchen too." Marge and Mary had already stacked dishes in their arms to clear the table.

"Michael, will you walk with me to check on Chance before you go?" Katy put her arms around left arm his as she asked. Sara smiled at her son as he looked at her in hopes of her permission to delay their leaving.

With concern in his voice Brent turned to Sara. "Is he going to be alright?" The tools had been placed in the truck beds and full attention was on Sara awaiting the answer to Brent's question.

"Truthfully, that will depend on a lot of really hard work and patience on Katy's part and a lot of Prayer too. It won't be easy, and will he be 100%? I can't say. There is muscle damage in a strategic area especially for a barrel runner." Sara nodded sideways as she sighed . . . "Katy has the fortitude, and she has been doing a lot of studying, so if he is going to recover, she will be the right one to see that he does."

As Katy and Michael approched the trucks Katy announced, "I have made a decision! My horse is going to be fine. There is no other alternative, and I am going to specialize in leg injuries when I get to into Vet school! Dr. McGregor at your service!" Everone took turns hugging and thanking each other as they prepared to leave. Michael pulled Katy close to him and whispered in her ear "That will be Dr. Moore if I have my way." As he held her close, Katy squeezed a little tighter and smiled. She understood that this was not a time to outwardly respond, she did so with a tighter embrace. She was still smiling as Michael and his family were the last of the trucks leaving the drive through the gates.

PART 8

The Investigation

"And for the local news, the investigation into the murder of Wes Grant at the rodeo grounds continues. Russell Barnes of the Barnes Rodeo Company has been formally arrested and charged in that murder. Barnes claims 'self-defense'. Detectives from Carnon have been brought in to assist in the investigation. We will have further details as they become available to us. Now for your weather forecast . . ."

"It's just not right, them accusing Mr. Barnes of killing that man. He was the one that was drunk and causing the ruckus after the Team Roping. I heard he was even more 'polluted' at the dance." Looking at her son, Sara felt a knot in her chest. "Did you see that man that night?"

"I guess he was just hanging around, sorta creepy actually, kept walking over to the Crow's Nest and pacing under it and then back to his truck and back to the Nest. Never came out to dance with anyone, it was like he was there for other reasons other than to dance. Why would you go to a dance and not dance? . . . weird, that's all."

"To fight. That's why he went. To fight. Probably had it all planned out, why with Mr. Barnes?" Brent shook his head and reached for another card; hopelessly losing at Rummy 500, he drew an ace. "Yes! I sure needed that!" Setting the ace, king and queen of hearts on the table and discarding the four of clubs, sitting back in his chair, he smiled.

"I'll take that four of puppies feet and with my other two, that's it! I'm out!" "Oh, but of course, you are Charles . . . of course, you are!" Brent fisted Charles, and they all counted their points. "Charles, that makes 545 for you, you win again . . ." "Why, thank you Mrs. Moore, for my winnings . . . I will just have to have one of the muffins you made this morning! . . . oh heck . . . lets all have one!"

As Sara brought the plate to the table the boys continued. "You saw Grant there? You gotta tell the cops what you know . . . it might help Mr. Barnes!"

"Yeah, man, you gotta tell em."

"What do you think, Mom?" Michael recalled the jeans that he had given Gram to wash with the torn pocket and the sight of that truck leaving the grounds . . . he still wasn't convinced of her actual wherabouts that night. "Do you think I need to go to the cops?" "They need all the information and evidence they can get to use in the investigation, be it in favor of Russell, um, Mr. Barnes or not. Yes, I think you should go to the station and tell them what you saw."

"But Gramp told me not to get involved in that which is not mine."

"That is true, but in this case to help prove a man innocent or guilty is 'justifiable involvement' as Gramp would say. What is important here is that the proper person be punished for the crime."

"OK, I'll go tomorrow. Who's going with me?"

"Going where?" Katy had slipped in the backdoor without discovery as the muffins were being devoured. "Got one of those for me? Where are you going?" "Seems I have been advised that I should make a statement to the cops about the night that Wes Grant was killed. That's where we are going tomorrow. I suppose you think I should go too . . ." "Yes I do. But not without me." She smiled at Michael as he reached an arm to Katy. When she was close enough he pulled her onto his lap. "Muffin?"

****

They parked the truck in the back row at the Police Station. "Think I'll wait here, just something about police stations and me, not a lot of fond memories" Leaning his back on the driver's door and facing Michael who was last out of the truck, John smiled at his grandson. Michael turned to his grandfather. "Sure you don't want to come in? I haven't the foggiest clue what to do in there, Gramp!" "You'll be fine. Just answer the questions honestly, no more or less than what they ask for. Pretty straight forward." "OK . . . Be back soon." Katy had put her arm in his; he patted her hand and smiled at her.

"Let's do this!"

Alone in the truck, John spoke softly as he watched them enter the glass doors of the old brick building. "Sorry kid, you will just have to do this on your own. Time to grow up a little bit more." He leaned his head back, closing his eyes he could see the memories of the Clint Barnes cattle rustling trial . . . "That's enough of that old man!" Taking a short look toward the station, he closed his eyes again; this time dozing off peacefully.

Looking up from her desk at the audible realization that the four teenagers were approaching, the station receptionist set her pen down and closed the ledger in front of her. She smiled at Katy. "Well, if it isn't the cham-p-on barrell racer! What brings you and this bunch of hoodlums here?"

Katy tried to keep from laughing as she answered, "Hello Mrs. Harrison. Good to see you again. Michael here would like to speak with the detectives that are working on the Wes Grant case." Katy held on to Michael's arm as she spoke.

"Oh, he does, does he? And just what makes you think the Detectives will want to talk to him?" She transferred her glare from Katy to Michael. "I saw him over at the Crow's Nest . . ." Before he could finish his sentence Mrs. Harrison held up her hand in a motion to hush him. "Detective Harrison . . . young Mr. Moore is here to talk with you regarding the Grant murder investigation." She spoke to the intercom on her desk as she continued to hold her glare on Michael.

Brent turned slightly and with his head behind Charles he whispered, "She's scary everywhere isn't she?" Charles nodded in agreement.
"What was that Mr. Thomms?"
"Um . . . nothing, ma'am."
"That's what I thought. Is there a reason why you and Mr. Hunter need to be here?" Charles and Brent looked back and forth from each other and Mrs. Harrison motioning with their hands, pointing to each other . . . Charles spoke first and Brent stumbled through his attempt to agree with Charles. "We are . . . uh . . . here because, well, we . . . heard him at the Rodeo too!"
"Heard who at the Rodeo?"
"That Grant fellow . . . he threatened Mr. Barnes."
"OK, boys, you can all have a seat while we get paperwork ready for your statements. And you, Miss McGregor, I suppose you want to make a statement now too?" Katy looked at Michael and then back to Mrs. Harrison. "Yes, yes, I do." As Mrs. Harrison pointed to the chairs in the waiting area, her gruff voice was again on the intercom. "Detective Borden, please join Detective Harrison in the front office."

Katy gripped Michael's arm a little tighter. It had been quite a while since she had last seen Nick Borden. Recalling the night she overheard her mother and aunt talking in the kitchen, she learned that he might in fact be her father. How was she supposed to react now when she saw him? Does he even know? If he does, why didn't he pursue knowing her? Michael did not know why Katy held to him, he thought it was just because she was worried for him. Placing a hand on hers he looked at her and smiled. "Thank you for being here, it means a lot to me. You seem to always come through for me."

Katy whispered in Michael's ear "Time for the truth . . . I think that Detective Borden might be my father."

"What?"

"Yeah, I overheard Mom and Aunt Cassie arguing one night. Don't know for sure, but maybe."

"You OK being here?"

"Yes, whether he is or he isn't has no bearing on why we are here right now."

Michael held her hands in his. "You are one tough lil cowgirl you know that!" Before he could kiss her, Detective Nick Borden was standing before the teenagers.

"Wow!" A puzzled look from Detective Borden jolted Michael from his stunned state. "I mean hello, sir, I am Michael Moore." "I know who you all are. All of you." He smiled directly at Katy. There was no mistaking the question of parentage. A tear slowly fell on Katy's cheek, unsure of whether she was happy or sad at the confirmation. To herself she thought "That will just have to wait until later. Right now, we have to focus on Mr. Barnes." She wiped the tear away.

Kent Harrison joined the group. "Lets all go into my office, shall we?" In a single file, the parade of friends followed him through the hallway. Detective Borden closed the door behind them. "Now, tell us why you are here." Looking directly at Michael, Detective Harrison spoke in much the same gruff voice as his mother.

"It's about Mr. Barnes."

"I got that from the receptionist."

"I saw Wes Grant at the Rodeo Dance."

Aware that they were interupting, Brent and Charles simultaneously said. "We did too!"

"And he threatened Mr. Barnes after the Team Roping! He was drunk, and he threatened him" Brent was speaking so quickly he was nearly out of breath.

"We all heard him!" Katy pushed her way into the conversation.

"Slow down . . . no, really . . . slow down . . . one at a time. Michael, let's hear what you have to say, we'll get to the rest of you in moment." His look of dismissal was nearly a chastisement and all four sat up straight in their chairs and were silenced.

"Michael, what do you mean you saw him at the Rodeo Dance?, Wait, let's back up to the Rodeo itself . . . You say you saw him threaten Russell Barnes?"

"Yes, Sir. It was after the Team Roping. He had a bit of bad luck with his partner and bein' drunk and all, he thought he was due a reride. That don't happen, sir"

"I know that, go on . . ."

"Well, when the men were dragging him out of there, he yelled to Mr. Barnes, "This ain't over Barnes" and he threw a fist in the air, and well, sir, he was gesturing profanity."

"And the rest of you witnessed this too?" Nick Borden looked directly at Katy. "Yes, sir, we did."
"Boys?"
"Yes, sir."

"So tell us about the Rodeo Dance." Detective Harrison had been sitting behind his desk in a high- backed leather chair, he now moved to the front of the desk and leaned against it. Detective Borden had his tablet out and was writing down what each of them said.

"Michael? The Dance?"

"Yes, the Dance . . . We were all just hanging out in the bed of the truck . . ." Snickering, Brent interrupted Michael.

"Yeah, well some of us were dancing our toes off! Miiiiichael . . ."

"Quiet, please, you will have your chance." Turning back to Michael, Detective Borden said, "Go on . . ."

"I saw Mr. Grant pacing back and forth from the concession to the Crow's Nest . . . a lot. He had something in his hand. I think it was a bottle or a can or something. He was walking sorta funny, I figured he was still drunk from that afternoon. He was flailing his arms all around . . . like my grandpa does when he is really mad."

"What time was this?"

"Well, when I wasn't dancing and when I wasn't . . ." Michael blushed. " . . . ah, having my attention on . . . Katy . . . I guess I saw him over there a few times like he was going back and looking for something."

"Or someone" Charles interjected out of turn.

"That's it! Separate these clowns. If we're going to take this seriously, we need to do this right."

With a hand motion to them, they rose from their seats and followed Detective Borden to the hallway.

"Mr. Moore, you wait here."

Katy turned back to Michael and smiled to him as if reassuring him he would be fine.

"Michael, may I call you Michael?" "Yes, sir."

"Now, Michael, I realize that this is a sensitive subject for you. Mr. Barnes has a bit of a history with your family, and it would only be right that you try to protect him. I certainly would in your shoes. This is a murder investigation, and no act of heroics will be tolerated. Do you clearly understand what I am saying here?"

"Yes sir, I do. And you are wrong if you think that I would help protect a man if I knew him to be guilty. My grandpa told me to stay out of it. He said what don't concern me, I need to stay away from. He's right. I don't want to chance compromising my rodeo career for the likes of Wes Grant or for Mr. Barnes either for that matter, but I sure as heck don't want Mr. Barnes to be accused of something that might notta been all his fault neither. Maybe, just maybe he's telling the truth about 'self-defense.' That's all I am saying."

"We have been gathering a lot of evidence from the scene, some of which we are still investigating. Did you happen to see anyone else around that area?"

"It was dark in the pens, sir. The light from the Crow's Nest doesn't get as far as the pens. I didn't see anyone else there."

"At the Rodeo, when the cattle are held in the pens, who looks after them? I mean, who runs the pens and moves the cattle in and out?"

"Sir?"

"Who works in the pens during the Rodeo?"

"The rodeo company's wranglers and handlers. Why?"

"Men? Women? Did you meet any of the wranglers and handlers from that rodeo company?"

"It was Mr. Barnes's company, sir. I only remember what they looked like, never got any names."

"Were there any women working for Mr. Barnes in the cattle pens?"

"Not that I know of, why?" A flash of heat seared through Michael as he remembered the 'feeling' he got when he handed his mother's jeans to Gram to be washed.

"Funny, that's all. A piece of a pocket from a pair of lady's jeans was found in one of the pens."

"Sir, if I am done, I would like to go now."

"You OK there, young man?"

"Yes, my gramp is waiting for us in the truck. He is probably wondering what is taking so long."

"You think of anything, you come right back here, you understand?"

"Yes sir." Michael was on his feet and rushing out of the office in a panic. As he was leaving the station, the others joined him. They had been waiting for him in the reception area. Startled by his urgency to leave they rose quickly and were out the door to catch up to him.

"Nick, that Moore kid knows something. Something big. I baited him with us finding the lady's jeans pocket, and you should have seen him squirm. We need to keep an eye on him and what was that look between you and the McGregor girl?" "Yup, keep an eye on him . . . hey, hold that thought, I'll be right back."

Sprinting through the entry door in pursuit of the teenagers Nick had hopes of speaking with Katy. While his body was in motion to reach her, his mind was racing with questions to itself as just how he would approach her. It was time to stop hiding from the truth that for so had been held back from the daughter he had been forced to love in secrecy. Hoping she was ready to hear what he was about to tell her, he called her name.

"Katy, wait up."

Michael stopped suddenly, he saw an uncertainty in Katy's eyes. "Oh . . . ummmm . . . What do you think he wants?" She spoke with a falter in her hushed voice. Michael felt the clench of both her hands on his arms as she attempted to steady her balance. "Michael . . ." Katy said, drawing the syllables of his name out individually. His heart pounding at hearing the urgency in her plea, he knew it was time for him to stand by for her as she had done for him so many times.

Unaware that Brent and Charles had joined his grandfather in the truck, Michael and Katy together turned to Nick as he approcached them on the sidewalk.

"Mr. Moore . . .?" Brent nudged the elder to awaken him. "Mr. Moore, we're back. At least two of us are." John sat up and straightened his hat. "Hello, boys . . . hey! . . . Where might the rest of you be?" Pointing with his right hand toward the police station, Charles spoke with concern in his voice. "Detective Borden has Katy and Michael . . ." Interrupting Charles, Brent leaned forward to the front seat and said "Mr. Moore . . . we all talked with the Detectives. They can't run out of the station and ask more, can they? Why do you think he stopped just them two?"

"Boys, guess we'll just have to wait for them to get here and tell us themselves." Turning his head back to the left and looking out the truck window in the opposite direction of the station, John sighed at the realization that Nick might be confessing to Katy what he had wanted to do since the day he had returned to Brandon. The McGregors had refused him his rights the night she was born. Nick fought the Court ruling but was denied as he was not married to the child's mother.

John recalled clearly how Nick swore he would find a way to change the laws. A small town of faithful families looks poorly on a man that seemingly took advantage of young woman, created a child, and then abandoned them both right after the birth. Most folks did not know his leaving was actually due to pressure from the McGregors. Determined to have a place in Katy's life, he attended the Police Academy in Januette he graduated with top honors. He then worked for the State Police Department until promoted to Detective and returned to Brandon hoping to show the McGregors and Katy he had truly become a man worthy of acceptance in her life.

John had seen many times over the years how Nick 'just showed up'at Katy's school events, or how he managed to get on the police safety unit at the Rodeos with Barrel Racing competitions. 'Man to man' he felt a sorrow for him. Nick had married the Yern girl, but that didn't last. He had not given attention to any others after his divorce; not that there weren't women that had hoped he would. It was a known among the older townfolk that Nick did love Callie, and she had refused him. Callie would not speak of it. The older women of Brandon were of the opinion that Callie had been threatened by her father all those years before his death with disinheritance if she married him.

Looking back toward the Police Station, he watched as Nick, Katy and Michael were engrossed in conversation. "Mr. Moore, what do you s'pose they're talking about?" Charles leaned over the seat, reaching for the radio tuner while looking out the window. "I 's'pose' we will know that when they are finished." "Yes, sir." Charles sat back next to Brent. They knew that it must be important and that Michael's grandfather knew more than he would say, but it would be disrespectful to continue asking him.

Michael held Katy's arm to steady her; he could feel her tremble as Detective Borden spoke to her. "I tried Katy . . . I did! The Courts . . . they wouldn't even try to understand. I loved . . . still love . . ." There was a pause in his voice. "Your mother. I wanted to marry her. Your grandfather would not hear of it. She was afraid of him. He wouldn't let me see her or talk to her. He said I wasn't good enough and would never make anything of my life. That's why I left. I left to go to school and the academy to be a man that your mother might want. I still attend classes on domestic law. I know you will soon be eighteen, and by then, it won't matter. You can decide for yourself. But Katy, I don't want what happened to me to happen to another man in a similar situation. It just isn't fair. I have tried to respect your mother and to respect you too. I had no idea if you knew, when I saw you in the waiting area earlier, the questioning expression on your face lead me to believe you may have suspicions. I am sure I am out of place here and will be chastised dearly for doing this . . . Yes. It is true. I am your father. I have loved you from before you were born . . ."

Katy placed her fingers to his lips. "My father . . . you *are* my father . . . I overheard my mom and aunt arguing one night but didn't hear the whole thing, so I wasn't sure. You are . . . my father." She turned to Michael. Tears flowing freely, she spoke slowly "He is my father!" Katy turned back to the man before her, opened her arms and wrapped them around his waist. With her head on his chest, she smiled at Michael. Nick sighed with relief that not only the 'secret was out' but that Katy had not run from him; in fact, she had accepted him. "Oh . . . my dear Katy, I know it is a lot to take in right now, but know I have always loved you and wanted you."

Stepping back, she looked at him and said, "I have seen you at my school games and at the Rodeos. I wondered why since you didn't live here anymore. You came for me . . . You came for me . . ." "Yes, I came for you." "Wow! Oh man! What am I going to tell Mom?" "If you want . . . we could go together." Katy clenched Michael's hand and asked, "What do you think?"

"Me? Uh . . . Katy, I think this is between you, your mom, and your father. I'm not so sure I should be there. I'm sorry." "He's right, Katy, and I will do what you want . . . do you want to talk with your mother alone or do you want me there too?"

Imagining in her mind the reaction of her mother, she was uncertain how to answer her father's question. "I can see you are not sure . . . why don't you think about it, and if you want me to be with you, here is my number at the station. Since you have already been here, there would be no suspicion as to your calling." Katy slowly reached her hand to his to retrieve the paper. "Thanks. I guess I sorta lost my words there . . . wow! Michael, I think we have kept your grandfather waiting long enough for there to be way more questions than I am ready to answer awaiting us when we get there." "Well, Brent and Charles have been looking at us for quite some time now, you know they will be curious!"

Walking toward the truck, Katy slowly turned back to the man standing in the shadow of the American flag. He raised his arm and waved to her . . . "Come on Michael, race you!" She spoke as she returned her direction toward the parking lot.

"Don't even ask. Please. Not yet." Katy settled in the center of the front seat, put her hands together in her lap. The sterness of her voice indicated to the others that it was a final statement not to be pursued. John Moore placed a hand on Katy's knee and tapped her leg several times. Katy looked at him to see him smile at her; she was certain that he knew what she didn't want to speak of. Tipping her head in response to him, he moved his hand to the gearshift.
"Time to blow this popsicle stand, don't ya think?"
"Good idea, Gramp!"

Brent thumped the back of Michael's head. "Get the radio, lover boy!"

****

"I thought I might find you here, how is Chance's leg doing?" Michael entered the barn holding a bouquet of wild flowers he stealthily picked from Mrs. Beeman's side corral on Route 9. Katy's attention was on the flowers as a smile befell her lips. "Those are pretty. They for me?"
"As a matter of fact . . . they are at that!" Michael extended the arm holding the yellow flowers to her. She reached for them and drew them near to her. "Thank you, they are beautiful. What do I owe this surprise of flowers and a visit? It is so nice to see you. Okay, maybe more than just 'nice' . . . it's really good to see you."

"Oh yeah? How good?" Michael placed a hand on her hair and set aside the lock that had come out of the barrette enabling him to see her entire face. "Really good." Katy wrapped her arms under his and holding the flowers behind him, embraced him with a fervor that even was a surprise to him. Kissing the top of her head was not enough for either of them. He gently moved her away from him and leaned to kiss her properly. "Katy McGregor, I have missed you very much." "And I have missed you too, Michael."

She turned toward the horse patiently standing on the cross ties. "He's doing a lot better than I had expected this early in the recovery. The muscles are not twitching like they had been and every once in a while I see him put direct weight on the leg. It is a really good sign . . . believe me." "Oh. I do, you know way more about all this than me . . . are you going to be able to run him this season?"

"I am not sure . . . I want to, but if I can't in order for him to heal proper, then I will just have to wait."

"But . . . your title . . . at the Rodeo . . ." "Not worth his life, just not worth his life. If I have to wait then I have to wait. We'll blow their minds next year!"

"You are going to be a great Veterinarian, you really are . . . you really love horses, don't you?" "Yes. I have spoken with the state school as well as a couple others. I am leaning toward Ohio State, but as your mother is helping with the expenses, I guess it will be up to her whether I stay 'in state' or not." "That's between you guys. I for one don't want you going too far away from me . . . But that is just my being selfish. Just so you promise to come back to me and don't let some rich fella with fancy horses and a big ranch steal your heart . . . I just couldn't bear losing you." Placing his right hand on her left, she looked up at him and said, "Only ring going on this hand is from you. I love you, Michael Moore, even so young, I know I love you."

"I love you too."

Latching the stall gate after returning Chance to his stall, Katy paused before turning back to Michael. Noticing her hesitation Michael became concerned. "What is it, Katy?"

"I haven't told my mother yet about the other day at the Police Station. I just don't know how. She is home now, would you go in with me?" "You don't think that the whole thing is more a private family matter? I mean, I will if you really want me to but I sure don't want your family thinking I am intruding."

"I need you there whether they like it or not, I need you with me." "Then, what are we waiting for? Seems like now is a good time, don't you think?" "I suppose. Waiting any longer is just going to create more of a 'situation' so yeah, it's time." Clasping her left hand with his right, together they closed the main door of the barn and walked toward the house.

"Hey you two . . . didn't know you were here Michael, come . . . join us for lunch. Callie will be down in just a moment." "Thank you ma'am, that would be very nice. Seeing as how I am a growing young man and all!" Michael laughed as he gestured with his hands of his tall physique and muscular arms. "Growing . . . yes, young . . . yes, as far as the man . . . well . . ."

"Aunt Cassie! Please . . . Not now!" Silenced by her outburst; Cassie and Michael stood as statues as Callie entered the kitchen. "OK, what is happening here? What have I missed out on? Hello, Michael, nice to see

you, hope my sister has been gracious enough to ask you to stay for lunch."
"Yes ma'am she has, thank you."

"Cassie?" Callie looked to her sister for an explanation for the rigid stance that she and Michael had taken. "Uh, lil miss smart britches here seems to be in a bit of a snit . . . care to tell us why?"
"I am sorry Aunt Cassie, really I am. I need to tell you something Mom . . . and . . . Aunt Cassie too." Katy sat hard in the chair she had been grasping onto for support; folding her hands in her lap and looking at her mother, she began to cry.

"Oh boy! This does not look good. Michael, do you have something to do with this? You darn well had better not have forced her to do things she didn't want . . . I won't stand for that. At least you are man enough to be here with her." The glare that Callie gave to Michael was not unseen by both Katy and Cassie. "Mom! No . . . geeze . . . No! He is not Nick Borden!" She knew the moment she said his name it was a mistake. "Mom. Oh man. I am sorry. I am sorry. That was a cruel thing to say. I am so sorry." Katy placed her hands on her mother's and plead with her for forgiveness. Michael had seated himself in the chair next to Katy. Looking at Cassie sitting opposite of Callie, Michael saw the realization in her expression that Katy knew enough of the truth to be here to talk about it.

Callie spoke first. "Michael, I am sorry for the accusation that I spoke to you and the way in which I spoke it. Obviously, it has been a concern of mine since the two of you became so involved. The mirrored happenings in Katy's life to those in mine at her age have left me a bit overprotective and nontrusting. Please, of all the young men that she could have chosen, I am grateful it was you. I really am." "No problem ma'am, it is more than understandable the concerns you have. And just to assure you, I love Katy very much, I would never ask her or expect her to . . . uh . . . you know . . . I am not like that. I respect her . . . I love her." "Good! Keep it that way, and we will all make it through yours and hers teenage years! Now, my lil punkin, what has you all in this snit your aunt says you are in. Hold it . . . You named Nick Borden . . . Oh my God, you know don't you?"

Unable to conceal the fears of her heart in her voice; the quiver of her lips gave away her true feelings. Sitting back in her chair she seemed to drift into a dreamlike silence. Cassie slowly removed herself from the table to pour her sister a much-needed glass of whiskey.

"Here . . . I'm thinkin' you could use this about now." Cassie sat down next to Callie and held her left hand. "It was going to happen at some point, you need to admit to the truth and let your daughter know what really happened with you and Nick . . . and Father. She's old enough now to understand, Callie, you need to do this."

"I don't know if I can."

"Mom, what is it? You can tell me. I love you, and whatever you need to tell me, I can take it."

"How did you know it was Nick?" Callie did not lift her head as she spoke; there was a solomness in her voice. Hearing her mother's pain, Katy knew she was about to open very deep wounds in her mother's past. She did not want it known that she had overheard the sisters' argument. "Have you seen him lately? I favor his smile and his eyes . . . and we have the same laugh. I have known of the rumors but wasn't sure until I saw him at the Police Station last week."

Abruptly, Callie interupted Katy. "The Police Station? What were you doing there? What was he doing there? I can't take much more of this . . ." She took a long draw of the whiskey. "He is a Detective there and is working on the Russell Barnes–Wes Grant case with Kent Harrison."

"He lives here?" Michael interjected "He hasn't been here all that long, he was over in East Dale for a while, got here a month or so ago. They got those two hotshots from Carnon working the case too. We . . ." Callie cut Michael short, "I want to hear this from Katy . . ." "Like he said, Mom, he's working the case . . ." "What does that have to do with you, and why were you at the Police Station? What do you know that you thought you had to go there?"

"Cool it, Mom, you act like I had something to do with the murder! No way! But we did see Mr. Grant over by the Crow's Nest, and he was acting weird, and we thought we ought to tell the Police. Maybe, just maybe Mr. Barnes is telling the truth that it was self-defense. I mean Mr. Grant did threaten him earlier at the Rodeo. I just thought we ought to tell what we know just in case they need it to investigate the whole situation not just what they saw at the end of it. Trust me Mom, it took a lot to go, but we knew it was the right thing to do!" "We?" "Yes ma'am, my gramps drove us all to the station. Me, Katy, Brent, and Charles."

"Is this true, Katy?"

"Yes."

"And that is where you saw Nick?"

"Yes."

Callie stood up, and leaned on the back of the chair. "Cass . . . I need a refill" Dutifully Cassie reached behind her to the counter where the bottle had been placed. Pouring only half a glass, she then returned the bottle to the counter. Callie reached for the glass and quickly drank the contents. "OK, I can do this!" She paced from the table to the sideboard and back several times all the while shaking her hands and head. Returning to her seat, placing her hands on the table in a clenched hold, she awaited the supportive nod from her twin sister and then turned to her daughter.

"Katy . . . I was so young. Like you are. Nick's family was new to the area, and no one knew anything about the Bordens. He was so handsome . . . and smart . . . and he had a new truck . . . Don't laugh, it was impressive, and all the local guys were envious. Katy, he looked at me. *Me*. Of all the girls that were so much prettier, he looked at me. He even left notes through the slats in my locker. I just couldn't believe he liked me. Cassie had eyes on him, and well, I didn't want to get in her way. But she knew he wanted me and backed off. She told me to try . . . I didn't know what to do.

"Then he asked me to the Spring Dance at school . . . your grandfather forbid me to go because the Bordens were strangers and he wouldn't let me go with someone he didn't know he could trust. I was heartsick. The night of the Dance I said I was going with my girlfriends and left before getting his permission. He was so angry. "When I got to the Dance, Nick was waiting for me and we danced every dance . . . he was so good . . . he was so kind to me . . . As crazy as it sounds, I think I fell in love with him that night. It was magical. I could hear the whispers all around us, and I didn't care. Neither did he until Father showed up and ruined everything. He dragged me out of there after threatening Nick right in front of the whole school. The mortification I felt was nothing compared to the embarrassment that Nick had to withstand after I was gone. Cassie went to him to try to talk to him. I know she did, he told me. She never did tell me she had tried to ease him, and yes, Cassie, I have known all these years that you did that. I should have thanked you years ago. I am sorry I waited so long."

"Callie, dear, Nick told me he told you . . . he thanked me enough for the both of you." She reached a hand to place it on the intertwined hands of her sister.

"Katy, we couldn't stay apart. It was really hard knowing I was lying to Father. Cassie did her part in a lot of cover-ups, and she too had to lie to him . . . I hated myself for asking her to, but she did. As the summer ended and senior year started, there was no turning back. I loved him. He loved me. I begged with Father to let me go to Prom with him. When father realized that we had kept seeing each other, he was furious and got in his truck and drove like a maniac to the Borden's house and demanded to speak with Nick and his father." Callie wiped tears away as she spoke. "Cassie and I followed him over there and hid in the bushes outside the house to try to hear what was said. You can only imagine the spar between to the two men and even Nick's mother intervened. It didn't end well. Father pushed Nick so hard that he landed on the chair at the window where we were hidden. "Oh man, the look on his face when he saw us hunched behind that bush . . . it was awful. I feared he would never want to see me again. Cassie told me not to cry and that we had to get out of there. I blew a kiss to Nick as she grabbed my arm and pulled me away.

"We got home only moments before Father did. Sitting in our chairs in the den, he stormed into the house, grabbed me, and pushed me into my room, throwing me on my bed. I curled up as tight as I could against my pillows in fear of the whoopin' I knew I was about to get. Cassie was screaming outside the door for him not to to hurt me. He had locked the door . . . we both knew she could be no rescue."

"I will never forget that night. I knew he was going to beat her and then me too if he even thought I had anything to do with it. But she never told him. Even through it all, she never told him of any of my involvment. She took all the pain. God, Cal, why? Why did you do that?"

"I knew he would beat you too. And you did what you did . . . for me, so I had to do what I had to do for you."

Katy had such a tight hold on Michael's hand that he had to use his other hand to ease the grip. He could see her eyes welling at the realization of the childhood her mother and aunt had had to endure, and what they must have had to bear to be able to keep her. Why did they not hate him? How could they have lived like that?

"Mom, did he . . . I mean . . . was he really going to . . ." Katy could not actually say the words to finish her sentence.

"Yes. He did." Callie 'choked' as she replied to her daughter's question. Only Cassie knew what their father did to them. It was a well-guarded family secret and now Katy knew too. And also, Michael. Callie sobbed as she looked at Katy, seeing the sorrow in her young daughter's eyes she reached her hands toward Katy. Withdrawing her right hand from Michael, Katy reached to her mother. Hands enfolded, Callie spoke again.

"We tried to stay apart. It did't work. Nick wasn't mad that I had seen him that night. After the commencement ceremony we hid under the bleachers planning our get-away. Father came looking for me, so we said to meet at Gordes Bridge at 9:00 o'clock that night. When I got there, he had left a note. Father had returned to their house looking for me, and again, there was arguing, and before it got physical, he had to promise not to leave the house. He had sent the note with the neighbor boy Brian, to put on the bridge. I got home to find Father in his chair. All he said was, "It is never going to happen. Not now, not ever. Go to your room and stay there." I ran to my room and locked the door. He never came in. The next morning was the beginning of his refusal to speak to me. No matter how I tried, no matter what I said, there was no changing how he felt about me. And no matter what he had done to me, he was my father and I felt as though he hated me. Cassie tried to console me, even said that if he no longer spoke to me, maybe he would no longer beat me either. That only made me fear for her all the more. I was doing chores in the barn one day when father was in town and Nick came to see me. We held each other for so long . . . He kissed me . . . he told me he loved me, and no matter what our parents said, it was our lives not theirs and that nothing would keep him from me. I believed him, with all my heart I believed him. It was that afternoon that you were conceived. It was the 'first time' for both of us. I had never felt so close . . . so a part of someone else, other than Cassie, of course. But . . . it was different. Nick and I swore to each other that we would be together. I gave my whole heart to him and he gave his to me. After he left, I stayed in the barn for hours, trying to make it look like nothing had transpired. Cassie came out to help me. When father got home and came in the barn, he didn't have a clue. Another 'sister secret' had begun. When I knew I was pregnant, I thougth of running away. I knew if I told Father, he would shun me from the ranch, and I would no longer have a family . . . I knew he would hurt me, and he might even try to hurt or kill Nick.

I ran to Nick's house and tapped on his window. I told him the truth and . . . and he was thrilled. He was happy . . . he said we would get married and start our family. Then Father showed up, and . . . well . . . Nick ended up leaving and staying with his aunt and uncle in East Dale, and they were told that absolutely for no reason was he to return to Brandon and that I was not allowed on their property. They were to call the Police if I was spotted anywhere near their house or in East Dale at all. He even had the Brandon Police involved. I was to go to school and bear the shame as my punishment. I was the only pregnant girl and you can imagine what I went through."

Shifting in her chair, Callie continued her confession.

"We did manage to get a few letters to each other in a circuit of friends willing to help. The pregnancy was not easy and I was often sick, and Cassie had to pick up the chores I couldn't do or she was . . . Oh God . . . he was ruthless. The letters from Nick stopped coming just before you were born. I was heartbroken. When I was in the hospital to have you, Father was there but stayed in the waiting area. Cassie was with me the whole time. When you cried, I looked in the doorway, and there he stood. Nick was there. Father grabbed him and called for Security. Nick swore he would come for us as he was escorted out of the hospital. Father came into the room, looked at you then held his hands out as if he wanted to hold you. I was afraid he would take you away from me . . . when I told him "no" he actually started to cry. He sat on the bed next to me, looked at me holding you, and through his tears said that I looked like my mother when she'd had us girls. He was so remorseful that both Cassie and I cried with him. He was never mean or hurtful to either of us after that day, and he loved you Katy, more than I could have ever hoped for. He told me he sent Nick away because he wasn't good enough for us. We deserved the best. We should have all that we wanted in life that he could not give to us, that he had taken away from us by how he'd treated us. He promised that night to seek help and become the father that he should have been all along. He told me to forget Nick Borden, he would find his way in another life, and that I had to concentrate on you and you only. I heard bits and pieces over the years about Nick. I think I even saw him a few times coincidentally at your school and a couple Rodeos. I had given my heart to him and was 'broken' all over again when I heard of his marriage to Elizabeth Yern."

"Mom, they are divorced. He went to the Academy for Police training and is still taking classes in Domestic Law. He said he tried to get rights through the Courts, but they wouldn't rule in his favor because you two were not married. Even though I am almost eighteen, he still wants to pursue this so no other man has to go through what he did. And, Mom, he told me he still loves you. He never stopped. Even when he was with Elizabeth. That must be why it didn't work out. He asked if I had wanted him to come with me to tell you . . . here . . . here is his number at the station . . ." Handing the card to her mother, Katy could see the hope in her eyes. Callie still loved Nick. To herself, she was imagining them all being a family, like it should have been from the beginning. "Mom, I wasn't sure about him being here, so I haven't called him, and . . . he doesn't know you still love him . . ."

"Cassie . . ."

"I'm way ahead of you!" She placed the bottle on the table in front of Callie. "Well sis, what are you going to do?"

****

"Shall we finish up here and catch a movie on the TV tonight?" Sara pulled the drying towel off her shoulder as she reached for the last pot in the dish drainer. "Oh, that would be great! I think they are showing *Sarah Plain and Tall* again. Not that John will want to see it . . ." "Don't be speakin' for me! I like that movie, it's good and wholesome, not like this other garbage the kids watch . . . *Dirty Dancing* . . . why in heavens should we let our young people see such perversion!"

"Oh, John . . ." "Don't 'oh John,' me, you know what all that body slithering gets young 'uns into!" "And here I thought you liked our 'closeness'!" Blushing, Mary wrapped her arms around her husband and kissed him gently. "Well, ahhhh yeah . . . but the young ones ought not be adoing this until they are properly hitched! That's all. I will check the TV guide for the movie listings."

"You just think that was a good 'save'! We will further this conversation later . . . I love you, Mr. Moore!" "I love you too, Mrs. Moore!"

Putting the towel on the counter, Sara hesitated before she turned to place the stock pot on the top shelf of the pantry. "What is it dear?" "I . . . ah . . . I thought Samuel and I would have what you have forty years into our marriage. It just isn't going to be. I don't know . . . sometimes I think about . . . maybe again . . ." As she tried to complete her thoughts the telephone rang and startled both women. "It's either for you or for Michael. I'll see you in the den."

When the phone conversation was over Sara joined John and Mary for the movie. "What is it, dear? Who was that on the telephone?" Mary had taken notice of Sara's bewilderment as she nestled into her favorite reclining chair. "Callie wants me to go to the Police Station with her tomorrow . . . she wants to talk with Nick Borden and needs me. Why me? Cassie usually does that sort of thing." "I've got time to get a soda before the movie starts . . . anyone else?" Both women nodded a 'yes' to him.

"Since John is out of the room, I can tell you that it is pretty evident that if you go with her, then you could see Russell Barnes. That's my guess. But hey, I am just an old woman . . . sitting here with my knitting, minding my business . . ."

As John was returning, he said, "Minding your own business! Mary Moore! I highly doubt that! Is the movie ready?" The two women smiled at each other and held back their laughter. "Yes, dear . . . hit the volume . . ."

****

Walking to the entrance area of the Police Station, looking around at the sparse furniture and noting the lack of technical equipment in the Brandon Office, Matt Brewer looked at his partner with a disapproving nod and then stood in front of the woman at the receptionist's desk. "Detectives Matt Brewer and Cecelia Lang, Carnon PD." Not impressed, Mrs. Harrison slowly raised her head from the paperwork she was involved in. "Yes, that is who you are! I am Mrs. Harrison, and you may be seated. I will call for Detectives Harrison and Borden."

As the two sat in the chairs along the wall, Mrs. Harrison gave Cecelia Lang another look. To herself she remarked "This ought to be interesting throwing a woman in with Kent and Nick . . . oh yeah, this could get mighty interesting." Placing her finger on the intercom, in her screechy voice she called for the Brandon Detectives to come to the lobby.

At the finish of the introductions, Kent showed the Carnon Detectives the small office that they could set up in while they were in Brandon. "Meet us in five in my office, we'll get started right away." Kent had vanished before either Matt or Cecelia could respond.

"He has an office, and we get a closet . . . they sure know how to treat their guests around here!" Cecelia had a large office with windows and her own private restroom on the third floor of the Courthouse in Carnon. Appraising the accomodations set for them in Brandon, she leaned on the left side of the table she assumed was to be a makeshift desk for the two of them. "Dibs on the left side! This is just about pathetic, I sure hope that this is no indication of the skill level around here. I won't be able to handle incompetence in a murder investigation." "Pipe down Cee, these walls can't be very soundproof, that old bag at the front desk might hear you!" As they both were finding amusement in their 'office', humorously noting the many descrepancies between the two departments, Mrs. Harrison arrived at their doorway. "Are you two quite through?"

Halted and appearing chastized both Matt and Cecelia found themselves face to face with the impressive aura of the elder woman. "I believe my son said to meet him in his office. Here, these are for you." She threw several file folders on the table marked "Barnes–Grant." As they landed and slid across the short expanse of table top, both Matt and Cecelia dove to the table to prevent them from landing on the floor. Having saved the papers from disorganization, they both turned to the doorway; Mrs. Harrison was gone. Cecelia looked at Matt. "OK . . . Thin walls . . . you're right!" Still laughing, they made their way to Kent Harrison's office.

"I heard you met our receptionist. Yeah, I know, she is rough on the outside, but a darn good addition to this office as she knows more history in this town and knows more about anyone here or how to get the knowledge there of than should be legal. Shall we get to work? Nick will be here shorlty, he has been detained in an unexpected meeting."

****

"Callie? You OK?" Sara placed her hand on Callie's arm and held her back as they approached the walkway from the parking lot at the Police Station. "You still haven't actually told me why we are here. Does it have anything to do with the kids coming down here the other day? I mean, other than that . . ." Callie gripped Sara's other hand with such ferocity that Sara stopped midsentence.

"Nick Borden is Katy's father."

"What!"

"Nick is her father. It is a long story. I needed you here with me when I talk to him. Sara, Michael knows the whole story, and I do mean the whole story. You need to know too, and I promise I will tell you but right now I have to try to hold it together when I talk to him. I still love him, always have and Katy seems to think that he may still love me. I have to know the truth." Looking at the ground and in a poor attempt at not weeping, Callie slowly repeated her words "I have to know the truth."

Taken aback by Callie's admission, Sara composed herself, took in a deep breath and pulled Callie in to an embrace. "Yes, Callie, I suppose you do." The embrace was broken when the Detectives from Carnon rushed past them to the entrance. "Well, while they go to their 'fire', lets get to ours!"

Standing just inside the doors, Sara and Callie waited their turn as Mrs. Harrison dealt with the Detectives. Callie tried to move toward her. Mrs. Harrison rose from her seat, walked to the hallway and dissappeared for several minutes. "I don't know if I can do this, Sara!" "Yes you can! You have to . . . remember you vowed to get the truth and this may be your only chance."

Mrs. Harrison returned to her desk.

"Next!" Callie looked at Sara. "Wow! Didn't expect that!"
"Not to worry, all the years of smoking must have worked her vocal cords pretty hard. It's time, Cal, you're up!" Sara nudged her forward through the hesitation until she reached the front desk.

"Um . . ."
"Yes, what is that you want?"
"Um . . ."
"Detective Nick Borden, you are needed at the front desk. Pronto!" Mrs. Harrison looked up from the desk. "Callie McGregor it is about damn time you set all this straight." Neither Sara nor Callie had ever seen Mrs. Harrison actually smile. "What? You don't think the whole town wants these two back together?" She was looking directly at Sara, "Why the hell do you think he came back here anyway?" Sara could see the tears forming in the corners of Callie's eyes. Looking at her friend, she said, "You might just get that 'happily ever after' you have dreamed of . . . you just might!"

They heard him walking in the hallway toward the reception area. Callie clenched Sara's arm as he approached the dividing doorway. He stopped on the other side before opening it and looked at her through the window. Moments passed in the silence. She could see him speak her name. Her breathing became more rapid and tears fell slowly from her eyes. Callie was entranced in their gaze. As he started to open the door Sara let loose the handgrip Callie had on her arm and motioned her to walk forward. Each took three steps at a walk and then threw themselves into the embrace they had for so long been waiting for.

―――

Nick stepped back, placed his hands on either side of her face and, through the quivering of his voice, declared his love for her. "Oh, Callie . . . I never stopped loving you or Katy. You have just got to believe me." "I do . . . I do believe you, I have loved you every day." He slowly leaned to her and with the passion awaiting for seventeen years, kissed her with abandon of who was watching them or where they were.

"About damn time! About damn time!" Mrs. Harrison shuffled the papers on her desk, smiled at Sara and said, "Suppose you want to see the Barnes fellow?"

"What? Huh?" Sara was startled by her statement.

"That's what I thought, go on through the blue doors to the Security Guard. Tell him you are cleared, he'll bring Barnes to the meeting room. You can talk in there. What's that look for? Why does everyone think I am so 'hard'? Go on now, while I'm still smiling!"

"Yes ma'am, thank you, thank you." Sara looked toward Callie and Nick. "Go on . . . I think they will be OK without you . . . won't even know you are gone . . ." Mrs. Harrison laughed as Sara opened the blue door to the prisoner wing of the building.

****

"So what you are saying is you think these kids know more than what they are telling you . . . you think this because the Moore kid got all nervous when you mentioned something about a pocket from a pair of ladies' jeans?" Cecelia had seated herself in the only chair in the room other than the desk chair. "Yes . . . he had held pretty good composure until I mentioned the . . . Oh, hey there, Nick, did the 'meeting' go well? Join us here, we have started discussing the Barnes–Grant situation."

"It is not a 'situation', Detective Harrison, it is a murder, and unless you start treating it as such, and get your little po-dunk head out of your ass and get some real evidence and real witnesses and real motives that we can work with . . ."

"Matt . . . hey . . . pipe down . . . geeze . . . we just got here, give the men a chance to catch us up to speed on what they have so far." Looking first at Nick and to Kent, Cecelia said "Sorry for my partner here, he is a bit agitated over having been assigned over here, and to be truthful, not to discredit you at all, really, but we are used to a more up-to-date system and frankly, you are 'small town' trying to work a case you may not have enough experience to handle."

"OK, stop right there. Time to set your minds at ease. Our 'lil po-dunk' town may have been able to keep from the horrors of your big city . . . we're actually rather proud of our record here. It is a good safe place to live and raise families . . . we are good people. Maybe we don't have the crime that you deal with, but personally I am glad for that. I live here too. Just because we have a quiet town doesn't mean we are any less qualified to handle this case than you are. Take a look on that wall . . . what the hell do you see. Yeah, I have credentials too . . . And Nick, he has been through the State Police Academy and is still attending Domestic Law studies there. Both of us worked in the city before coming home, so don't think we aren't up for this. I am sure I can speak for my partner as well . . . I am . . . we are . . . offended by your assumption that we are not as capable as the two of you of working on this case. Now, let's get to work so you can go back to your big city."

"Coffee, anyone?"

"You have impeccable timing Mother, you really do!" Kent smiled as he took the tray and set it on the desk. "Nothing to do with timing . . . everything to do with the whole station hearing the raucus in here. You are here to work together, you best figure out how you will solve that problematic situation before you attempt to solve the murder case." She was out of the room as she finished her sentence.

Glancing toward Kent, Matt looked above his glasses. "Your mother? Nope, this isn't at all 'po dunk' . . . oh nooo" Nick rushed to step between the two men. "She's right . . . If we are going to get this finished, we can't even start if you two can't work together. You are here because the State has been concerned as this is not the first time that Grant, or Barnes for that matter, have seen the inside of a jail cell. So could we just please accept it that we are working together and move on? I mean really . . . this is just . . ."
"I get it, I get it, I'll back off."
"Good, now . . . Kent . . . maybe you ought to continue from where you were when I walked in."

****

Walking down the narrow corridor to the next doorway she would have to go through, Sara felt a chill on her skin. The silence was almost eerie as she could not even hear her own footsteps on the linoleum tile floor. Instinctively she clutched her purse to her chest as she opened the second door. Directly on the other side was the Security Officer's desk. The dissarray of accessories were noticed, but not until she caught her self mesmerized by the size of the man facing her from behind it. He stood as she approached him.

"Sara Moore . . . I presume. The receptionist said you would be coming in . . . have a seat over there in booth 3. I will bring the prisoner out to the other side. The phone on the wall is for your conversation. You will need to leave your purse here and empty all your pockets."
"Whhhaaat?"
"It's the rules, ma'am. I am sorry, but if you want to see the prisoner, you have to put your purse and pocket contents in the basket."
"YYess, sir." She placed what he wanted in the basket next to the sideways nameplate that she read quickly as he placed his hand on it to set it back straight. "I will just be seated now, Sergeant Blakeman, if that would be OK . . ." "You sit, I will get Barnes for you." She was surprised when he held the chair for her. "Thank you." Sara sat on the hard plastic chair watching as the massive man dissappeared through a locked door on the other side of the glass. She hated that he referred to Russell as 'the prisoner'. He is a man, still innocent until proven guilty according to the Constitution. He should not be accused of maliciousness without justification of it.

The door slowly opened. Russell walked toward her and stopped as the door closed behind him. The clanging of the latch startled Sara yet her eyes never left his. "You have ten minutes, Barnes . . . ten minutes." He sat in the chair opposite her and smiled through the glass partition.

Russell reached for the receiver. Sara followed his lead. "You are here." Sara smiled at him. "Are you all right? How are you being treated?" She felt silly having asked him such common questions.
"Sara . . . I am glad to see you, really . . . I am. I just didn't expect you to come."
"Russell, the kids have spoken with the Detectives, they saw a lot more than they originally admitted to. The case is far from over. I don't know how long you will have to stay in here. I am so sorry for that. What I do

know is that the Detectives from Carnon are here, and the possibility of believing it to be self-defense is actually on the table now . . . Thanks to Michael, Katy, Charles and Brent."

"What about you . . . Sara . . . what do you believe?"

"I saw . . ." He stopped her before she could say any more. "No . . . you can't . . . You can't be a part of this, Sara. I don't want you hurt any more for any reason. I haven't spoken a word about you being in the pens that night . . . they don't know . . ."

"But . . . I saw him"

"No!"

"Russell! It could help you . . ."

"And hurt you . . . I won't have it." He stood up, pushed the chair back and was in motion to replace the receiver on the wall. "Russell, wait . . . please . . ." Her pleading voice pulled at his heart, and he sat back down. "Let me get my brother here to represent you."

"Why would you do that? I can't pay . . ."

"We'll worry about that later . . . I need to know you are represented by someone I trust."

He sat back in the chair, shifting his head side to side. "Sara, do you really think he will do it?"

"He has to, he's my brother!"

"OK then, thanks . . . But I will find a way to pay him . . ."

"Time's up, Barnes, back to your cell, tell the pretty lady goodbye!" He put his hand to the glass. Sara placed hers up to it. "Thank you, Sara."

"I'll be back soon, I promise." Sergeant Blakeman pulled him through the doorway backwards Russell kept his eyes to her until the heavy steel door was closed between them.

Sara stood still; her mind consumed with thoughts of how she would approach Mark. How would she convince him to work on Russell's defense?

"Mrs. Moore . . . Hello . . . Get your things. You need to leave now."

"Yes, Sergeant Blakeman." As she turned toward the door, she could hear him clear his throat.

"Ma'am, if it makes any difference, I think it was self-defense. That Grant fellow is known for his temper and his grudges. After the Rodeo, the guys were here at the station talking that Grant had threatened Barnes, and well, they even speculated what might happen. If your brother needs me on the witness stand, just ask."

Taken aback by his turn of nature, Sara slowly placed her hand on the doorknob then stepped back to be able to see him. "Thank you. Would you do something for me?" She didn't give him time to respond. "When I return, could you maybe not refer to Russell as 'the prisoner'? I can see the pain in his eyes when you call him that. His current state of punishment is yet to be for a proven reason and he has to live shadowed by the 'probable cause' accusations each day he is here." "Yes, ma'am, I think I could do that for you." "Do it for him. Good day, Sergeant Blakeman." She opened the door and again was in the silence of the barren hallway.

Kent Harrison was standing at the coffee table behind his mother's desk refilling the carafe as Sara hurriedly walked toward the double glass doors leading to the outside of the station.

"Mother, who was that?"

"That was Sara Moore, she was in seeing Russell Barnes."

"What? Michael Moore's mother?"

"That would be correct, great detective work there!"

"Mother, be serious, what was she here for?"

"I told you, she was in seeing Russell Barnes. They have a history."

"A history? What kind of history?"

When the account of the tragic cattle drive had concluded, Kent set the carafe on the tray and began his retreat to his office. "Hmmm, interesting, very interesting. Get the Moore kid back in here, there seems to be more we need to talk about."

****

"Mom?" Michael was in the kitchen making a lunch for himself. "You in the laundry room? I'm going over to Katy's today, if that's OK . . . she says Chance is really improving and she wants to show me some newfangled treatment she has come up with."

"Callie mentioned she was free lunging[33] him already, whatever she is doing must be right! Give her a hug for me and ask her if she has applied to any schools yet"

"OK, will do. I'll be home for supper. Love you."

Sara entered the kitchen just in time to see him close the screen door behind him. The remnants of his lunch-making on the counter. Sara smiled as she thought "Well, at least he knows to take food with him. Hope he took enough for everyone." She sponged the cutting board and replaced the bread to the drawer bin.

Looking through the window over the sink, she could see John and Mary working in the garden. She hoped they would remain outside while she called Mark in East Dale. She brushed her hands on her jeans and cleared her throat before speaking to herself. "Just do it Sara, just do it." She started to answer herself as she reached for the wall phone and was startled by the sudden intrusion of the silence as the phone rang.

"Hello?"

"Mrs. Moore, Mrs. Sara Moore?"

"Yes, this is she."

"Mrs. Moore, this is Mrs. Harrison from down at the Police Station. Detective Harrison would greatly like it if Michael would come back to answer a few more questions."

"Is he in some sort of trouble?"

---

[33]   Exercising a horse in an arena using voice commands and body language; no connecting line or rope between the horse and the person.

"No. Kent, I mean Detective Harrison, has been working the case and feels that Michael could have more information to help them with the investigation."

"Michael is not here today, when is he needed there?"

"Tomorrow will be fine. If he comes home today before 3:00 p.m., call the station. Detective Harrison may be able to talk then. Thank you, Mrs. Moore."

"Yes ma'am. I will let him know."

Sara leaned her back on the wall and slowly slid to her knees. "Why do they need him again?"

"Sara, honey, who was on the phone? Are you all right?" Standing up, dazed at not having heard Mary come into the kitchen, Sara regained her composure. "That was Mrs. Harrison down at the Police Station. They want Michael to come back in for more questioning."

"It seems our Michael is in this pretty deep. Wouldn't have anything to do with the connection of Russell and our family, do you suppose?"

"Mary, I have no idea. How's the garden doing?"

"Good, but John is parched. I came in for some ice tea. Would you like me to pour you a glass too? You look like you could use one."

"Thank you, yes."

When Mary had returned to the garden, and Sara was certain that she would not be interrupted again, she dialed Mark in East Dale.

"Good morning! You have reached the law offices of Miles, Miles & Welderman, my name is Barbara, how may I direct your call?"

"Hello Barbara, this is Sara Moore, is my brother there?"

"Hi Sara, he sure is. I will patch you to his office. How have you been? Haven't heard from you or anyone from over your way in a long time."

"Been good, guess if you're a law firm and haven't heard from us all must be all right!" Feigning a light-hearted tone, Sara wanted to talk to Mark before she changed her mind.

"Suppose you're right. I will patch you through. You take care, Sara. Say hello to the family for me, would you?"

"I will, thank you." She heard the clicks of the switchboard as the call was transferred to Mark.

"Mark Bloom."

"Mark . . ."

"Sara?"

"Yes."

"Wow . . . sis! To what do I owe this surprise to? Is everything OK over there?"

"Mark . . . I . . . I need your help. Before you go asking all kinds of 'lawyer questions' . . . let me explain, then you can yell at me all you want."

"OK, just tell me you are not in trouble."

"It's not me. It's Russell Barnes."
She could hear Mark 'choking' to clear his throat before she was sure he was about to interupti her.

"Let me finish, please."

"Russell Barnes, OK . . . go on . . ."

"Mark, he's been in that jail for weeks . . . They won't release him . . . 'probable cause' or something like that. The investigation is far from over, and they haven't been able to formally charge him with anything, and he is still there. They said something about circumstantial evidence too. It is wrong." She paused and spoke again. "It is wrong, isn't it?"

"Sara, where is his attorney in all this? I know you have some sort of feelings toward this man, I know you do. I understand you wanting to help him. Sara, that is for his counsel to take care of. I am sure the laws are being upheld."

Discouraged by his passive attitude, Sara slumped into the kichen chair by the wall. "Mark, he has a rookie public defender. How is he going to get a fair shake when the guy supposedly helping him has never defended anything more than a shoplifting case?"

"Sara . . . I . . ."

"Mark, please . . . You have to help him. Please."

"I can't."

"Mark, he is only guilty of self-defense . . ."

Interupting her, he said, "I know you want to believe that Sara, but that is for the investigation to determine."

"No! Mark, you don't understand . . . I was there. I saw everything."

"What? You were there? Sara, why haven't you come forward on this?"

"Michael doesn't know I was there. Actually, no one other than Russell knows I was at the Dance. I was hiding in the pens when I saw the fight."

"Oh lord, Sara, you know what this means . . . you are withholding . . ."

"I know . . . But Russell won't let me get involved. He wants to have it all cleared without my involvement. He knows how it would look—and not be truthful at that either . . . Mark, OK, so it is more than Russell that needs you, I need you too."

"You lied. You said you were not in trouble when in fact you could very much be. Just the implications alone . . ."

"Please, Mark, I am sorry, who else can I trust? I need you." She was crying as she sat in the chair leaning over into her lap.

"Bad timing, sis. Bad timing. That is going to be a really high-profile case and I am up for partnership here at the firm. I take this and it goes poorly, I can kiss that promotion goodbye. Probably my job here as well, for that matter. I just have to think about this. I love you but . . ."

"Mark, think about it . . . If it is going to be that big of a case and you win, you are a shoo-in for that partnership! All the more reason to take it, so you have the opportunity to really prove your worth. There shouldn't be any thinking to do!" Sara was relieved to have an angle to play that would be convincing to him to take the case. "Please Mark, please."

"What about payment? This won't be cheap . . . How do I know he's good for it?"

"Between the two of us, we'll get that sorted out. Thank you, oh, thank you! This is going to be good for everyone . . . I promise."

"Don't promise anything Sara, I know I can't. But I will take this to the Board of Directors for approval and call you with the answer. That is the best I can do right now."

"Thank you. I love you. Call me as soon as you know so I can tell Russell."

"I'll call as soon as I know. Might be a day or so, but I will call you. Take care of yourself, Sara. I love you too."

She was wiping the tears from her cheeks as she lifted her head at the sound of the disconnection tone. To herself, she said "He'll do it, I know he will. Thank you, Mark! Russell, you're going to be all right!"

PART 9

The Old Red Oak

Michael reined Capp in as he approached the cattle lot gate behind the McGregors' main barn. The trail between their ranches was becoming well worn and more adapted to faster riding. Capp had learned all the rocks, ridges, and dips along the way. Michael smiled as the two of them had learned a bit about jumping over the downed trees; he was still baffled by his mother's fondness of the sport. Gramp had teased her often that "hooves belong on the ground, not in the air . . . that is what wings are for, and a horse don't have no wings!" Still smiling, Michael muttered "Well, Gramp, guess Capp has a pair of wings after all . . . won't tell Mom though, she'll want to put him in her arena."

"Won't tell your mom what?" Standing in the doorway of the barn, Katy smiled at Michael. Capp stepped forward reaching to her with his muzzle in anticipation of the treat he was certain to receive as he did each time they came over. "Looking for your carrot, big boy? Here you are, you gotta bow for it today!" As Katy reached under Capp's foreleg, he obediently lowered his head and tucked under his chest to nab the carrot from her hand.

"Gee, Katy, where's my treat?" "Well, cowboy, dismount that saddle and come get it!" He quickly was standing in front of her. "Ready!" "You always are!" She stood up on her toes, put her arms around him and as he bent to kiss her, she snapped back and turned. Before she could get out of his arm reach, Michael had caught her and pulled her in to him.
"Hello my someday-going-to-be Mrs. Moore."
"I like the sounds of that!"

Leading Capp around the tractor in the barn, Michael and Katy held hands. "He's recovering remarkably, he really is. Wait till you see him in the round pen!" Michael removed the bridle from Capp's head, replacing it with a halter and lead and then tied him to the post.
"You can put him in the side corral if you want. Not too much mud over there!" While he unsaddled Capp, Michael watched Katy as she walked over to the round pen where Chance stood nickering to her. Michael knew she had the same love for horses as did his mother. Katy and his mother often had the same reactions and insights to the behavior of a horse as well as the emotions of one. The deep desire to learn as much as possible about everything 'horse' Michael thoughtmust definitely be a girl thing. He was content to ride, rope, and round-up. The 'fancy stuff', as his dad called it, was just that . . . fancy stuff.

Capp trotted into the corral and settled to grazing.

"Holy cow! Katy . . . Chance looks good! Like he's ready to race again!"
"Oh, he is far from that, but he is improving everyday. Watch this . . ."
Katy moved to the center of the pen. She lifted her left arm and the horse positioned himself on the rail and started to trot forward clockwise. "He doesn't limp at the trot anymore! Can't let him canter yet, but the trot is good!" "Mom said if anyone could fix him, it's you! She also asked if you had applied to any schools yet . . ." "As a matter of fact, I have! I will tell you on our picnic!"

Right now, I will show you what I am doing with his leg. They had returned to the barn and put Chance in the cross-ties to enable Katy to explain his recovery to that point. "Here, put your hands around the forearm, do you remember how it felt the day of the storm?"
"Ahhhhh . . ."

Katy placed her hands over his when he had them positioned on Chance's upper leg. "Feel that?"
"Sorta, I guess" Michael was reluctant to admit he was not nearly as adept at the physiological aspects of a horse's leg as she was.
"I know it's hard, if you can't that is OK, the damage is quite deep and difficult to feel unless you know right where it is. I can assure you the healing has been awesome. Way quicker than Dr. Peterman thought it would be! I work on this every day, sometimes more than once. I have to do the best I can for him. He has always done his best for me."

Katy reached into the cupboard on the wall and brought out a 'mitten' that she had devised for working on Chance's leg. "See this, this is the massaging mitten I came up with for working the deep areas of his muscles."
"You can use that on me anytime!"
"Hush . . . silly!"
"Just wash it first, OK?"
"Stop, I am trying to show you this . . ."
"Yes, ma'am."
"Anyway, I have been deep-tissue massaging him with my mitten at least once a day and treating him with natural anti-inflamatories. I just don't want him on Bute continuously for an extended period. So I have come up with an herbal solution of devil's claw and buckwheat."
"Hold on here, 'Doc' . . . devil's what and buckwheat? Where did the flap jacks come in?"

"Devils claw . . . it is an herb that is anti-inflamatory as well as anti-spasmodic. The naturalists call it 'nature's bute'. It has been used for tendon and ligament damage, arthritis, joint injury, even navicular. It gets deep into the tissue walls and the buckwheat helps to improve the blood supply to the injured area by strengthening the capilary walls and nuetralizing excess toxins . . ."

"Whoa, speak in English please . . . I am not following you at all!"

"I blended herbs for the benefit of the site itself and the expedition of healing . . . how's that?"

"OK . . . Katy, you are amazing . . ."

Michael stepped back as she finished the massaging of Chance's leg. As she ran the mitten over his shoulder, wither, back, loin, croup, and followed down the hindleg. Michael positioned himself next to the horse's haunch. "Next?"

"Nope! Need to massage the other side, what you do on one side you have to do on the other for symmetry."

"Again, the big words!" She kissed him as she walked to the 'off' side of the horse and finished the massage. Placing the mitten back in the cupboard, she said "Chance, buddy, sit tight, think I will show Mr. Cowboy here what's behind the barn."

"I like the sound of that!"

"Easy there, stud . . . better yet, Chance you're coming with us to really show him."

Katy held the lead rope in her right hand and Michael took hold of her left. Capp picked his head up from grazing to watch as the trio approached a ditch beyond the corral fence.

"This is Chance's swimming run. I figure the racehorses have been using the theory for years, it must work for more than cooling out after a race. Hydrotherapy is beneficial for so many reasons. In Chance's case, the exercise he needs is combined with the cooling. He gets the resistance conditioning for his muscles without the concussion. He gets stronger every day and I know this has a lot to do with it. Watch him, he loves it."

"Did you build this?"

"Yes we did. Mom helped with the tractor and with the dirt we dug out, she built a raised walkway for me along the side. I went with a straight design as it was easier for me to do alone. Got lucky with the footing, as by the time we were down eight feet, it was all rock. Mom is a whiz on the tractor and she really did get the shallower ends pretty smooth. Watch him . . . he loves it!"

Katy let the rope out. Holding the looped end, she walked Chance to the edge of the water lane as she started up her walking ramp. "Time for your midday swim!"

"Wow! He really does like it! He went right in! How hard was it to train him to do that?" Michael turned to look at Capp. "What do you think . . . you wanna try it?" Capp snorted a response of discontent. Both Katy and Michael laughed at his attempt to convey he wanted no part of it. When Chance was through the 'pool', Katy used the sweat scraper on him to get the water off. "Only bad thing is I don't have anyway to keep the water clean, so I have to pump it all out once a week and refill it." "You thought of everything, didn't you? I am impressed."

"Let's get him put away and then I can impress you with a picnic lunch."
"I'll take your picnic over my smooshed sandwich any day!"

****

"Did you call the Moore kid? I'd really like to talk with him again." Kent brushed past his mother's desk without stopping as he spoke. "His mother says he is not home today. I told her if he gets home before three to call, if not then to call in the morning."
"He's probably at the McGregors. If I was to bet, I would say he is rather smitten with her."
"Good detective work Kent, what was it . . . the way he stumbles over himself when he looks at Katy?"
"Who's looking at Katy?" Nick Borden entered the reception area unnoticed from the prisoner hallway. Kent paused his step to turn to look at Nick. "You sure do jump at the mention of the McGregor girl . . . What's up? And don't 'nothing' me, we are partners, I know when you are holding out information."
"Not here, in your office." Nick passed Kent and hurried toward his office. Exchanging glances with his mother, he said, "This ought to be good!" "If you really don't know by now, then yes, you are in for a shocker."

Kent entered his office to see Nick seated in the chair. He repeatedly tapped his fingers on his knees and was blankly looking out the window. Walking around the desk and to his chair, Kent held his gaze on the nervousness of his partner. "OK, the badges are set aside, 'friend to friend' here, you need to tell me something?"

"She's my daughter."

"Holy cow! How long have you known?"

"I was and still am in love with Callie McGregor. I knew when she was pregnant. I was at the hospital. It is complicated. Her father, he well, chased me off. Thought I wasn't good enough and after I ran, I thought she would think me only a coward. Time and years went by, didn't change how I felt about her or about me either for that matter. I thought she would never have me again, so I married Elizabeth. We all know what happened there. I knew I had to come back to Brandon. When I got here, well, I kept telling myself I had to wait for the right time, and then Katy comes to the station the other day and I spilled it to her."

"Oh man . . . How'd she take it?"

"Better than I thought, she even went to her mother, and believe it or not, Callie still loves me. I think this just might work this time. With her father gone, there is no fear of his wrath, and I know Cassie has always been in favor of us. Just can't think of any reasons now why not to get back together."

"That's why you were late for the meeting with Brewer and Lang! And now I know why my mother keeps teasing me about my detective skills. She knew didn't she?"
"Well, yes . . . lots of folks know, it wasn't a secret! I wanted to marry her and was not shy about it. Can we get back to work now? Did I hear you say something about Michael Moore?"

"Get your camera, we're heading over to the Rodeo Grounds. I have questions about who might have been in the pens that night, and the kid got real shaken when I questioned who all has access during a Rodeo. I'm thinkin' we missed something over there, and I plan on finding it . . . before our 'friends' from Carnon take credit . . . Get where I'm coming from?"
"Yeah, sure enough do, you and I are going to solve this case . . . our way!"

****

Michael and Katy sat with their backs against the old Red Oak tree that had stood for over a hundred years at the edge of the second horse grazing pasture. Underneath them was a red checkered blanket for protection from the dirt at the base of the tree. The blanket her mother and father had used in their courtship of secret picnics under this very tree now acted as a table cloth for the same picnic basket they had used and Katy had filled with sandwiches, apples, cookies and sodas.

"Yup!"
"Yup what?"
"Yup . . . impressed me again, Katy McGregor!"
"It's the tree!" Katy could not hold back a slow tear.
"Whoa, what's that for?"
"My father would bring my mother out here when they were young. Kinda makes me sad, that's all." "No 'sad' today . . . won't have it!" Michael pulled Katy to his lap, placing her right leg to the outside of his left to have her straddle him. Placing her hands on his face, she leaned to him and surprised him with their first 'French kiss'.

Michael leaned forward while embracing Katy, moving his hands up and down her back. Aware that she, too, was sighing with each breath, he could feel the warmth rise within him. She moved slowly over him as they rocked to the rhythm of their breathing. Their lips parted, yet they moved not back from each other. "Katy . . ."
"Yes." He kissed her again, the passion escalating, he moved his hands to the edge of her shirt.
"Are you sure?"
"Yes." Katy moved his hands to help him, reassuring him of her desires for him as well as his for her. Katy sat back, lifting her arms to assist in the removal. He was gentle with his hands on her. She too could feel the warmth rise in places she had never known to be deep within her.

"You are so beautiful . . . So beautiful." Reaching behind her for the bra hooks, Katy saw the wanting in Michael's eyes. "Oh, Katy . . . I do love you."
"I love you too." She set the bra on the ground beside her. He was paralyzed by her beauty. He slowly removed his gaze from her eyes and looked to her breasts. A whisper of a gasp was the only sound he could utter. Katy reached for his hands, pulling them to her she placed them on

her breasts for him to hold. "Oh! Katy . . ." He looked at her eyes and then looked at his groin, he looked back at Katy to see the pleasure in her smile.

Katy leaned forward and started to undo the buttons of Michael's shirt, never taking her eyes from his. "It appears I am at the last one . . ." When she finished the last button, she paused, took in a deep breath, lowered her right hand, and placed it on the zipper of his jeans. Katy closed her eyes as she felt the pulsing of him. Removing his hands from her, he took his shirt off. "Katy . . . I haven't . . ."

"I know. Neither have I. Lets enjoy each other's bodies now and learn." Sliding down his legs past his knees, all the while opening the belt buckle, she then slowly undid the buttons of his 501 jeans. With closed eyes, Michael tipped his head back, the sun shone warmly on his face as she carefully removed his jeans and underwear. He felt the heat upon his naked body. He was tipping his head back to look at her as she was lowering her head toward his groin and began to kiss his upper thighs and genital area.

"Oh god! Oh god! That feels good! Oh, Katy!" His breathing intensified as the rush of power did the same in his loins. Reaching a hand toward her, he touched the side of her face as she lowered her mouth over his engorged penis. He felt his hips rising and falling as if he was trying to find her while she moved up and down on him. "Katy . . . I . . . uh . . . I . . . it's happening . . . it's . . . hap . . ." He did not finish the word as he ejaculated.

"Kiss me, Katy McGregor, kiss me again and again, forever . . ."

"Forever." Katy moved up on his legs, placing her groin over his, she could feel the revival of him under her. Michael reached to her jeans, slowly undoing the button and sliding the zipper open. Katy rose to her knees as he started to pull the belt loops downward. She stood, and as he watched her, she let the garments fall to the ground. Michael had never seen a woman without all of her clothes. He had seen pictures from the waist up, but not the waist down. He caught himself staring at her pubic area, he looked back at her smile and then felt again the rise of his penis.

She stood over him, so close that he could feel the heat of her skin. Reaching to her waist, he drew her to him. He knew what he wanted to do, but he knew it was wrong. He knew if he did not stop now, he would not be able to. He loved Katy and in that love, he respected her. Michael placed his right arm around her and twisted the tangled bodies to reverse positions. He had to carefully place himself between her legs as his penis was again engorged, and he knew he had to control himself.

Katy placed her hands on the back of his head as he held his face over her pubis. She opened her legs and bent her knees.

"Michael, place your hands under me." He did so and began kissing her as she had kissed him. Katy reached her arms above her head, her hips rising and falling, the slow moans of pleasure as he explored the hidden places of her womanness.

"There, Michael, right there. Oh, Michael . . ." Her hips thrust forward as she climaxed.

They lay next to each other on the blanket, both looking up at the tree limbs swaying in the breeze. "Katy, are you OK? I mean, are you sure we were . . ."

"We are perfect."

"I almost couldn't stop. I am sorry, but I have to say I like it. Guess that is why you are supposed to wait for the right person."

"We are right. But not yet for the . . . you know . . ."

"No, not yet. I had no idea it was like all that. Suppose we ought to get dressed, sure hate to cover you up, you are beautiful."

"Yeah, well, how you gonna get back in your jeans?" They laughed as she teasingly fondled him and then pulled away as she felt his arousal happening. "No fair, I have a distinct disadvantage here, don't I?"

"That you do, and now I know the real reason you are called 'Mountain Man!'"

****

"Where have you two been? Capp has been pacing the fenceline of the corral for an hour. Long picnic out at the big Red Oak?" Panicked at the possibility of having been discovered, Katy grabbed Michael's hand. "It's such a nice day . . . we just enjoyed the afternoon."

"Don't worry, I didn't follow you. I wouldn't do that. I am glad you had a nice picnic."

"Do you think your mom knows? I'm dead if she does. Just plain dead."

"Calm down, she didn't follow us, she said so. It is time you start heading home though. Let me help you saddle Capp."

Michael rode the trail home in a daze of mind pictures, emotions and a lot of questions. He realized he was talking aloud as he attempted to assure himself that he hadn't done wrong by Katy. Capp maneuvered the trail unguided with precision and cadence. Without realizing the time passing, Michael was startled when the horse halted at the gate. "Good boy! Glad you got us home OK . . . I sure wasn't much help!" Rex barked at the sound of the latch as it closed; acting as an affirmation of their arrival home. "Hey, buddy . . . good to see you too. Come on in the barn with me."

****

"You did what? Sara, I just don't think that is a good idea!" Michael stood hidden from view on the back porch. His grandfather was in what sounded like a rage and he did not want to become involved. He did manage to see his mother sitting in the end chair of the kitchen table closest to the sink and his grandmother seated on her right as Gramp stood, leaning on the other end chair. Remaining unseen, Michael overheard what his grandfather was upset about.

"John, what else was I to do? I know that you do not like Russell, I get it. I even get why, but . . ."

"No 'but'! He is the son of that no good cattle thieving son of a bitch, and I won't stand for . . ."

"John! Watch your language"

Mary interrupted him briskly in a chastising tone that Michael had never heard before. He backed to the porchwall, trying to get farther out of a possible discovery of his presence. Waving his hand at Rex, the dog understood and sat at Michael's side.

"John, you said it yourself . . . He is the *son* of a cattle thief. Why are you punishing the son for the actions of his father. He was there when I needed him and whether or not you can understand, I owe a great debt to him. You weren't there." Sara slammed her right hand on the table to the shock of both Mary and John. Standing between the chair and the table, Sara tried to hold back the tears as she felt the pain and the appreciation all over again of that day out on the range when Russell came to help her with Samuel.

"I . . . I . . . This I can do for him. I know you don't agree with it, but for me, I need to do this, for him, I need to do this and for Samuel. Yes, for Samuel too, this is the right thing. If you can't support me, please at least don't fight me on this, please." Sara fell back into the chair, put her face in her hands. Through her weeping, she looked first at Mary and then to John. "I love you both so much. Never would I do anything to cause you to be shamed . . ."

"Oh dear, dear . . ." Mary placed a hand on Sara's arm. "We are a family. A strong family." She took John's hand and drew him to them. Sara did not see the exchange between the elders.

"Sara, if you really feel that this is what you need to do, and I see that you do, you obviously know him better than we do, you care about this man, don't you? For reasons I just can't grasp, you are determined, and well, I will just have to try trusting you in this. I, we, support you and will help in whatever you need." Sara stood, tears of hurt had changed to tears of happiness as she and John embraced.

"Like I said, we are strong." Mary put her arms around Sara and John joining the embrace.

"Thank you. It means a lot to have you with me on this. I can't get through it with out you both. I just can't."

"Is there more you need to tell us? Is there more to the reasoning behind your getting Mark to represent Russell than you are saying? I am not being accusatory, just curious . . ."

Before Sara could answer John's question, Michael bolted into the kitchen followed closely by Rex. "Oh boy! This looks like I have interrupted . . ." Michael did not want them to know he had overheard. John motioned for Michael to have a seat at the table. "Your mother has informed us that she spoke with your Uncle Mark . . . she has the idea that he should be Russell Barnes' legal counsel at his hearing and trial." "Will he do it? Mom! Will he do it! Oh, that would be great. I knew it would be OK. I just knew it! Thank you, Mom . . . really, thanks . . ." Throwing his arms around his mother, Michael kissed her cheek.

"Slow down there, champ . . . he hasn't agreed to anything yet . . ."

"Oh, Gramp, you know Mom's persuasiveness tactics. He'll be here by the end of the week!" The four laughed as John agreed with his grandson.

"The Police Station called for you today." Michael's expression changed at his mother's announcement. "For me. Why?" "Don't know, something to do with the case, they said if you get home before three to call them. As late as it is now, you ought to wait until tomorrow. Maybe by then, I will have heard something from Mark, and we can go together."

"I'm heading to the barns for chores, be back in for supper. Thanks again Mom, for talking with Uncle Mark." Motioning for Rex to join him, the pair skipped out the door toward the barnyard.

****

"Good Morning Mrs. Moore . . . young Mr. Moore . . . I suppose you both know which direction to head. I will ring the prisoner wing for you, Sara and let the Detectives know you are here as well, Michael."
"Thank you, Mrs. Harrison." Turning to Michael, Sara smiled. "Be honest, answer all their questions, this needs to get done. It just needs to get done. I will be back shortly." Nervously, Michael smiled back at his mother. He had evaded questions the last time and was not sure just how to do so again. "Tell Mr. Barnes I said hello."
"I will."

Kent Harrison appeared in the doorway. "Good to see you Michael, care to join me in my office?" "Yes, sir." He turned to follow the detective as Sara walked toward the door of the familiar barren hallway leading to the prisoner wing.

"Hello again, Sergeant Blakeman."
"Well, well, hello to you too."
"I know, put my stuff in the basket . . ." Sara removed her purse from her shoulder and placed it in the basket. "How is he?" She was hoping the same feelings of benovolence remained that he displayed when last she was there.
"He is a little depressed, but for the most part, OK I guess."
"I have good news to tell him, hope it will cheer him up."
"Have a seat, I will bring him out."

Sara sat on the same hard chair in booth number 3. While waiting for Sargent Blakeman to bring him out from the cell area, the anticipation of Russell's reaction to her being there as well as the news she had brought regarding Mark gave her cause to fidgit. Hearing the clang of the steel door beyond the chair opposite her, she rose up from the seat as Russell stood motionless with his eyes fixed on hers at the realization of his visitor's identity. Sergeant Blakeman must not have told him who was there. He smiled and Sara could see the pleasure in his eyes.

Sara spoke first. "Hi"
"You look good."
"You look thin."
"I'm on a new diet."
"Mark will help you."
Simultaneously they sat in their chairs, never losing eye contact. Russell put his hand up to the glass. Sara slowly reached hers to his.

Neither noticed the smile on Sergeant Blakeman's face when he heard that Mark would represent Russell. In a low tone so as not to be heard, he said, "All right . . . Barnes, you are going to be a free man soon. And that you should. Hope you realize what this woman has done for you."

"Wow! Really. How did you do it? How did you get him to agree? I have no way of knowing how I am going to repay him . . . Sara, he can't possibly do this pro bono, I can't let him. Oh man! Mark is really going to do this for me . . . well, I am sure it is more for you, but none the less, he is actually going to help me. Thank you. You just don't know how much I thank you! If this wall wasn't here I would really like to . . ."

"Hold that thought, Barnes, I think that can be arranged!" Sara and Russell looked at Sergeant Blakeman as he rose from his chair, approached the divider wall and then opened a door. "Make it quick, I get caught and it won't be good!"

Russell came around the wall, smiled at Sara and placed his hands on her face and quickly kissed her, and then with his arms around her, enclosed her to him, holding her in an attempt to convey to her how deeply he felt at her belief in him.

"It's going to be all right, Russell, it just has to be."
"Thank you."

"OK, that's it, sorry, back to your side of the wall, Barnes"

As Sergeant Blakeman locked the door, Sara placed a hand on his arm. "Thank you."

"Get him cleared, just get him cleared." The big man returned to his desk.

"Michael is here with the Detectives again. Seems he is rather popular around here these days. He wanted me to tell you hello." "He's a good kid. Good rider too! Is he still smitten with the McGregor girl? Katy, is it?"

"Yes . . ."

"Mrs. Moore . . . the front desk called and said that your son is finished with the Detectives and ready to go home."

"That's my cue . . . I'll be back as soon as I can with more information from Mark. You will be out of here soon . . . Soon."

Retrieving her purse from the basket, Sara turned back to wave at Russell as he passed through the doorway to the cells.

While Sara had been in with Russell, Detectives Harrison and Borden were relentless with their questioning of Michael.

"We need you to go to the Rodeo Grounds with us. You need to tell us if you saw anyone else lurking in the holding pens. Michael, if you know anything to help solve this, you are obligated by the law to disclose all information you may be holding. Don't try to judge the relevance, that is our job. Talk."

"Easy, Kent, he's a kid not a drug dealer. Michael, what Detective Harrison is saying is . . ."

"I know what he is saying, and I know what he is implying . . . Yeah, I know a couple big words too . . . You want me to go to the grounds, I will. I don't have a problem with that. What I do have a problem with is that you have me back here and no one else . . . Why is that? There were four of us here the last time, were there not? So why only me?"

"I'll be in the squad . . . Nick, you want to answer him, that is fine, just get him to the car." Kent was through the office door, pushing past Matt Brewer. "We're going to the crime scene, wanna join us?" Before he could answer, Nick and Michael were in the hallway approaching him. "Uh . . .

problem?" Matt waved his hand in Kent's direction as indication that the question referred to the curtness of Nick's partner.

"He thinks that Barnes is hiding something, and now that he has a hotshot attorney from East Dale coming over, if we don't find out what it is first, then Barnes will hide behind his lawyer and we may never know all the truth. Kent is a perfectionist when it comes to his job and he despises it when he gets blindsided or has to deal with 'privileges' when an attorney is present."

Michael turned away from them, fisted hand against his chest, arm bent at the elbow, he pulled down and smiled. "Yeah! Good girl, Mom!"

"God bless you!" Michael grinned at the thought of Matt thinking he sneezed. Nick 'coughed' and pushed Michael's arm, letting him know that he agreed with Michael's gesture.

"Hey . . . Mom! They are taking me to 'the crime scene'." "I thought you were ready to go home."
"Mrs. Moore, with your permission, we would like to have Michael show us where he was and what he saw the night in question. As he is underaged, we need your permission as well as your presence when we do so." "Detective Harrison, you are correct in that he is underaged, and with that, I will not have you questioning him without my permission and or presence regarding the legal aspects of your investigation. Do I make myself clear?"

"That's what I need . . . The sister of the hotshot being the mother of a key witness . . . why me? Yes, ma'am, you are clearly understood. Just bear in mind that they approached me, us, in the first place . . . without your presence. I have taken that into consideration and feel the neccesity to continue doing so."

Matt and Cecelia had joined them in the lobby. "Does he badger everyone like that?"
"Not everyone, Cecelia, just most." Nick motioned to Michael to move toward the door. "He does get the truth, and he does solve situations he's just got his own way of doing it. Come on, Michael, don't think keeping him waiting will sit too well." Sara, Michael, Matt and Cecelia followed Nick through the door to the parking lot.

The drive to the Rodeo Grounds was devoid of conversation; each person in the car had thoughts of their own regarding the purpose of the return to the 'scene'.

Detectives Brewer and Lang arrived five minutes after the Brandon department. Michael watched his mother as she turned toward the stock pens. "Mom . . . you OK?""Yes, just picturing in my mind that night at the Dance and how you surprised everyone, that's all." He had never known his mother to lie to him, but he knew right at that moment that she had. He pulled her arm, bringing her to face him out of earshot of the detectives.

"Then why are you looking at the stock pens? What are you not telling me or the cops? Mom . . . please . . ."

"I . . . I can't. I really am sorry. I promised."

"Promised? Promised who? Does someone have something on you and making you keep quiet? Mom . . . tell me."

"It's not like that. I just can't say anything right now. You have to trust me. You just *need* to trust me."

"OK, Michael, we're ready for you now. Follow us . . ." Kent Harrison kept his eyes on Sara as Nick instructed Michael to show them just where he was and what he saw. Walking from the parking area around where the dance floor had been set up and then to the stock pens; the Detective stayed behind the group to observe the body language of both Sara and Michael.

"What are they doing?" Matt held back from the others to be close enough to Kent for a private conversation. "Hey, Matt, here's my thoughts. Watch Mrs. Moore a while, she keeps looking at the pens and the Crow's Nest . . . does she seem nervous to you?"

"Maybe a little, why?" "Remember we found the pocket off a pair of Lady Wranglers in the third pen over . . . my guess is that the pocket belongs to a pair of her jeans. I'm thinking she was in that pen and saw what happened. The kid got real defensive the first time he was in for questioning when we mentioned the find. That's why I wanted to bring them here, I need to know."

"Good instinct, Kent. She have something to do with Grant or Barnes?"

"Barnes."

"Barnes?"

"Yeah, goes back to when her husband died. Long story, later . . . now we have to figure her involvement in this case."

"Found something!" Cecelia had walked through to the last stock pen and was kneeling on the ground. "What could you have found that we did not. Our team has been all over this place!" "Well, you missed this!" She had been hand-digging and retrieved a revolver buried by the corner corral post. Lifting it with a pen, she smiled as she displayed her find. Sara had been standing in front of Michael, and at the sight of the gun she nearly lost her balance. Taking hold of Michael's arm behind her to steady herself; an inaudable gasp filled her lungs as she regained her stance. Kent glanced at Matt and nodded to him to take notice.

"We'll have this dusted and see if any prints are still on it, check the number . . . see who the owner is . . . unless, of course, anyone here knows anything about it?" Kent's accusatory tone was not unnoticed. "Bag it, Nick. Let's move over to the Crow's Nest."

Walking beside Michael, Nick asked Michael about what he saw that night. "Honest, sir, mostly I was with Katy and the guys and only saw Russell, um, I mean Mr. Barnes a little bit. Yeah, he was over here, I saw him on the stairs, and I saw him walking toward the pens."

"Did you see him with a gun? Do you think the gun Dectective Lang found was his? Did you see him bury it?"

"Whoa, slow down . . . I never saw a gun! And besides that, it wasn't a gun that killed the guy anyway, that has already been proven, so why all the questions about it?"

"Maybe he knew that Grant was going to be there, and he hid it ahead of time to be ready for him, things got out of hand, and he never used it as originally intended. Guy got lucky with a rock shot to the head instead of just shootin' Grant."

"No way Mr. Barnes intentionally killed him, no way! Mom . . . tell them . . . tell them the kind of guy he is . . . They don't understand! He didn't do this on purpose! It was self-defense! It was self-defense!"

"Calm down, kid, no one is guilty yet of anything. We will get to the bottom of this, we will. I think we're done here, for now. We can come back later if we need to. Let's get these two back to the station so they can get home. Thanks for all your help and input. Really, thanks."

"Mom?"

"Lets just go home, Michael."

Again, silence in the car on the way back to the station.

"Nick, come in here, would ya?" Nick was in the doorway looking toward the lobby instead of where he was going and bumped the wall. "Shut the door."

"Oooookay . . . what's up?"

"How the hell did she find that gun? We were all over that place! She was out ahead of us the whole time . . . You don't suppose she planted it there and then dug it up like it had been there all along, do you?"

"Kent, no way . . . I mean, she's on our side, right?"

"I'm not so sure anymore of anything. Too many 'variables'. I am curious as to who the piece is registered to and how fresh the dirt is around it. You make sure our guys look at it and not theirs. Got it?"

"On it."

"Good. I don't like how this is going. Don't like it at all. A gun! This changes everything."

****

Charles, Brent, Katy, Marge and Mary were on the porch when Sara and Michael returned from the Police Station. Rex jumped at the sound of the truck and barked at their arrival. "Hey there, boy! You keeping our company entertained until we got home?" Michael reached to ruffle the hair on Rex's back. Charles put a hand on Michael's arm. "We heard you were called back in . . . what's up?"

"Took us over to the grounds again. As much as I hate the reason for all of this, detective work is pretty interesting. Criminal law . . . hmmm . . . I might just think about this! The V-E-T and the D-E-T . . . what do you think?" He smiled at Katy when he spelled the V-E-T. Brent laughed and slapped his knees. "Yeah, right, you? Mrs. Moore, are there any cookies in the jar? Sure could use one of your famous choc-o-lotts a chips about now!"

"Come on in kids, the jar is full."

"Did I ever mention I love your mother?" Brent had his right arm over Michael's left shoulder.

"Yes, Brent, many times!" The friends hurried as they entered the house.

Sara placed the cookie jar in the center of the kitchen table; six hands were reaching for it before she even had the lid off. Stepping back smiling, she looked from one to the next of the friends innocently being kids while on the brink of losing that youth to become the young adults they thought they already were.

Michael saw the smile and the moisture in her eyes. "Mom . . . You OK?"

"Absolutely, what I see here I love so much. Milk, anyone?"

"Please!"

Seated in his favorite recliner, John pretended to concentrate on the newspaper. Folding the pages and lowering them to his lap, he patted the chair next to him, indicating he wanted Sara to sit with him. "John, it was awful. I hated being there where it all transpired. Those Detectives, they were hounding us, and frankly, they made me very uncomfortable."

"They are just doing their job, Sara. How was your time with Russell?"

"He is very thankful that Mark is going to help him. He insists on paying him and, well, he may have to sell the Rodeo String to do so. He loves that string, he was hoping to reestablish himself and regain the trust and respect of everyone by proving he is not a part of his father's legacy."

"If the man is innocent, it would be a fair price to pay."

"If? You still don't believe him do you?" Sara stood, looking in John's eyes.

"I do." She threw the pillow she was holding into the chair and left the room without another word.

She heard the friends in the kitchen planning a ride to the Red Pasture.

"How's Chance's leg?"

"Doing good, Mrs. Moore. He isn't ready to run the barrels yet, but I have been working him easy in the arena. I am going to try him tomorrow on the ride to the Red Pasture."

"Go easy on him, you'll know what he can handle."

"Thanks, Mrs. Moore." Sara walked out onto the porch, sat in the chair swing, and looked upon the crimson sky of the setting sun. Off in the distance, she heard the squelch of a hawk. "Hello, Samuel, good to know you are here."

PART 10

The Trial

"Today starts the trial of Russell Barnes in the Wes Grant murder case. All eyes are on the Brandon Courthouse where Attorney Mark Bloom is set to prove the legitimacy of the 'self-defense' plea of Barnes. We will keep the listeners apprised of the proceedings as we are made aware of details. Now for the weather . . ."

"Big news for a small town. There are reporters from all over coming in for this. You sure you are OK, Michael? They are going to call you to testify, and if you think it was tough before, just wait." "I'll be fine Gramp, Uncle Mark has warned me what to expect and told me how to answer their questions and how to act on the witness stand. Brent is a nervous wreck that they might call him and so is Katy, but since her father is one of the Detectives, Mark said they may not call on her. Charles . . . well, he's ready for anything, like usual."

"Well, good luck, son."

"Aren't you coming? Gramp, I need you there."

"No, son . . . not today. We'll see . . ."

"You think he did it intentionally . . . Mom was right, I overheard her . . . she says you don't believe him. You're wrong, Gramp. You're wrong."

John was seated in his chair, his heart broke as he listened to the dissapointment in his grandson's voice. He turned to speak to Michael but was too late, the door of the kitchen had closed before he had the chance. Mary came in and sat beside him, placing a hand on his.

"John, sometimes you have to let go of that damn 'Code' of yours and listen to your heart." She rose and was gone from the room. John sat in his chair staring at the painting Milly Toole had done of the 5 of them when Michael was 6. "What can I do Samuel? How do I make this right?" As he wept silently, Mary looked on from the kitchen doorway.

The parking lot at the Courthouse was filled to capacity as Sara searched for a space large enough for their truck. Michael sat in silence as he read the sides of the television station news vans that lined the outer edges of the lot.

"There, Mom, over there behind the Channel 4 news van . . . I think we'll fit there."

"Good eyes, Michael!"

"Thanks Gram, and thanks for coming."

"Where else would I be?"

Mary leaned her shoulder onto Michael's and with the slight strength left in her hand, she then squeezed his lower arm and looked in his eys and smiled. "I love you, Gram." Michael put his arm around her and hugged her from the side. "I love you too." Sara knew what it meant to Michael to have his grandmother there in support of them as well as the hurt at his grandfather not attending.

"Who loves the woman that parked this beast, Huh! Look at that!" In unison all three laughed in an attempt to over ride the nervousness each held in their own way for what lay ahead of them and for Russell.

"Ready?"

"Mom . . ."

"I know, I know. I am so very proud of you. So is your grandfather. Just because he isn't here doesn't mean he isn't proud of you. He loves you very much. You have a job to do today and you will do it, and do it well. Tell him all about it when we get home. Now, we have to help Russell."

Michael opened the heavy wooden door for the women. "Holy smokes! I had no idea a wooden door could be so thick and so heavy! Ooo . . . look at the carving on it, it is really detailed. Those old guys sure knew what they were doing back in the 'olden days' . . . huh?"

Mary and Sara simultaneously nudged him forward. Mary laughed as she took her hand off Michael's back. "Watch what you say about the 'old guys'!"

"Oh, Gram, the men that carved that door are wayyyyyyyyyy older than you! Why, I bet they were long dead before you were even born!"

"You, my dear grandson, have inherited your grandfathers ability to slither out of about anything!" Sara giggled and turned to Michael. "What she means is 'good save'!" Sara placed her arm in Michael's left and Mary was in his right; the three walked the grand hallway to the courtroom. Sara and Mary let go of their hold to get seated while Michael held back in the waiting area.

"Oh, Katy, am I ever glad to see you!"

"What about us? Do we still count?" Charles, Brent, Marge, and Mary stood behind Katy.

"Of course, good to see you ladies, glad you are here for us, this is going to be rough to say the least."

"Hate to interupt you but . . . they are calling everyone into to the courtroom. Michael, you all need to get seated." "Yes, Mom." Michael leaned toward Katy, placing her hands in his, he hesitated slightly and drew her to him. Stepping back, with a quiver on his lips he kissed her.

"It's going to be OK Michael, really . . . and hey, you said you wanted to be a detective, maybe now you can see how it all works."

"Maybe, maybe be a detective . . ."

"We best go in and find your mother."

At his mother's right, Michael settled into the wooden pew-type seating of the old courtroom. He realized he was looking around at the walls, the ceiling, the floor, and most of all, the Judge's bench that was on a platform allowing the Judge to see over the entire room. The effect intimidated him. He focused on the ornate hand carvings surrounding the windows and the rails of the chair backs in the witness stand. The jurors' seating was much more comfortable in appearance as those chairs were upholstered and had armrests. Also, their area was safely situated behind the waist-high half-wall as if removed from yet still inclusive in the room. Michael thought to himself: "Russell's fate would he held by the men and women that would soon occupy what he had learned was reffered to as the 'Juror's Box'."

Sara watched her son in his mesmerized accounting of all that he was taking in. "It's a bit overwhelming now that you are in here, isn't it?"

"Mom, it's awesome, and at the same time, it scares me."

"It is supposed to. You are supposed to 'feel' the justice system here. There is a respect in this room. You know how you have a 'code,' an honor, in your rodeo, heck in ranch life . . . well, there is a 'code' here too. The attorneys work within the boundaries, and justice will be sought and carried out."

"Please, those in the gallery, be seated. We are ready to begin." Mary reached for Sara's hand and held it tight as the bailiff instructed everyone to prepare for the trial. Mark entered followed closely by his assistant, William Pettere. William was burdened with the briefcase and folders containing the case files and information Mark would soon disclose in his defense arguments. The young intern carried himself with authority and with a respect for the attorney he admired. Two deputies escorted Russell to his seat between Mark and William. Hoping to see her, Russell quickly perused the gallery. When their eyes met, Sara smiled and nodded her head for his assurance of her support.

Mason Henry, the County Prosecuting Attorney stood behind the lectern, checking the microphone. Using a hand signal, Mark indicated to William and Russell to cease speaking. Mark had learned the hard way this 'trick' to get a chance to overhear the defense strategy. Mark had not planned on the use of the lectern, when Mason had completed his 'check', Mark carefully held both sides of the old wooden structure and as he began moving it looked at a surprised Mason Henry. "I hope you didn't want to use this . . ."

"Ah . . . no, that is fine." Mark smiled as he set the lectern to the other side of the prosecution's table.

Katy gasped as the jurors entered the courtroom and proceeded to their seating in the jury box. David Engle entered first and sat in the foreman's chair. Stunned by her reaction, with an 'asking of why' in his facial expression, Michael looked at her. Softly, she whispered, "He owns the stockyards in Clinton. A lot of rodeo castoffs go through there. He'll buy and sell anything lame or sound. My mother and aunt have tried to get him closed down a couple times."

"Why would they let a guy like that sit as foreman in a trial like this? Do you think Mark knows?"

"Shhhsh."

"Mom . . ."

"I heard, he has to know, they are thorough during selection. We will just have to trust Mark."

"All rise!" The bailiff stepped forward from the wall as the door opened and the Judge briskly walked to his bench. Standing before the courtroom, he peered at the jury, then the persons in general seating, then to Attorney Henry and finally settled his focus on Mark. "The Honorable Judge Theodore Mann." The voice of the bailiff was deep and loud as the Judge seated himself in the high-backed black leather chair.

"State Case 752-189 Brandon County vs. Russell Barnes." The sound of the gavel as it hit the oak desktop echoed throughout the courtroom. The silence was immediate with all attention on the Judge.

"Will the Defendant please rise." Mark and William had reached full stance as Russell composed himself. "Mr. Barnes, do you fully understand the charges against you and the procedures about commence in this Court of law?"

"Yes, Your Honor, I do."

"Then we will proceed. Mr. Barnes, you have been charged with the murder of Wes Grant." The Judge turned his focus on the jury. "Ladies and gentlemen of the jury, it will be your duty to listen to the testimony of both the prosecution and the defense attorneys in this case without prejudice or bias and to decide without a shadow of doubt a verdict of guilty or not guilty. There may be testimony deemed objectionable and to not be concidered in your decision. You must disregard testimony when instructed to do so. You must be able to conclude with a unanimous decision. You will remain sequestered until your verdict has been met. We will have opening statements now. Mr. Barnes, you may be seated. Mr. Henry . . ."

Russell sat with perfect posture and composure. He looked upon the persons of the jury. A small bead of sweat slowly fell past the nape of his neck as he felt the debasing glower of the men and women that would be deciding his fate.

Mason Henry slowly walked toward the jurors.

"Ladies and gentlemen, we are here today because a man is dead."

He paused as he looked at the jurors individually. "A man is dead due to the actions of the man sitting at the defense table." He pointed to Russell as he continued to speak. "Russell Barnes has admitted to picking up a rock and 'bashing' the side of Wes Grant's head. Those are his words . . . 'bashing' . . . to me that sounds like he meant to do just that. He claims . . . claims it was a move made in self-defense, yet no weapon or evidence of weapon other than the rock he used to strike the victim was found anywhere at the crime scene to give relevance to his statement.

"There is evidence, however, of previous altercations between the two men all of which were physical and threatening in nature. Throughout the course of this trial, I will present to you the facts leading up to the events of that night, and you will undoubtably agree that his actions were pre meditated and felonious in nature. It is my request that you listen to the testimony and agree that Russell Barnes is guilty in the murder of Wes Grant."

He again looked each juror in the eyes as he stated his final words, locking eyes on David Engle before returning to his chair at the prosection table.

"Mr. Bloom."

Mark took in a deep breath as he nodded to the Judge, then to Henry Mason. Standing in front of the table, he hesitated, smiled at Russell, and then faced the jury box.

"Hello, ladies and gentlemen. My name is Mark Bloom. The man sitting to the left of the defendant is my assistant, William Pettere. We are here today to clear any misconceptions regarding the innocence, or guilt of Russell Barnes. Mr. Barnes admits to the fight with Mr. Grant, what the prosecution failed to mention is that Mr. Barnes did not start the altercation. Mr. Grant did. Mr. Grant assaulted Mr. Barnes, and so Mr. Barnes had no choice but to protect himself. There are persons that you will hear from in the course of these proceedings that through their testimony, you will understand the truth. Mr. Barnes acted solely in self-defense and had no prior intention of harm . . . of any kind actually . . . to Mr. Grant. In fact, Mr. Grant regularily attended the Rodeos that Mr. Barnes supplied stock.

"The death of Mr. Grant is not to be taken lightly, no death is. However, in this case, his death was of his own origin of doing. 'Murder' did not happen that night. Mr. Barnes, in fact, was unaware that Mr. Grant was on the Rodeo Grounds the night in question or that he would even be present there for the Dance as he had been physically removed by Sheriff's Deputies earlier in the day after the Team Roping and instructed not to return during all events of the Rodeo, including the Cowboy Dance held at the conclusion of the day.

"So you see, ladies and gentlemen, Russell Barnes in no way went to the Rodeo Grounds with the intention of killing Wes Grant. Mr. Barnes was in fact taken by surprise when Mr. Grant approached him. You will hear testimony and statements verifying all I have said to you. You will come to know the truth of the events leading up to and including the arrest of Mr. Barnes and the injustice that has befallen him as being accused of such a heinous crime. I look forward to assisting you in your journey to justice."

Mark smiled at each juror and then lifted his arm and pointed at Russell. "He is a man falsely accused." Mark turned and walked back to the table, nodded to the Judge and sat down.

"Mr. Henry, you may begin." Judge Mann sat back in his chair, placing his right arm in front of him on the desk, he had his hand on the gavel handle.

"The prosecution calls Mr. Robert Doens."

"Oh my! This is digging deep."
"Mary, why do you say that?"
"Sara, that is Bob Doens of the Double D Ranch. He and his brother . . . well . . . Clint Barnes stole cattle from their ranch. He sure as heck isn't going to have good things to say about the Barnes name." To herself, Sara thought: "First witness, and I'm worried already." She noticed Michael had been holding Katy's hand on his thigh. Sara knew this day would be difficult for her son to understand, and enduring the accounts of the witnessness, he would have to take great pains to hold his emotions to himself. Sara reached over to Katy's hand and smiled at her as she gently grasped the hands of them both. Her eyes told them that trust in the truth would get them through this day.

Mr. Doens had sworn his oath on the Bible to tell only the truth and was sitting in the witness chair.

"Mr. Doens, would you please tell the court the nature of your livelihood."

"My brother and I run the Double D Cattle Company."

"And just how is it that you know the defendant, Russell Barnes?"

"Why, him and his no good father and a few others, they stole cattle from us and moved 'em south of the state line."

A murmur of reactions from the jurors started the same murmurs in the gallery of spectators.

"When did this thievery occur, Mr. Doens?"

"I'd best guess seven or eight years ago, say does that mean that Clint Barnes is due outta the joint soon?"

"Your Honor . . ." Mark stood to express to the Judge his discontent as to the nature of the witness's response to the prosecutor's question. "Mr. Henry, please advise your witness to refrain from outbursts and to stay with the question asked of him."

Bob Doens turned to the Judge. "I'm sorry, Your Honor, I'll do better. I promise"

"Proceed."

"Mr. Doens, when your cattle were returned to you after the incarceration of Clint Barnes, what would you say was the attitude of Russell Barnes at that time?"

"Objection! Your Honor, he is asking the witness to diagnose the behavior of another man. Unless he is a certified physician, he cannot possibly be able to do so."

The Judge turned his attention to Mr. Henry.

"Your Honor, I am simply trying to establish the behavior pattern from past incidences and how they similate with the patterns displayed in this situation"

"I will allow the testimony, Mr. Doens, answer the question."

"He was a hothead punk. Yellin' and cursin' the whole time. The man in charge of the whole deal didn't want him involved, but the Court said he had to be. I remember a couple times Barnes tried to push through the barriers to let 'em out of the stock pens. That would have been a real mess if it wasn't for that big foreman guy puttin' him up against the side of the chutes and punchin' him out. Oh man, Russell, he come back at him fists a flyin'. He was mad as a hornet. Telling everyone he wasn't done with them all yet. They'd know soon enough who he was and that everyone had ought to keep an eye on their stock. We was all real happy to see that truck roll back on outta there with him safe inside it. We didn't want the kind of trouble he was fixin' to get into"

"In your opinion, Mr. Doens, is Russell Barnes a man capable of a violent act?"

"Yes, sir. I would say that he sure is. I seen it myself!"

"Thank you, Mr. Doens." Mason Henry returned to his seat.

"Mr. Bloom, do you wish to cross-examine the witness?" As the Judge asked Mark, he had already started thinking of his questions to Bob Doens.

"Yes, Your Honor, I do."

"Mr. Doens, you say that this incident you spoke of happened 'seven or eight' years ago. You seem to remember a great many details concerning the defendant and his involvement in a very high-profile case, of which your ranch was a major focus. Your ranch was, in fact, the main reason for the apprehension of Clint Barnes, is that not right?"

"Yes, I suppose so . . ."

"And yet in all it's importance, you cannot remember when this transpired. Seems to me, Mr. Doens, if you cannot recall the actuality of those facts, if your memory is unclear for that, perhaps your memory is unclear as to just who it was you saw. Or thought you saw in this tirade you speak of. Mr. Doens . . . are you absolutely sure . . . sure that it was Russell Barnes that you saw that day on your ranch?"

"I . . . ah . . . yeah . . . it was him. He was there."

Mark turned to the Judge. "Your Honor, I have here a document signed by the Sheriff's Deputy assigned to the wherabouts of Russell Barnes on the day of the cattle returns. The Double D was one of four ranches to have deliveries that day. I have signed proof that Russell Barnes was not at the Double D. In fact, as the cattle were returned to the Doens, Russell Barnes was willingly assisting the delivery of cattle to the Henderson Ranch, forty-five miles away from the Double D."

"Your Honor . . ."
"Sit down, Mr. Henry. Mr. Bloom, may I see that paper . . .?"
"Yes, Your Honor."
Pleased that he had made an impression on the jury as to the validity of this witness's testimony, Mark handed the paper to the Judge.

"Hmm, this is all in order . . . Mr. Bloom, do you have any further questions for this witness?"

"No, sir."

"The witness may step down. Mr. Henry . . ."

"The prosecution calls Mr. Kenneth Winton."

The bang of the swing gate as Ken finished closing it echoed in the Courtroom. The jurors and gallery alike instantly looked at the gate and then at Mr. Winton as he swore his oath and walked to the witness seat.

"Mr. Winton, do you know why I called you here today?"

"Yes, I do, sir, as a witness for the prosecution of Mr. Barnes."

"Yes, that is right. Would you please tell the jury and members of the court just how it is that you have personal knowledge of the character, or lack thereof, of the defendant."

"He had an affair with my wife."

Sara watched the reaction of the female jurors as he continued his explanation. The information was new to her also, she only knew his wife had died in childbirth, or at least that is what he had told her. Not wanting to doubt Russell, she reassured herself that Mark would 'cross' and get the whole truth. He just had to.

"And . . . this affair with your wife . . ."

"She left me for that no good sonova . . ."
"Mr. Winton . . ."
"Sorry, she left me for Russell Barnes, and . . . and she was dead within a year. I loved her and wasn't even allowed at her funeral. He killed her. I know he did. She would still be alive if he hadn't taken her from me."

"Objection. Speculation, Your Honor, there is no way to guarentee she would still be alive having there been many years from that time frame to the present."

"Sustained. Mr. Henry, keep your questions pertinent to this case."

"Yes, Your Honor. Mr. Winton, in your opinion, if it had not been for the subversive actions of the defendant . . ."

"Objection again, Your Honor, the witness will have to answer on speculation."

"Sustained. Mr. Henry, if you cannot ask your witness a direct question that will have a direct answer regarding this case, I will have to ask you to sit down and turn the witness over for cross- examination."

Mason Henry felt the heat of anger rise within him as the judge openly chastised him before the courtroom. He knew he would be up against a tough defense attorney and had heard that Judge Mann was intolerant of wasted time. He knew he needed the opportunity to show that Barnes had a temper as well as a tendency for violence and was not being permitted to do so. He knew even then, so early in the trial that he was going to have to 'up his game' and blind side the Defense. He knew exactly what he had to do.

"No further questions, Your Honor." The expression of surprise was not limited to the Judge. Mark shook his head and looked at William; quietly, he spoke past Russell . . . "He's up to something. Get ready"

"Your Honor, if I may?" Mark stood and walked dilegently to the witness.

"Mr. Winton, what was the nature of your ex-wife's passing?"

"I . . . ahh . . ."

"Are you not sure, Mr. Winton?" Before he had a chance to answer, Mark had already addressed the jurors. "Mr. Winton's *ex*-wife died in childbirth as did the daughter she was birthing. The then Mrs. Barnes had a heart condition that was unable to withstand the strain of bearing a child. Mr. Barnes was in the delivery room and held his wife as she died. That, ladies and gentlemen is the truth in her passing. A tragedy. An absolute tragedy. Mr. Barnes had nothing to do with her death."

Sara was relieved that Mark had proven Russell innocent of the accusations of Ken Winton for the trial as well as for herself. Her sigh was not unnoticed by Mary as she patted Sara's hand.

"Thank you, Mr. Winton." Mark returned to his seat.

"The witness may step down."

"The prosecution calls Miss Louise Smith"

Brent leaned to Charles. "What's she got to do with this? She was drunk at the Dance and messing with Osborne." William overheard Brent; leaning to Mark, he relayed the information. Mark quickly glanced at the witness list, and he smiled as he saw Peter Osborne's name after Bonnie Roberts.

"Good afternoon, Miss Smith."

Louise smiled at Mason and pushed back her hair. Leaning toward him, she intentionally straightened her skirt. It was very apparent to anyone looking at the jurors that the men were fully focused on the witness.

"Miss Smith, can you tell us your wherabouts on the night of Wes Grant's murder?"

"Objection! The crime of murder has not yet been determined!"

"Sustained. Be very careful, Mr. Henry, I am growing weary of the advantages you are trying to take of my Court."

"My deepest apologies, Your Honor. Miss Smith, again I ask, where were you the night that Wes Grant and the defendant, Russell Barnes, were involved in the altercation that ultimately lead to Wes Grant's death?"

"I was at the Rodeo Dance."

"Did you see Mr. Barnes there?"

"He was in the Crow's Nest."

"Please, Miss Smith, explain to the court what the Crow's Nest is."

"Gee, everyone knows that is the announcer's booth above the arena."

"Now, Miss Smith, how is it that you know he was in the Crow's Nest?"

"Well, I . . . I was taking a break from dancing . . ." Several young men in the gallery grunted as she was explaining her whereabouts.

"Taking a break? Just what do you mean by that?"
Charles fisted Brent's thigh, under his breath. "We can tell you that!" Several teenaged boys reacted to the question, disrupting the quietness of the gallery.

"Order, order in the courtroom!" Displeased, the Judge looked directly at Charles. Charles pulled his arms to his side and faced the floor. He felt a nudge from Mike Venet who was sitting behind him.

"I had been dancing and was thirsty. I went over to the concession stand to get a soda. I saw Mr. Barnes walking over to the Crow's Nest. I never actually met him, but I was told he was the one that owned the rodeo stock."

"So you didn't actually speak to him?"

"No, but I saw him go up the stairs and then he looked out of the front like he was looking for someone."

"How long did you see him 'looking for someone'?'"

"I don't think it was very long, I got my soda and when I turned back to look again he was gone."

"Did you see him leave the Crow's Nest?"

"No."

"Miss Smith, would Mr. Barnes have been seated out of your line of view, say, in the chairs up there?"

"I guess so, there are a couple old ones up there."

"You saw Mr. Barnes go up to the Crow's Nest, look upon the grounds as if seeking to find a specific person, he then, to the best of your knowledge, remained hidden out of view."

"Yes, sir."

"Thank you, Miss Smith."

"No questions, Your Honor." To the surprise of the jury, Mark chose to not cross-examine. William leaned over. "What?"
"Wait, I have a plan."
"OK, you're the boss."

Bewildered, Mason Henry called his next witness. "The prosecution calls Mrs. Bonnie Roberts."

"Mrs. Roberts, you were at the Rodeo earlier in the day were you not?"

"Yes."

"In what capacity were at the Rodeo?"

"I organize the livestock, vendors, hire the judge and keep the points tabulations for the competitors."

"So you actually hired Russell Barnes and his stock?"

"Yes."

"And the pens? Did you also hire the men that worked in the pens?"

"Yes."

"Only men, Mrs. Roberts?"

"Yes, we hired eight men . . ."

"Then I am confused as to why this was found in the area where you say only men were hired to work." He held up for the jury and the Judge to see the hankie that Sara had lost that night. "This is clearly a woman's hankie, don't you agree?"

"Yes."

"How is it that a woman's hankie would be in an area that only men as you have stated would be present in?"

"I don't know."

"Is it yours, Mrs. Roberts?

"No, no, it is not"

"Then perhaps, there was someone in the pens later, someone that lost this hankie. Perhaps, this hankie is a memento kept of sentiment, by someone hiding, awaiting his chance at vengeance . . ."

Sara could not breathe. She felt weak, her heart was heavy, and the fear of the true holder of that hankie being disclosed consumed her. Russell had wanted her to remain out of all of this, but how could she now that her hankie had been discovered?

"Your Honor, the defense has not been made aware of this piece of evidence!"

"Is that true, Mr. Henry? Have you not properly submitted this 'hankie' into evidence?"

"Sir, with all due respect to yourself and to this court, I have just learned of it myself."

Mark knew he was lying, this was his plan. Why? How was he going to tie a token of sentiment to the connection of Grant and Barnes?

"Your Honor, I would like to see this hankie."

"By all means . . . Mr. Henry . . ."

As he reached his hand out, Mark saw the initials embroidered in the corner of the aged linen. His grandmother had given this to Sara on her fifth birthday.

"Mark, are you OK?" William placed a hand on Mark's back to steady him. "You look like you've seen a ghost!" "I have." Mark wanted to ask the Judge for a recess, but the attention it would bring to the 'evidence' he did not want; preventing just that is what he absolutely had to attain. He would speak with his sister at a better time.

The reaction of Mark Bloom was exactly what Mason Henry was hoping for. The clear possibility of Russell waiting in hiding had been established not only in the jury's minds, but in Marks mind also. Mason was not aware that Mark Bloom knew more about the hankie than he did.

"Thank you, Mrs. Roberts, your witness . . ."

"Mrs. Roberts, you state that you only hired men to work in the pens . . . correct?"

"Yes."

"Were there any female participants in the Rodeo that might have been in the area?"

"There was a team of girls in the roping. So yes . . ."

"So the possibility of this hankie being one of theirs is very real?"

"Yes."

"Would you say very possible?"

"Yes."

"Would you say most probable?"

"Your Honor, how many ways does the defense have to ask the same question?"

"Mr. Bloom . . ."

"My apologies, Your Honor. No further questions."

Mark sipped from his water glass the moment he sat in his chair. He knew exactly who the hankie belonged to, and yet he had to convince the jury that it was anyone other than Russell Barnes. To himself, he said "Oh man, Sis, what the hell do you have to do with all this?"

"The prosecution calls Mr. Peter Osborne."

"Do I have to swear on the Bible, I don't believe in all that bull . . ." The disgusted look on the bailiff's face as he turned to the judge for an answer was indication to Peter that he had said the wrong thing. Everyone in the courtroom reacted to the comment, causing a disruption that Judge Mann forbid to continue.

"Order, I will have order!" The gavel hit the desk with ferocity, the courtroom quieted instantly.

"Young man, this is a court of law, this is my courtroom, you will not be disrespectful to God in this room, do you understand? You have a right to your faith or lack thereof, but in this court, you will respect the law, and the law says you must solemnly swear to tell the truth. Do you swear to tell the truth or face the consequences?"

"Yes, sir, I do."

"Do you understand the meaning of perjury?"

"Yes, sir. I tell the truth or I go to jail."

"That about sums it up, proceed . . ."

"Mr. Osborne, you were at the Rodeo and the Dance, were you not?"

"Yup, I was."

"Regarding the defendant, what did you witness at the Rodeo?"

"Mr. Barnes was getting a lot of heat from Mrs. Harrison about signing papers and stuff."

"Stuff?"

"Yeah, he was supposed to have checked the timers and lines, things like that. The judge was pretty mad at having to stop the roping 'cuz the eye quit. I heard Mrs. Harrison say that Grant would have a legal case against the Rodeo if he wanted too. She told Mr. Barnes he needed to take care of the situation."

"What do you mean 'take care of'?"

"I dunno, just to take care of it."

"Then what did you see?"

"Then I saw Mr. Grant get all mad at Barnes for not letting him have a reride. He threatened Mr. Barnes."

"Threatened him?"

"Yeah, said it wasn't over . . . he really was mad. Guess Mr. Barnes thought he was going to sue like Mrs. Harrison said he might. Guess that's why he whacked him."

"Your Honor, objection . . . Speculation . . ."

"Sustained. Mr. Osborne, state just facts please, no 'guesses'."

"Moving on to the Dance, Mr. Osborne, did you see the defendant at the Dance?"

"Yeah, he was still real mad. I could tell by the way he was walking really fast and didn't stop to talk to anyone. Who does that at a dance anyway? He just went right to the Crow's Nest."

"When did you see him at the Crow's Nest?"

Peter turned to the Judge. "Do I really have to answer that?"

"Yes."

"I, ah, was over in the pens."

"And you saw Russell Barnes in the Crow's Nest?

"Yeah, and I heard him up there too, sounded like he was arguing with someone."

"Arguing with someone? Did you see anyone else up there with him?"

"No, but I know when I am mad, I talk out loud a lot, maybe that's what he was doing."

"You heard . . . and saw . . . Russell Barnes in an angered state in the Crow's Nest just before the altercation with Wes Grant?"

"Yes."

"Thank you."

Mark stood, collecting his thoughts and then walked to the witness.

"Mr. Osborne, were you alone in the pens at that time?"

"Ahhhhh." He looked at the Judge, received a stern glare and nod and knew he had to answer.

"No, sir, I was not."

"You were not alone, so your focus was not solely on the happenings in the Crow's Nest. What were you focused on, Mr. Osborne?"

"I'm sorry, Louise, really . . ." Peter looked at Louise Smith. "Louise and I were . . . ah . . . 'fooling around' you might say."

"Fooling around, Mr. Osborne, it hasn't been all that long since I was your age, and when I was 'fooling around', as you call it, my attentions were not anywhere other than on the girl." There was an audible agreement with a hint of laughter from the gallery as well as the jury.

"Please, tell us . . . how is it that a young man involved in 'young man things' had his attention on the Crow's Nest. We have all seen Miss

Smith . . . With all respect to you, Miss Smith." Mark turned to Louise seated in the back of the room.

"We were looking for the cloth she lost. She said she had found it earlier and thought it was really pretty. Like her grandma would have. Wanted to give it to her the next time she saw her. While we were looking, that's when I saw Mr. Barnes."

The relief that Mark felt could not be explained. He had the opportunity to clear Sara.

"Your Honor, may I show the witness the hankie that has been entered into evidence?"

"Yes, you may"

"Thank you." His hands shaking, Mark picked up the bagged item and presented it to Peter.

"Yeah! That's it! Hey Louise, they found your cloth!"

"Thank you. No further questions."

"The prosecution calls Detective Cecelia Lang."

Stunned by Cecelia being called as a witness, Kent and Nick shifted in their seats. Neither wanted to hear their names called forward. The fact that the 'visiting' Detective was a witness for the prosecution was very unsettling to them. Kent leaned to Nick. "I told you she didn't seem right. I still haven't quite put my finger on it, but I will. I just don't like her. Nick . . . look!"
"What?"
"She's wearing Wranglers."
"Shit, Kent, the pocket piece we found looked just like that. You might be on to something!"

"Detective Lang, you have assisted in the investigation of this case, have you not?"

"Yes, I have."

"Can you summarize what you have discovered and what you know as fact in this investigation."

"The death of Wes Grant has classic signs of premeditation. The defendant has displayed an unsavory character on many occassions, he has had his livelihood threatened, one man holding the ability to destroy his business and any possible advancement in a community of people he is desperately trying to gain access and trust. The defendant had undeniable motive. And he had opportunity. The Dance presented the perfect cover for his activity. The noise, the commotion of the dancing, and yes, the 'young people doing young people things' would all be distractions to anyone present. Mr. Barnes wanted to make sure that Mr. Grant would not be able to ruin him."

"Was there any other deciding factors in your conclusion?"

"We found Mr. Barnes's gun at the scene."

The courtroom fell silent. Mason knew he had the attention of everyone there. This was it, his moment to shine against the great Mark Bloom.

"You found a gun registered to Russell Barnes . . . is that what we heard you say?"

"Yes, it was buried in the corner of the last pen closest to the Crow's Nest."

"Can you please tell this court, the reason why this information was withheld until now?"

"We had to wait for ballistics to validate the ownership and verify fingerprints on the weapon. As of yesterday, the results were still not in."

"When did you receive the results?"

"This morning."

"And what were those 'results', Detective Lang?"

"The gun belongs to Russell Barnes."

Mason turned to the jurors, saying: "The gun belongs to Russell Barnes." Returning to the witness, he asked, "Detective Lang, how long have you been a Detective, and how many cases such as this have you investigated?"

"I have been working as a detective for ten years and have focused my work on the Behavioral Criminology."

"Can you explain to the court 'Behavioral Criminology,' Detective Lang?"

"Simply put, I have studied the 'why' a person commits a crime and the emotional and behavioral factors leading up to the crime."

"And have you accessed this crime?"

"Yes, sir. This particular course of events is very typical of a person that was abused as a child and forced to participate in crime as a youth. I have seen this behavior many times. In this case, Mr. Barnes felt the threat of his escape from his 'past' and knew only the need to eliminate the reason. In his mind, he had no choice."

"Thank you, Detective Lang."

Triumphantly, Mason Henry looked at the jury and then to Mark. Quietly, he mouthed to Mark, "Got him now!" Mark returned with "Not so fast . . ."

"Detective Lang, how familiar with the cattle rustling case are, or were you?"

Mason stood, saying: "Your Honor, he is asking the witness about a completely diffferent case as he himself has pointed out in these proceedings!"

"Your Honor, I am trying to inform the jury of the connection of this witness to the description of the background behavior she states influenced my client's actions."

"Overruled, be very careful, Mr. Bloom."

"Thank you, Your Honor"

"Detective Lang, please, answer the question." Mark had thought how she might answer and had prepared his continued questioning for either a response of nonaddmittance or inclusion of the case.

"I was on the investigation."

"Your experience level at that time, how would you consider that?"

"Sir?"

"Is it not true that at the time of the cattle rustling investigation, you were still a 'rookie' as those new to police work are referred to."

"Yes, I suppose so."

"Then how is it that so early in your career you were able to determine the 'Criminal Behavior' of a then very young Russell Barnes? How could you have possibly known he was criminally influenced by his father's actions? Is it not possible that a young man could see, through the actions of the law, that perhaps, he as a young man would not want to reflect his father and, in fact, would do just the opposite . . . is that not a possibility, Detective Lang?"

"I suppose so. I have been studying this behvior for years, it is 'classic'."

"You suppose so? Is there a more definitive answer, Detective Lang?

"Yes, it is possible."

"One last thing, Detective Lang, did ballistics find any current fingerprints on the gun? Or if it had recently been fired?

"No."

"Thank you, Detective Lang."

Mason stood as Mark thanked the witness.

"Your Honor, I wish to ask the Court's permission to redirect, sir . . ."

Judge Mann looked at the clock on the back wall of the courtroom; it was 4:25 p.m.

"Redirect is granted, however, due to the late hour, we shall recess until tomorrow morning at nine o'clock. You may begin your redirect at that time. Ladies and gentlemen of the jury, you will remain sequestered. My apologies to those of you that this will cause inconvenience. Your needs will be taken care of as you have previously made arrangements for."

"All rise." The deep voice of the bailiff instructed the room as the Judge stood and removed himself to his chambers.

The gallery emptied quickly. Sara waited for a chance to see Russell before they lead him back to his cell. She only caught a quick a smile before Mark interrupted. "You, have some explaining to do." The urgency of his voice startled her.
"Mark, I can explain . . ." Before she had a chance to speak more, William stepped to Mark and said, "Hey, you gotta hear what Kent and Nick have to say!"

Mark looked at Sara, saying: "We'll talk later"
Pleading, Sara said, "Mark . . ."
"Not now, Sara, not now!"
She fell back to the seat and wept into her hands. Mary came to her, putting an arm under Sara, lifting her to her feet. "It's time to go, dear, we'll be back in the morning. Come on . . ."
"Yes, time to go . . ." The words were faintly audible as Sara took a last look at the doorway that Russell had been escorted through.

Mark, William, Kent, and Nick were seated in Kent's office. "OK, here goes, you ready for this?"
"Yes, I need some good news."

"Grant and Lang have a connection . . ."
"What?" Mark had his full attention on the conversation. "Yeah, seems our little detective used to ride a little rodeo herself."
"Go on . . ."

Young Cece ran the barrels on a big Palomino. Grant wanted the horse, and when she wouldn't sell it, he drugged it just enough so that when it was turning the last barrel, the poor thing tripped and broke a leg.

Grant ran into the arena and shot the horse in front of Cece. Said he was with the Rodeo Company and no one questioned him. Needless to say, Cece was devastated and enraged at the same time. I'm thinking she has been wanting revenge a long time!"

When the explanation concluded, Mark stood, saying: "Get warrants for her place, Grant's place, Barnes' place . . . and my sister's too. Good work, gentlemen. Do your jobs tonight, and we'll do ours tomorrow."

Nine o'clock the next morning, Court was reconvened. Mark had several different folders on his desk than those he'd had the day before. Mason Henry returned with an assistant.

Proper initiation of the reconvening of the case concluded, Mason stood and said, "Your Honor, at this time, I would like to beg the court's forgiveness and state that at this time, I do not choose to redirect Detective Lang. I realize that it is out of order, but I would like to reserve that right until later in the procedings as she is an officer of the law and her testimony is of great importance. I respectfully ask that you grant this most unusual request."

"You are very correct, Mr. Henry, as this is not the true nature and course of Court proceedings, I am most interested as to why you, a well-mannered and learned member would request such an action."

"Your Honor, my associates have advised me that there has been further investigation, and I wish to be apprised of such, prior to continuation of my questioning."

"Granted."

Mark stood up from his seat and said, "Your Honor, it is true, the investigation here in this county has continued even as the case has gone to trial. The local Detectives were not and are not completely in agreement to the findings of Detectives Lang and Brewer. New information has come to light, and at this time, I would like to ask the Court that further questioning of Detective Lang by both the prosecution and the defense be stayed until later in the proceedings."

"Gentlemen, approach the bench."

Mark and Mason stepped side by side to face the Judge close enough for their whispers to not be heard beyond the three men.

"This is most unusual, and I am not particularily entertained by this disruption, Mr. Henry. Mr. Bloom, am I to assume you wish to further question the witness?"

"Yes, Your Honor. I am in agreement with the request of my collegue. I do however question his motive. I can only assume he feels he has lost his advantage with her and will try to regain it later. There is no regaining later, her testimony will be an asset to my defense of this case. If he holds the belief that he has the ability to discredit my defense, I ask only that I have the chance to recross at that time."

"This may be a the most unusual decision of my career. I only grant this request on the opinions and statements of you two attorneys and will have that on record so as eliminate myself from recourse. Is that understood?"

"Yes, Your Honor, thank you." Mark had taken a huge chance asking the Judge for such a favor, and it had worked.

"Yes, Your Honor." Confident in her testimony and her credibility, Mason could not understand what Mark thought he could use to discredit Detective Lang as a witness for the prosecution.

"It would seem that the prosecution has completed their witness examinations. Mr. Bloom, you may proceed."

"The defense calls Mr. Michael Moore."

Sara placed her hand on Michael's thigh. "Tell them only what they need to hear. Tell the truth." As Michael rose, he heard the backdoor of the courtroom open. Peripheral vision allowed him to see his grandfather enter and sit next to his mother. Breathing a sigh of relief, he knew he would endure this. Gramp was here; that meant he believed the truth.

Michael's height challenged that of the bailiff. The smile from the weathered face of the uniformed man eased the burden on Michael's dread of this moment. When the Oath concluded, he had a newfound confidence. While Michael spoke his declaration, Mary placed her hand on John's, and with a slight squeeze, she leaned to him and whispered,

"He knows you're here, and you have given him strength. You are a good man, John. Thank you." Their hands still clasped, they watched as their grandson took his place in the witness box.

"Good morning, Mr. Moore."

"Uhhh, hello?"

"Relax, son, this is a time for you to tell the truth. That should be a natural thing for you as you are regarded highly by your peers and by the community. You are an honest and forthright young man."

Michael sat in silence, not knowing if he was supposed to respond or not. He chose not to.

"Mr. Moore, please, tell us how you know the defendant."

"All of it?"
"Yes, all of it."
"OK . . . when I was ten, my parents went to the North Grazing Lands to bring the herd home way past time. My father's horse fell and died in a ravine, my mom, she got my dad back up the mountain, and they finished riding to the herd. When they got there, my father . . ." Michael was trying to speak, emotion overcoming him, he paused before continuing. "My father died in my mother's arms" John put his arm around Sara as she fell to his shoulder. Michael was looking at his mother, with tears in his eyes. Everyone in the room felt the 'loss' as Michael spoke. "Mom said that as she held Dad, a man was riding through, and he came to help her."

"Who was that man Michael?"

"Mr. Barnes."

"What did Mr. Barnes do when he rode to your mother?"

"He helped her roll my father in a blanket, got him on the pack mule, and he lead the mule as my mom and Rex and Bandit, our dogs, pushed the herd home. He rode drag and side all the way back to the ranch."

"Had you met Mr. Barnes prior to this day?"

"No. He was a stranger that helped my mom."

"A stranger that helped a woman in need far from her home. That was a very benevolent act, wouldn't you say?"

"Benevolent?"

"Doing something good for someone with no want or need for a return favor."

"Yeah, then that would be right. He helped when they got back, and Gram offered a room in the house for the night, but he insisted on staying in the barn. Said we needed our time as a family without a stranger interfering. Gramp offered him the bunkhouse for as long as he needed."

"How long did he stay?"

"He left during the night."

"Ladies and gentlemen, I ask you, are these the actions of a cold-hearted man? A man that would kill someone? I think not. These are the actions of a man with a compassionate heart and understanding of 'right time and place' and when and when not to be involved in situations that are not of your choosing."

Mark turned back to Michael and asked: "Michael, have you had dealings with Mr. Barnes in the years since you first met him?"

"Yes. He has the Rodeo stock that was used this year."

"Have you conversed with Mr. Barnes at the Rodeos?"

"Yes, we have spoken a couple times."

"Have you ever seen him angry or threatening?"

"No, never."

"It has been mentioned that there is a possibility that he is a vengeful man, would you agree or disagree with that?"

"Disagree. Absolutely. All he ever did was help us. Mom was sure lucky that he was there."

"Thank you, Mr. Moore, you have been most helpful.

Mark returned to his table as Mason approached Michael.

"Mr. Moore, don't you think it odd that a man who was willing to help your mother, out of nowhere, and then wanted not to stay in your house but was willing to stay in your bunkhouse and then snuck off in the middle of the night? Isn't that what a man that was hiding something would do, a man that didn't want his identity discovered because he had taken part in the thievery of some of your ranch's cattle, a man that had ill intent on his ride and then came upon your mother and had to change his course?"

Taken aback by the accusations that Mason had been throwing at him rapidly, Michael looked at Mark for guidance. Mark nodded at him and smiled. Michael had no idea how to answer.

"May I have a glass of water?"

Mason fulfilled Michael's request and spoke to him again.

"Mr. Moore, please, answer my question."

"First off, Mr. Henry, I have no idea as to why Mr. Barnes was out there that day. I am just thankful that he was. As to any ulterior motives, how could I possibly know that? My father learned from his father that actions speak louder than words, and his actions told me that he wanted to help my mother, and when he got her home safe, he wanted to leave us to our private time. He knew he should do that. So if you want to think he was anything other than a man that helped us, you can, but I never will, and I bet my mom won't either!"

Mark lowered his head as he grinned, then raised it so Michael could see the approval he had for his answer.

Mason retreated to his table, feeling that at every turn he was being defeated. Just when he thought he was gaining ground, it was swept away again.

Judge Mann spoke to Michael, "Son, you may step down now." The Judge smiled at Michael, intending to let him know he had done well.

"The defense calls Mr. Jason Dewain."

Charles leaned to Michael and said, "That's the Judge from the Rodeo!" With a questioning sound to his voice, Michael looked at Charles and asked, "Yeah, why?"

Mark had changed his tone of voice when he started to question Jason Dewain. "Mr. Dewain, you were the Judge at the Rodeo the day of Mr. Grant's death, is this correct?"

"Yes."

"When the Team Roping had to be stalled for technical difficulites with the timer eye, it was your decision to make to replace it with the 'break away', is that true?"

"Yes."

"In your opinion, Mr. Dewain, what was the reasoning, or cause, of the technical failure of the timer eye?"

"The wires had come loose off the rails of the boxes and had been stepped on by a horse. Let me tell ya, that kid could sure ride! Like he had an angel with him, that horse of his was none too happy and tossed him about like a seasoned bronc!"

Charles nudged Michael. "You did have an awesome few bucks, dude!"

"Who was this rider you speak of?"

"Michael Moore. Won't ever forget that ride!"

"Michael Moore. Hmmm, so if Mr. Barnes was responsible for the timer equipment, after hearing Mr. Moore's testimony, do you think that Mr. Barnes would have purposely tampered with the wiring just prior to Mr. Moore's ride?"

"Barnes? No way. He wasn't even around the Team Roping boxes. I saw him over in the pens talking with some of the guys working the ground even before the teams got started. Mr. Barnes is a good man. He loves his stock, and he loves the sport. The kids were all real happy to have fresh mounts and cattle to work and ride. Everyone was happy, and that don't happen too often."

"Thank you."

Mason rose but remained behind his table; he asked only one question. "If you were judging the events, how did you know the whereabouts of Mr. Barnes? If in truth your attention was on the Rodeo events, could there have been moments, many moments at that, that you did not in fact know where he was?"

Mason did not give ample time for a response. "Thank you, no further questions."

Mr. Dewain returned to his seat in the gallery with a defeated expression.

"The defense calls Deputy Nate Sherwood."

"Mr. Sherwood, were you at the Rodeo Grounds at all during the day of events?

"Yes, sir."

"In what capacity were in attending, in other words, were you there as a spectator or were you on duty ?"

"I was assigned to work at the Rodeo that day, sir"

"Mr. Sherwood, as an officer on duty, were there any incidences of which you become involved with at the Rodeo?"

"The Grant fellow, he had taken to drinking, which is not permitted on the Rodeo Grounds and was visibly intoxicated and with that was causing quite a commotion."

"Was he threatening anyone?"

"Everyone! The guy had it out for Joe Hinder, for the judge, for Barnes . . ."

"Joe Hinder?"

"Yeah, his partner in the Team Roping. Joe's horse got scared and wouldn't stay in the box. Got the team disqualified."

"And Wes Grant was angry?"

"Yeah, seemed to think that he should get a reride with a new partner, that doesn't happen, ever. He sure was mad, cursing at Joe, flailing his whiskey bottle, then he saw Mr. Barnes, turned his blame on him. Guess because he owned the stock and the equipment, whatever, Grant threw the bottle at him about the time that me and my partner got to him to escort him off the grounds."

"When you say escort him off the grounds, was that just for the rest of the Rodeo?"

"No, sir, we told him he was not to return at all and that included the Dance."

"So when he did go to the Rodeo Grounds at the time the Dance was happening, he was, in fact, there illegally?"

"Yes, sir."

"Was Mr. Barnes aware that he has been told not to return that evening?"

"Yes, he was standing there with us at the gate, he had to be there as he had legal responsibilities to the grounds commissioners."

"It would appear, Mr. Sherwood, that Mr. Barnes would not have devised a plot against Mr. Grant because he had clearly heard you tell him he was not to return. Mr. Barnes was not looking for Mr. Grant when he was in the Crow's Nest, simply, he was looking upon the celebration of the participants of the day's Rodeo. A man overlooking teenagers having fun. Thank you, Mr. Sherwood."

William slid a paper to Mark as he sat down.

Approaching the witness, Mason Henry tapped his forefinger on his cheek. "Mr. Sherwood, in your experience, when an apparently dunken man in an agitated state is ordered off a property, does that man respect that order or does that man reject it and return anyway in order to 'save face'?"

"I am not sure what you are asking, sir."

"When you ordered Mr. Grant off the grounds, what was his response to you?"

"He said, 'You can't keep me away, I can come back if I want, this ain't over.'"

"And Mr. Barnes heard this?"

"Yes, I would think so."

"Then Mr. Barnes could have thought there to be a good chance that Mr. Grant was going to return. In fact, Mr. Barnes was sure of it, wasn't he?"

"I don't know, he left as soon as Grant was over the threshold of the gate."

"You may return to your seat, Mr. Sherwood."

Mark had put reasonable doubt in the minds of the jurors, and Mason had turned their minds back in the testimony of one man. Mark read the note, turned to William, and then with his eyes on the Judge, announced: "The defense calls Detective Kent Harrison."

"Detective Harrison, tell us what you have learned in regards to the investigation of the death of Wes Grant just in the short time of this trial?"

"It appear as if someone other than Mr. Barnes has motive for killing Mr. Grant."

"Do explain."

"This is difficult, you have to understand this from my perspective. There is a trust and a bond among law enforcement, and I just . . ."

"I understand your hesitancy, Detective Harrison, but the life of a man is at stake here, and you are under oath."

Kent Harrison knew just how to 'play' the Jury.

"Detective Lang used to ride a little Rodeo herself."

"Go on . . ."

"Grant and some fella named Wayne Mont had a Rodeo School over in Sesta. Little Cece Lang attended that school. Grant wanted to buy her horse, and she wouldn't sell him. He drugged the horse before a run in the practice ring at a local Rodeo, and as the Palonimo turned the last barrel, he tripped. When he fell, he injured his leg. Grant ran out to the horse, claimed he was with the Rodeo Company and shot the horse right in front of her."

"And . . ."

"Lang was at the Rodeo here when Grant and Joe Hinder D-Q'ed, and she saw the drunk Grant threaten Barnes, seems she also overheard him being advised to do what needed to be done in regards to preventing legal action."

"And why does this raise concern with you, Detective Harrison?"

"When we were at the scene, she miraculously found a gun. Our team had been all over those pens, and I do mean thoroughly, how she found that, I'm thinking she had it all along and made it look like she had just found it."

"How would she have possibly had a gun registered to Mr. Barnes?"

"We searched his residence last night and found the gun cabinet lock had been forced open. There was a woman's hairpin on the floor next to it. Grant lives alone."

"What prompted this search of Mr. Barnes's home?"

"When Detective Lang was called forward to testify, we noticed she was wearing Lady Wrangler jeans. The pocket we found in the pens was the same. We searched her house in Carnon and found a pair of jeans missing a pocket."

Sara realized that it was Cecelia Lang she heard in the darkness that night.

In the last row of the gallery, Cecelia Lang was slowly edging sideways in the seating toward the door. Sergeant Blakeman had stood sentry throughout the trial; he would not permit her to leave. All eyes were on her. She had nowhere to turn, no recoupment of innocence.

Standing now looking at the room in front of her in the blur of her tears, Sergeant Blakeman placed a hand on her upper arm. She looked back at him and then to Russell.

"You gave me the perfect cover, you told me you feared he would return, I knew he would. He killed my horse. I have waited a long time for a chance to get him back. How was I supposed to know that you would be at the Crow's Nest? I wanted him dead. You got to him first! Dam you . . . you killed him when he should have been mine!"

"Order! Order in the court!" Judge Mann was on his feet leaning over the bench.

"You killed him!"

Sara knew she had to speak, knowing it would be cause of a lot of explanation later, she had no choice.

"It was self-defense! I was there!"

"Sara!" Mark shouted at her.

"I was there. Please, Your Honor, let me speak."

"Counselors?"

A simultaneous "Yes" was heard by all in the room.

"Come forward, ma'am, you must take the oath and be seated."

The court stenographer was desperately resetting the paper in her machine with a trained swiftness.

"I swear on my heart and to God above what I am about to say is the truth."

"I was there. In the pens. I went to the Dance for two reasons, to see Michael surprise everyone at knowing how to dance and also to see Russell Barnes. I got there and hid under the bleachers to watch Michael and Katy."

Sara smiled at Michael, a slow tear on her cheek.

"When I was under the bleachers, I saw Russell heading for the Crow's Nest, he went up the stairs, and I saw him looking for me. I made my way in the darkness through the pens. I kept hearing someone else there, but couldn't see who it was. I got to the end pen and saw a man I did not know standing by the big rock. When Russell started to come down, the man crouched behind the rock and came at Russell from behind. They fought, and Russell was on the ground. The other man was hitting him as Russell lay on the ground, Russell found a rock and hit the man in the head, and he fell to the ground. When Russell had realized what he had done, he too fell to his knees. I could hear him crying.

"When the police got there, he saw me, and he must have known I was going to come out of the pens, and he looked at me and said "no". I ran back through the pens. I fell once and scraped my knee to where it was bleeding, and I guess it was then that I lost my grandmother's hankie. The one that Louise found. It is mine. I got back to the truck, checked to make sure Michael had not seen me and drove home."

"It was your mother's truck we saw." Charles leaned to Michael.

The Judge turned to Sara and said, "Mrs. Moore, you have withheld information, do you realize this?"

"Yes, Your Honor, I do."

"This is very serious, Mrs. Moore. A man has been on trial for a crime you know he did not commit."

"Yes, Your Honor. Russell would not have me involved. He told me that he knew the truth, and the important thing was that I knew the truth. With the histories of our families, he wanted to protect me from the scorn. He knew that the hope of him being believed is but slim, and he would not have me caught in that as well. Your Honor, Russell Barnes is a good man. He did not 'murder' Wes Grant."

Mark stood, pride in his sister at a height he could not shield. "My sister is right, Your Honor, In fact, the proof of self-defense is undeniable, what we also know now is that Cecelia Lang did in fact conjure a *plan to murder* Wes Grant."

"Sergeant, detain Miss Lang. Mr. Henry, do you have any words?"

"Your Honor, in the charge of murder, the state rests its case. However, sir, the fact remains, a man is dead. I would ask you to pass judgment against the defendant within the laws regarding self-defense circumstances."

"If it will make you happy, counselor, as this entire trial has been plagued with nonconformity, the defendant, Russell Barnes, is sentenced to one day probation. Case dismissed!"

The echo of the gavel hitting the wood of the bench seemed to be undetected as Sara rushed to Russell.

PART 11

Two Pieces of a Knot

Rex met the truck as Sara pulled into the driveway. Hank and Baron, the two young Border Collies followed closely behind as the elder dog barked at the homecoming.

"Rex, we are just as glad to be home as you are to have us!" Sara knelt to hug the friend that she shared so many years with. "You are a part of my heart, you know that?" To Sara's delight, Hank and Baron had bonded with Michael. She now laughed at the antics of the youthful play of 'air fetch' the boy and two dogs were busied at. "That used to be you my friend, that used to be you." Sara reached to him and kissed the white triangle on his forehead. "Getting a little grey these days boy, trying to catch up to me?" As if he dog understood the implication of his getting older, he jumped back, quickly yipped, and ran to join Michael, Hank, and Baron.

"Tough, isn't it?"
"Yes, Mary, it is. I don't want to even think about life without him. When Bandit died I . . ."
"I know dear, just don't think about it today, OK? Today, we have reason for celebration, and I for one am starved, and I happen to know that there is a rather scrumptious ice cream pie in the freezer!"
"Shhhhsh . . ."
"Did I hear ice cream pie?" Michael was running toward the house with three dogs in tow as Sara placed her arm around Mary's waist. Mary reciprocated; the women walked together to the house in silence, each in their own thoughts of all that had happened to get to this moment.

"Gramp better hurry up and get home. He's gonna miss the pie!" Michael had a large piece on the plate in front of him. As Sara started to slice a piece for Mary, the backdoor flew open. "We knew there would be something good here! And something good just turned into something great!" Charles stood next to Sara and kissed her cheek as everyone laughed and the new arrivals seated themselves around the table. Sara sliced pie for everyone, leaving one portion in the pan for John.

"Where's Gramp? He should be here by now."
"You know your grandfather, he'll be here when he is ready."
"Gram, he'd better hurry, that last piece is looking pretty darn tasty!"
"Not so fast there, young man, I believe that piece is mine!" Walking to Mary, John bent over to kiss the top of her head, a communication between them known only from so many years together. Mary reached her hand

to his on the back of the chair. Sara could not help seeing the 'knowing' smile Mary gave to John.

There was no mention of the whereabouts of John Moore that delayed his arrival home.

"Gramp . . . thank you."
"For?"
"For being at the trial today when I had to testify."
"Seemed like the right thing to do."

"What changed your mind?" Sara recalled the evening when she and John exchanged cross words regarding how John felt about Russell. Sara truly was curious as the 'change of heart' John had to have had to be at the trial.

"You really want to know?" "I think we would all like to know!" Mary spoke before Sara had the chance.

"Remember during the trial that Mark said they had Russell's place and that lady detective's place searched . . . well they came here too." The eight forks of the others seated at the table were placed on plates in unison.

"You three had gone to town when the cops showed up here. Believe me, I was not happy, but they had a warrant. Kent Harrison explained everything to me. How they had found the torn jeans pocket, they wanted to search your dresser Sara . . . seems young Michael here had gotten a bit nerved up when questioned about you the first time the kids all went in. He was looking for anything to connect you with Russell.

"They had suspicions regarding the Lang woman and sure were happy to find that you only wear Levi's. He even went into Michael's room. I asked him why he would even think . . . oh, I was just not very nice, let's just leave it at that. He explained they truly believed Russell was innocent, and when Mark got here, he told me how Russell had done everything he could to keep you two out of the trial. He even said Barnes would rather go to prison than have you, Sara, be falsely accused of anything and then have to bear the shame that was not yours to carry. He didn't want any association with him to affect Michael's rodeo career. Mark even said that . . ."

"Mark was here too?" John placed his hand on Sara's. "Yes, Sara, Mark was here too. He loves you and had to know for sure after the deal with the hankie shocking him. He just didn't want to be blindsided again."

"I'm so sorry, I should have told you I went to the Rodeo Dance. I didn't want Michael thinking I was checking up on him." Sara grinned as she turned to her son. "You were great! And Katy, you went with it, and the two of you owned that floor. I was so proud and not able to tell you. One of those times when I had to hold it to myself and I will never forget."

"Neither will we! How he kept that secret is beyond me! The Mountain Man can dance!" Brent and Charles began to laugh and were soon joined by everyone at the table.

"John, do you understand now why I never turned my back on Russell?"
"Yes, yes, I do." The two embraced as Mary wiped a tear from her cheek.

"I suppose we ought to start talk about this year's cattle drive. Sara, have you checked the forecasts?" John had changed the subject upbruptly from Russell and the trial to the upcoming cattle drive down from the North Grazing Lands.

"As it does seem as though my approval of the time frame seems to be the deciding factor as to when we head out, yes, I have been keeping an eye on the weather systems. As a matter of fact, we have three days to prepare, not much time, but we can manage it. There is a window of five days of good weather and a little warming trend too, so I am proposing we leave on Friday, Saturday at the latest."

Michael glanced at his grandmother and then his grandfather with a concerned look in his eyes he then paused as he looked at his mother with a smile. "We?"
"Yes, . . . we, I want to go this year."
"Mom, you haven't gone since Dad died . . . are you sure?"
"It's time. I'm ready. I need to." Sara lowered her head, collected her thoughts, and as she rose up, she looked at John and then Mary. "I really want to go this year." Her somber tone changed to anticipation. Smiling, she sat back in her chair.

Looking at Brent and Charles, Michael tipped his head toward Mary and Marge. He moved his eyes as if asking the boys if they wanted him to ask his mother if the girls could attend the drive this year.

"Mrs. Moore?"
"Yes, Charles."
"Mrs. Moore, do you think it would be OK if Marge and Mary ride this year too?"
"Have you asked them?"
"Ahhh . . ."
"Could we? Could we please?"
"Ask your parents. This is a lot of work, girls, but I have known you two long enough to know you can handle it. Why don't you call them . . ."

Marge dialed their home, a brief conversation with her father granting permission ended in she and Mary jumping repeatedly for having been given permission. Turning to Sara, she said, "Oh, thank you! We won't dissappoint you, I promise." Marge turned back to her sister before returning to the table. Michael had concerns for Katy. "If Chance isn't ready, we have a horse you can ride."

"He's ready, more than ready, got his shoes back on last week!"

Leaning back in his chair, John looked over the 'meeting' at the kitchen table. Listening as each person contributed ideas and plans, he smiled at Mary. She reached her hand to his, stood up and without removing her hold on him, she placed herself behind him. Leaning her head to his shoulder she whispered in his ear, "She's back . . . Our Sara is back." He reached his other hand up behind his head and found her cheek. "Time and love, dear, time and love."

A knock on the door followed by the appearance of Mark ceased the talk of the drive and focused on his arrival and opinions of the trial.

"I brought this for you, Sara . . ." Mark reached to his pocket and then placed the hankie in her hand. "Oh my, thank you. I thought it was gone forever, and now I have it again. Oh, thank you so much!" Crying, she hugged her brother until he pulled away. "Judge Mann could see how much it meant to you, and as it really was never entered into 'evidence', he let me bring it to you."

Sara, I'm heading back to East Dale tonight."

"So soon? Can't you stay another day or two? We're heading to the North Grazing Land on Friday, stay until then . . . please?" Mark looked at Michael. "Did she just say 'we'?"

"Yup. She's going with this year."

"Good to hear. Good to hear. Now I know for sure you are all right."

"Mark, what about your fee? We haven't talked about that yet."

"Barnes sold his stock, we're square. You know, Mr. Moore, Russell is probably going to be needing a job . . . don't suppose you could use a hired hand around here?"

Sara did not see the wink and exchange between her brother and her father-in-law. "Just might, never know!" John winked back at Mark.

"I need to get going, sis, I love you. Take care and be careful on the drive. The weather ought to cooperate for you, and by the looks of all your help here, this is going to be a successful adventure!" Michael stood to shake Mark's hand and then hugged him. "Thank you, Uncle Mark, it was awesome what you did for Mr. Barnes."

Everyone at the table stood to say their goodbyes, the horn of the car honked. "That would be William, anxious to get home to his girlfriend."

"You know you could use one of those yourself, little brother!"

"When the time is right, I do have a special girl I date, we'll see."

"I love you, Mark!"

"Love you too, Sara." Sara stood at the backdoor and waited until she could no longer see the taillights of Mark's car before she returned to the table.

****

"Well, old girl, think you still got it in you?" Jazzy lifted her head as Sara slipped the halter on. "Guess that's a 'yes'. I might need a little help out there from you. You ready?" A nicker from the mare gave Sara the strength to return to the North Grazing Lands. "Then it's time we get to it!"

Looking around the tack room, she slowly walked to Tonk's bridle. Michael had cleaned it within days after it had been removed from the only horse ever to wear it. Running her hands over the leather brow band, she stopped at the knot that connected both sides. She remembered Samuel whispering to her: "Two pieces tied together to form one . . . that's us, Sara, we're one." As she passed her hand from the brow band to the reins, she said, "Yes, Samuel, we were one. I still love you and always will. You told me to find love again. I think maybe I just might have." Turning to the rack with her saddle, reaching her arms under so as to carry it readied for setting on Jazzy, she closed her eyes. "Ride with us today, Samuel, ride with us." Rex followed Sara and Jazzy out of the barn toward the holding pen.

Unbeknownst to Sara, Russell had been in the end stall brushing Buck. He knew she would want the cross ties, and well, Buck wasn't too keen on any tie other than the traditional one rope to a post so Russell had remained in the stall. He would have let her know he was there, but when he heard her speaking, he knew it was not his place to interupt her thoughts.

Marge and Mary arrived and unloaded their horses; leaving them tied to the trailer while waiting for Charles and Brent. Katy was next to get there, she had ridden over on the trail that Michael and Capp had made between the two ranches.

"Wow! Katy . . . he looks good! You sure can heal a horse!"
"Thank you, Mrs. Moore. Even Dr. Peterman said he'd never seen any recovery like it. He said if I needed a letter of recommendation for a school, he's be glad to write me one!" Sara stood next to Katy, putting her arm over her shoulders. "I meant what I said, kiddo, we will help you financially. And not because of Michael, because of you. Promise me, after we get back you will start really looking into schools."
"Yes, ma'am."

The group could hear Charles's truck turning in the driveway. "You'd think he's get that darn muffler fixed!" "Oh, Gramp . . . That makes it 'cool'!" "I guess I am just an old man beacause I highly disagree with you!" The statement gave cause for laughter amongst everyone.

"OK . . . What's so funny? Not my truck . . .?" Charles and Brent joined the others as they gathered at the gate.

John and Mary stood in the barnyard with Rex at John's side. A slight whimper indicated his want to be a part of the drive, yet his obedience of Sara when she told him to stay. Sara knelt down to him and put her arms around him. "You need to stay here with Gram and Gramp, they need you to protect them." Standing, she faced the matriarch and the patriarch of the family she loved so dearly. "We'll be back soon. All of us. I love you."

Mary took Sara's right hand. "You ride safe, you ride smart, keep an eye on those young ones." John moved to Sara, saying, "I'm proud of you. I love you." "I love you too. Time to go."

"Mount up!" Rex barked his farewell. Hank and Baron placed themselves next to Sara and Michael. John opened the gate, and the riders passed through and headed to the Red Pasture. All fell silent as a hawk flew overhead, circling the riders, and then flew ahead of them to the open pasture. Sara smiled as she cued Jazzy into a jog.

"Well, Mrs. Moore, what do you think about the ranch starting a new business?"

"I don't have a clue what you mean . . . what else would you want to do? You have been a cattle rancher your entire life! I don't understand . . ."

John was about to explain when the sight of the hauler trucks turning into the driveway caught Mary's attention. "What . . . John Moore, what is this all about?"

"Remember how I was later getting home after the trial . . ."

'Yessss."

"And remember how Mark had said that Russell sold the Rodeo Stock to pay his fees . . ."

"Yessss."

"I bought the stock."

"You did what?"

"Now hear me out . . . Russell Barnes proved to me who he is. He could have dragged this family through a lot in that trial and wouldn't. He showed me the man he really is. And frankly, he loves our Sara, and I think she may love him too, and if that really is the case, then if we want to keep her here, we have to accept him as a part of the ranch. You have seen how Michael loves his Rodeo and . . ."

"You can stop now . . . I get it. John Moore, I love you!"

Mounted, Russell rode to John and Mary. He dismounted, stood before them, took off his hatand placiedit on his chest. 'Ma'am, sir . . . I just wanted to say thank you again." Mary hugged him, stepped back and smiled at him. "That is John and Mary, please, you are part of the ranch now." "Russell, we have this all under control here. My suggestion to you is that you get back on that fine horse, kick it into gear, and catch up with the ride!"

Placing his hat back on his head, he turned on his heels, placed his foot in the stirrup and remounted Buck. "Yes, sir! I mean, John"

Mary and John Moore stood at the end of the holding pen, Rex at his side. John put his arm around Mary's waist as she put her arm around his. Tipping heads together, they could see Sara and Michael at the Red Pasture gate, he had opened it for his mother, and she was heading through . . . in a silouette against the morning sky, Michael had turned and seen Russell approaching. From their distant stance, the elder Moores could see their grandson motion to his mother to stay where she was as he rode to the others. Sara stopped to close the gate when Russell approached her. John and Mary watched as Russell dismounted, and as he stood next to Sara, she leaned to him. He took hold of her, gracefully pulling her from the saddle, a moment of pause, and then they embraced.

John and Mary held each other a bit tighter, and as Sara and Russel remounted, the elder Moores kissed, then looking back to Sara and Russell; knew that the 'life' of the ranch had returned as the riders held hands, galloping through the Red Pasture. The hawk flew at Sara's side, circled and then swooped to John and Mary before disappearing on the horizon.
